NEVER *Sleigh* NEVER

GIA STEVENS

Never Sleigh Never: An Enemies to Lovers Christmas Romcom by Gia Stevens

www.authorgiastevens.com

Published by: Gia Stevens

Editor: My Notes in the Margins, Davenport Edits

Publisher: Wild Clover Publishing, LLC

Cover Design: HEA Studios

Print ISBN: 978-1-958286-22-7

V100825

This is for Brad.
You taught us to be brave. Be fearless. To follow our heart.
Go live your best sheep life!

While this story is a romantic comedy there may be situations that are triggering to some. For a list of those content notes please visit my website and scroll to the bottom of the blurb.

Brie

Brad's gentle brown eyes stare back at me. For most, it would be horrifying to see Brad on the other side of the window, but not in Mount Holly, where it's a regular occurrence. His short, stubby tail wiggles with happiness. At least someone's excited to see me in the mornings. Unlike my ex, whose morning greeting involved a grunt, a blanket over the head, and possibly a fart if he was feeling generous. Mornings weren't his thing, but is it too much to ask for a little tail wag? Brad disappears for a second before reappearing with a mouth full of straw from my flowerbed.

"Oh, I see. You only came for breakfast." I cross my arms over my chest. After he's finished chewing, his mouth falls open, and he *baaa*s before trotting off toward my neighbor's yard. Again, just like the ex, he gets what he wants, then leaves. I sigh, grab my phone from my robe pocket, and open *Mount Holly's Shenanigans*—our town's unofficial social media group where Brad's escapades are chronicled like Bigfoot sightings. Sure enough, the morning feed is full of him.

Brad is a sheep that belongs to Henry at the Reindeer Ridge Tree Farm. Unfortunately for Henry, Brad likes to live his best sheep life. Escaping fences, barns, and trailers has been his life's work, and he has masterfully evaded every single one of them. At first, it was a nuisance. Now, my week just isn't the same without a Brad sighting.

Brie: He just left my backyard and headed east.

I hit send and set my phone on the counter. Unlike the rest of the world, I *love* Mondays. Most people dread going back to their nine-to-fives and spend the next four days counting down until it's the weekend again, but not me. Mondays are a new start. But this one is extra special. This Monday is the kickoff of Mount Holly's annual Holly Jolly Festival. Not only will this Monday be my bitch, but so will this festival. It will be the festival to trump all festivals. Mostly, I need this year to be the best event this town has ever experienced. If not, I'll have to pack my bags and leave town with my tail tucked between my legs. Perhaps that's a bit dramatic, but it'll be humiliating to ask my dad for a job at his hardware store. Again. He can't fire me twice, right? Crossing my fingers, I hope I don't have to find out. Thirty-two days until Christmas. Let the countdown begin.

I pull a coffee mug from the cupboard and lift the lid off the coffee container. Peering inside, I stare down at a dusting of coffee grounds. Oh yeah. That's what I forgot to get at the grocery store the other day. One minor blip won't ruin my Monday. This only gives me an excuse to visit Sloane at Sip and Sleigh. Not that I needed an excuse. I was going regardless.

After getting ready for the day, I hop into my SUV and head toward Mistletoe Street in downtown Mount Holly. The bell above the door of Sip and Sleigh jingles as I step inside, the warmth and chatter washing over me. Mount Holly's resident coffee shop owner and one of my best friends, Sloane, effortlessly serves coffee and pastries to eager patrons. The familiar melody of Mariah Carey's holiday hit mingles with the rhythmic hiss of the espresso machine's steam wand. Her auburn hair flops back and forth from the bun on the top of her head. I don't know how she gets up before the sun every morning to serve coffee to the town, but I'm glad she does, otherwise I'd have to make my own specialty coffee. As much as I've tried, even with the help of a fancy espresso machine that now collects dust after one use, no one can make coffee as good as Sloane. She's a magical coffee wizard. After she finishes serving the customer in front of me, she drops her hands to the counter, a wide smile gracing her lips.

"How did you know this is my favorite song?" I tease.

She laughs. "I think you're the only person whose favorite song is not only a Christmas song but also 'All I Want For Christmas Is You.'"

My love for Mariah Carey runs deep. Her voice is iconic. "Doesn't it just make you want to get up and twirl around and dance and throw confetti?"

"Nope. But I'm happy you're happy."

"It just makes my Monday even better." I unravel my scarf from around my neck, letting the ends dangle over my shoulders.

Sloane spins around, grabs an extra-large vanilla caramel latte, and holds it out to me, a bright smile covering her face. With both hands, I grip the compostable paper cup. The moment the lid's under my nose, I inhale caramel heaven. "Have I told you lately that you're my absolute favorite person ever?"

"Every morning."

I meet Sloane's gaze. "This morning, I especially mean it. Brad stopped by, and it wasn't to bring me breakfast."

"Dammit Brad. He's so selfish."

I nod along.

"He's had a rough three years. It will be good for him to be surrounded by family." Irene Dahlby's voice cuts through the rest of the chatter as she sits with the other six Gossiping Grannies, Gigis for short. They're Mount Holly's Golden Girls. Retirement has given them extra time to spend their mornings chatting about all the gossip in Mount Holly. They are the first to learn what's happening in town, and they are also the first to tell everyone else, regardless of whether the information is true or false. You want the juicy news? They're dripping like a freshly brewed pot of coffee. Lucky for me, Sloane always gets the secondhand gossip to share.

"So, what's the topic of today's conversation?" I nod at the ladies huddled around the table, sipping their coffee.

"Apparently, someone's moving back to Mount Holly." Sloane shrugs.

My lip curls in disappointment. "They need better gossip."

"Like the herpes outbreak of twenty-twenty-two?" She lifts a brow.

"Yes! That was good gossip. Who knew that when Samantha dumped her boyfriend and slept with Peter, they'd both end up with herpes?"

"Only Peter didn't know until he had an outbreak and later traced it back to Michelle, who was sleeping with his dad."

"You forgot Michelle also got pregnant. The herpes outbreak was quickly forgotten. The next question then became was the baby Peter's kid or his sibling?"

"At least it kept Dr. Montgomery busy."

"Compared to that, people moving in and out of Mount Holly is weak. Unless it's Paul Rudd, because that man has somehow defied time and doesn't age. I want to know if he moves to town so I can question him about his secrets." I point to the corner of my eye. "These crow's feet are not getting any smaller."

"I couldn't agree more. About Paul Rudd. Not the crow's feet."

Behind the counter, coffee mugs rattle against each other as if the Polar Express were barreling down the tracks, except there aren't tracks running through town. I spin around. A semi-truck rumbles down Mistletoe Street like it owns the place. My brows knit together. This isn't a common sight in a town with a population of one-thousand-two-hundred-fifty-one and one rebellious sheep. Following the semi-truck are two pickup trucks towing cargo trailers. Did they take a wrong turn off the highway? That's the only logical explanation for why they're rolling through Mount Holly. After the third truck passes, silence settles in. It's eerie. Like the calm before the storm. Just when you think it's over, but in reality, it's a false alarm. The storm is only building momentum. Then another semi noses into view, this one is hauling a twenty-foot metal Christmas tree strapped to a flatbed. All the noise inside Sip and Sleigh drains away as I push outside and onto the snow-covered sidewalk. The icy wind smacks me in my face. Truck after truck drives past like a scrolling marquee.

If they want the highway, they need to turn east, not west. As the last truck drives by, I fixate on who's behind the wheel. My heart rate spikes. All the air pushes out of my lungs. Oh no. No, no, no. Logan fucking Crawford.

I whirl around and duck my head, praying he didn't see me. Would he even recognize me? It's only been eighteen years since I last saw him. In person, anyway. As the white pickup truck passes, I peer over my shoulder as he follows the convoy of other trucks. I check my phone—one hour until I need to be at town hall. A split second later, I make the worst decision of my Monday. I follow. Shoving my phone into my pocket, I race down the sidewalk and jump inside my SUV. Turning over the engine, I shift into drive and make a U-turn onto the road and follow the parade of trucks through downtown and toward the outskirts of Mount Holly. I follow closely enough so I won't lose them, even though it would be hard to lose a convoy of trucks, but I also don't want to make it obvious I'm following them.

To say I hate Logan Crawford is an understatement. I despise, no loathe, no *despisingly loathe* him. It started in elementary school, continued through middle school, and escalated in high school. We were both top of our class. But of course, he was valedictorian because he not only excelled with his grades but was also the captain of the hockey team, which added three state championship trophies to the school's display case. So I'm sure it was easy for teachers to give him a pass or extra credit because he was such a great athlete. By not being top of my class, I missed out on a scholarship opportunity that would have been a full ride to my first-choice college. Instead, I settled for my second-choice school. Even before that, he had to one-up me at every opportunity. For our middle school fundraiser, I raised a respectable $1,200. He had to outshine me with $2,100. I got an ACT score of 34. Of course, he had to get a 35. Needless to say, after graduation, he left town to go to Boston College on a full-ride hockey scholarship. I stayed in Minnesota with a scholarship that paid only a fraction of my tuition.

My SUV creeps to a stop next to an open field on the side of the road across from the Reindeer Ridge Tree Farm. Henry, the owner, usually used it for overflow parking, except it's gone untouched for the last few years. The rumbling of heavy machinery pushing snow around echoes over the rolling hills. Mesmerized by what's happening, I pull the handle on the door and step out onto the road.

"What the hell is he doing?" I whisper, rounding the hood. Squeaking brakes cause me to whip around. An oversized box-style truck stops inches from my rear bumper. I race around to the back. A big, burly guy in a tan jacket and a black knit cap jumps out, slamming the truck door.

I point at the sliver of daylight between our bumpers and then glare at the guy. "Hey, you're a little close, don't you think?"

"Just parking my truck."

"Perhaps you could throw it in reverse and park it so you're not mounting my car like it owes you dinner."

He strides toward the rear of his truck, then thumbs over his shoulder. "You'll just have to pull forward."

I stomp my foot. "Fine!"

The steady beeping of a truck reversing mimics the throbbing in my temples. I spin around to the bright white reverse lights getting closer. I hoof it toward the front of my SUV. "Hey! You can't park there."

Another guy, skinnier than the first but wearing the same tan jacket and knit cap, steps out and shuts the door. "Well, I can't park in there since they're moving snow. I gotta park somewhere."

I peer down at the tiny gap between our bumpers. Oh my god, they trapped me in. My vehicle is in a three-way it never wanted. "What the hell?" I throw my hands up in the air.

"You got plenty of room." He shrugs before strolling down the makeshift driveway.

"You can't be serious! Someone should take your license away if you think that's enough room! Maybe I'll call Carson and have you towed instead!"

Asshole Number Two meets up with Asshole Number One, and they merge to create a super asshole and continue ignoring every word I'm yelling.

I stare at my front bumper. Granted, it is more room than Asshole Number One left me, but certainly not enough to get out. As I stomp down the shoulder and around the front of Asshole Number Two's truck, I yank out my phone, scrolling for Carson's number. Head down, I round the bumper and step into the road—

"Brie!"

Time slows. A hand clamps on my forearm and yanks. I lose my footing and stumble just as another truck screams past. My phone slips from my hand and crashes into the gravel. Wind from the near-miss blows my hair everywhere, and I slam into… flannel. Warm, steady, soft flannel. My eyes flutter open. I get lost in a fresh, clean linen scent. Is this what heaven smells like?

"Are you okay?" The voice is soft, but my spine recognizes it before my brain.

I tip my chin up until I meet mesmerizing hazel irises. My gaze drifts down his slightly crooked, sloping nose to the dimple of his left cheek. Every muscle in my body stiffens. Not heaven. Hell.

His fingers brush against my back, breaking me from

my trance. I shove my way out of his grasp. "What are you doing?" I can't keep the venom out of my tone.

He stumbles back, brows lifting. "Saving your life? I guess next time I'll let the truck hit you."

My mind's a jumbled mess. I was just in Logan Crawford's arms. My hands on his chest. A truck nearly turned me into roadkill. "Well, the truck was going entirely too fast. And it wouldn't even be here if it weren't for you," I spit out.

"Wow. So this is my fault now?" He crosses his arms over his broad chest.

"Yes. Yes, it is. It's exactly your fault." I mimic his pose.

He rolls his eyes. "Please. Explain."

"If you never came back to town and started doing whatever you're doing with all the trucks," I wave at my currently trapped vehicle, "and caging me in, this wouldn't be an issue. What are you doing here, anyway?" With my hands on my hips, I bore my gaze into his, but he doesn't back down.

He shrugs. "I thought Mount Holly could use some extra holiday cheer this year, so I'm organizing a carnival."

A Christmas carnival? Not in my town. "We have enough cheer, thank you very much. It's called the Holly Jolly Festival. And I am this year's event coordinator." I point to the field. "Whatever you think is happening here is not approved. I suggest you shut it down."

"Just because you asked doesn't mean you always get what you want."

"The festival is important to me."

"And my carnival is important to me. What's your point?" He lifts a perfectly sculpted light brown brow. "I'm not shutting it down because you said so. Besides, I didn't know an event coordinator held such weight in this town."

My nostrils flare. He has a point, but I don't like it. "Well, I'll find out, and I'll get back to you."

He flashes me a dimpled smile. "You do that then."

I rub the center of my forehead. "This is just like high school all over again. You come in and ruin everything. Because you have to be number one. Logan Crawford, best at everything."

"You said it. Not me. Also, tell your parents I say hi. Actually, I need to stop by the hardware store. Your parents still own it?" Before I can tell him to get lost, he finishes, "Never mind, I'll tell them myself."

I huff, pivot, and stomp away.

"Hey Brie!"

I freeze.

"Watch out for speeding trucks. I'd hate to rescue you twice." I whip my head around and glare at him. He winks. "I'll do you a favor and move this truck so you can leave."

"Don't do me any favors. Moving the truck is common curtesy. Not a favor."

"Just say thank you."

"To you, never."

"You're welcome." He climbs into the truck, turns the engine over, and pulls forward, giving me just enough room to squeeze out.

Not wanting to waste another second, I jump into my SUV and step on the gas, driving in the opposite direction of town, but I don't care. I'll take the scenic route back. I just need to get away from Logan. My hands tremble as I grip the steering wheel. This isn't how the kickoff to the holiday season was supposed to go down. It was to be joyous and exhilarating, not like I want to commit murder. I whip the steering wheel right, brake hard, and skid to the shoulder. Park. Inhale. Hold. And exhale a primal scream that probably startles a crow three counties over. Sadly, it still doesn't make me feel better. My phone chimes with a message. Glancing down, a smidge of comfort washes over me. My other best friend will help me wallow in this catastrophe.

WILLA

Checking in to make sure you didn't get kidnapped by the Grinch in a white windowless van claiming to sell Christmas decorations.

BRIE

No van. But worse.

WILLA

Ooo. What can be worse than a kidnapping?

BRIE

Logan fucking Crawford.

WILLA

Yikes. I bet you wish it was the van.

BRIE

Yep.

WILLA

Your breakfast sandwich is getting cold. Come to the diner and I'll make you a new one. Then you can tell me what Logan has to do with anything.

BRIE

My Christmas Wonderland turned into a Christmas hell.

Willa's strawberry-blonde hair is pulled back into a ponytail, her signature work look. *The Jolly Biscuit* stretches across the front of her gray shirt. She greets me from behind the counter with a to-go bag of my usual turkey sausage patty, egg white, and pepper jack cheese, on a whole wheat English muffin.

"So, I hear you're making out with Logan Crawford on the side of the road."

My mouth falls open. "No! My lips would never touch his."

"Mrs. Hanson says otherwise. She said she saw you two embracing in a lip lock on the side of Snowflake Lane by Reindeer Ridge."

"Mrs. Hanson needs to get her eyes checked, because none of that happened." The gossip runs rampant through town, and today it seems to be spearheaded by the head Gigi herself.

"But you did run into Logan."

"Unfortunately. And by the looks of it, he's not passing through town. He's building a Christmas carnival."

"Ooo. Competition." She leans on the counter, resting her chin on her hand.

"No! Not competition. More like a pain in my ass." I rub my temples. A headache tap-dances behind my eyes. "What time is it?"

"8:55."

"Shit. Shit. Shit. I'm going to be late! And it's all Logan's fault!"

"Fine. I'll let it slide this time, but the Deer tonight. Because I need the rest of the kiss story, and it's raffle night."

I drop my shoulders and glare at her.

She holds her hands up in defense. "I heard kiss. Until you tell me the full story, it's a kiss."

I roll my eyes. "Is it too early to drink now?"

"It might be best to wait until at least noon."

"I'll call you later." I spin on my heel and wave my hand over my head. A gust of icy wind smacks into me as soon as I land on the sidewalk. Mondays can swan-dive straight into the frozen Winterberry Creek.

Brie

Stupid Logan for making me late. Okay—technically, *I* made me late, but it's because of Logan. Without wasting another second, I shoulder through the heavy steel doors of town hall, boots squeaking traitorously as melting snow tattles on me. As I dash up the stairs two at a time I pray I can shave a couple seconds off my tardiness. It doesn't matter. If Mrs. Kingsley checks the surveillance video, she'll know I'm sneaking in like a teenager past curfew. I round the corner to my desk and tiptoe like the floor's made of bubble wrap. I freeze. The only sound I can make out is my heart thumping in my ears. With trembling hands, I pull open the bottom drawer, hoping to keep it from clicking, and slowly slide my purse inside. Gently, I shrug out of my coat and hang it on the coat rack behind me. Pinching my eyes closed, I lower myself to my chair. The shaft squeaks as my weight pushes down on the metal. Slowly, I continue to ease down, until I'm fully seated. My ears are on high alert for any sounds of movement. When the coast is clear, I exhale.

"Brie! Come in here for a moment," Mrs. Kingsley yells from her office down the hall.

My teeth grind together as I silently curse myself. "I'll be right there!" I shove my chair away from my desk and swipe the strands of hair off my face. The soles of my boots continue to squeak on the tile floor as I stroll toward the door leading to her office. Before I reach the doorway, I pause, straightening my hair and saying a silent prayer that she doesn't know I arrived late. I peek my head around the doorframe. "Yes, Mrs. Kingsley, you wanted to see me?"

Without looking up, she says, "You're late."

Dammit. "Uh. Yes. Sorry. Henry's sheep Brad got out again. You know how he is. Wanderlust is in his blood, and Mount Holly is his playground. Of course, when you need him to move, he doesn't." I deploy the widest, most innocent smile in my arsenal. No carnival talk yet—not until I have a battle plan.

She drops her pen to her desk and glances up, meeting my gaze. Not a single hair is out of place or a piece of lint on her blouse. She's fully composed as always. I'd love to see her let loose. I bet she'd be a riot. But a blizzard in hell is more likely to happen.

Her lips purse, then relent a fraction. "Unfortunately, I've had an encounter or two with that sheep." Her fond memories of Brad are quickly forgotten as she pushes a stack of papers toward me. "I need you to look over these contracts for the festival. Remember, this year I'm putting you in charge. If you can pull it off, my position—when I retire after this year—is yours. I know you've waited a long time for this."

I bite back my smile and grab the stack of contracts from her desk.

"Yes, Mrs. Kingsley." *Waited a long time* is cute for *eight years of hauling folding chairs and solving frosting emergencies.* The entire town has been whispering about her retirement for three years. Plus, I'm the only logical replacement. I can practically predict her sneeze schedule. The position is as good as mine.

"And if you don't…" she adds.

A sucker punch to the gut nearly drops me to my knees. There should be no "if you don't."

Her beady stare bores into mine. "It will be up to the town council if they want to hire an outside agency to handle all future events in Mount Holly."

"An outside agency?" A cold sweat prickles my skin. "But Mrs. Kingsley, do you think that's the best plan for Mount Holly? They know nothing about our town." I can't keep the panic out of my voice.

"Perhaps that's exactly what this town needs. An outside perspective. Someone to bring excitement back to our small community."

My shoulders deflate. "We have enough excitement here," I mutter. The 4th of July parade last year drew the largest crowd Mount Holly has ever seen. Granted, it helped that the Women's USA curling team joined our parade since a woman on the team grew up in a neighboring town. The autograph line stretched down Mistletoe Street, and Willa nearly camped overnight.

There's been no mention of an outside agency until now. Sure, there have been a few—or several—mishaps during the previous festivals that happened on my watch, but an outside agency? I grit my teeth, fighting the urge to lunge across her desk and shake the answer out of her. But Mrs. Kingsley is five foot nothing and has made grown men sob into their mittens. I don't want that to be me today. "Yes, Mrs. Kingsley. I'll get started on these right away."

"Good. I have high expectations of you. We don't need another… inflatable incident."

I wince. "No, ma'am. I'll triple-check the tie-downs myself."

Last year, a blizzard rolled through Mount Holly, causing the Santa and Frosty giant inflatables to loosen. By morning, the ties twisted together, causing Santa to thrust his hips against the backside of Frosty every time there was a slight breeze. All the children of Mount Holly now believe Santa likes to give hugs from behind. By December twenty-fifth, the townsfolk of Mount Holly, but I'm pretty sure it was Mason and Simon even though they both denied the act, thought it would be hilarious to add tiny plastic snowmen in Santa hats surrounding the inflatables.

"I expect nothing less," she says crisply. "This year, you're in the driver's seat. Make the Holly Jolly Festival the best we've ever seen, and I'll know you're the right successor."

I nod along. No pressure. No pressure at all. Especially when I have Logan Crawford in town. The golden boy, the hometown hero, the hockey legend himself, competing with his own Christmas carnival. "Sure, no problem. I will make sure that this year's Holly Jolly Festival will be the best this town has ever seen."

"That's the spirit. Of course, I'll be here to oversee anything if you have questions or concerns. But otherwise, I believe these are yours." She turns around, rises to her feet, and collects three overflowing three-ring binders. She steps around her desk and drops them into my hands on top of the contracts. The heavy weight threatens to make me topple over as my arms struggle to hold everything. I know exactly what these are. The Holly Jolly Festival Bibles. All the vendor information, marketing, business plans, budgets, and attendance records. Everything that makes the Holly Jolly Festival function.

She returns to her desk chair and gives the computer monitor her full attention, essentially dismissing me.

For the second time today, my stomach falls to my ass. I spin on my heel and exit her office, clutching the binders and papers to my chest. This wasn't news I was expecting. An outside agency knows nothing about this town. They wouldn't understand the small, tight-knit community we've built here. They'll only ruin it with all their big-city glitz and glamour. For the past eight years, I've worked as the assistant event coordinator. Eventually, I thought I would get the job. I'm not saying the town council should give it to me, but why not promote from within? I know all the inner workings of every event planned in Mount Holly. Especially the Holly Jolly Festival. It shouldn't be given to some outside agency who has never stepped foot inside the town's limits. Sure, there may have been one or two, or ten minor mishaps in years past, but they've never been because of negligence on my part. I can't control the weather. Maybe Santa had a thing for Frosty that finally came to fruition that cold and windy night. That could make for some good fanfic. I thumb through the stack of contracts. New motivation unlocked. I'll make this year's Holly Jolly Festival so dazzling the council won't even think of the outside agency.

At my desk, I drop the binders and exhale. I know I need to jump into the deep end of event planning, but my brain is currently a snow globe someone won't stop shaking. Bending over, I yank open the bottom desk drawer and pull out my phone. Glancing over my shoulder, Mrs. Kingsley's door is now shut, so I slink down the hall like a raccoon who knows where the good trash is. Once in the restroom, I call Sloane. She's always the voice of reason. Maybe she can talk me out of smothering Logan with my scarf.

After a few rings, she answers, "Sip and Sleigh."

"Do you ever have one of those nightmares that you can't seem to wake yourself out of?" I pass the three closed stall doors as I pace to the other side of the restroom.

"Um, sure. Yeah."

"That's me right now. Except it's not a nightmare. It's my life!" I freeze and pinch the bridge of my nose.

"What has you so frazzled? Especially for a Monday. I thought you always make Mondays your bitch."

"Currently, this Monday can suck it. It's not even noon, and I already want this day to be over. Actually, the week. No, month. Let's fast forward to next year." I wear a hole in the tile as I pace back and forth.

"Where are you? It's kind of echo-y."

"I'm in the bathroom because my boss can't hear me."

"What happened?"

I sigh. "Where do I begin? For starters, I just found out if I don't nail this Holly Jolly Festival, she's going to pass it over to some out-of-town firm who knows nothing about the town. We all know they're just going to ruin the whole spirit of our town and the holiday. The Holly Jolly Festival is the backbone, no, the heart of Mount Holly." It used to be the top festival in the state. Sadly, over the years, the joy and excitement diminished.

"I grew up three towns over and even I heard about it."

I throw my hand in the air. "See! That's how popular it was. Eight years ago, when I joined Mrs. Kingsley as the assistant, I offered fresh ideas to draw a crowd. Gradually, each year got a little better. We added more activities and games and rides. Together, we brought back the tradition of the Holly Jolly Festival to Mount Holly." I blow out a deep breath, remembering some of the more memorable mishaps. "Now I can't say that each year since I've been here hasn't been without a few hiccups. Like when the reindeer thought Mistletoe Street would make a good runway."

Sloane snorts. "I remember when the mini sled dog race turned into a mini dog orgy."

I pinch my eyes closed. "I never thought No Humping Allowed would become a rule, but here we are."

"Don't forget, turkey frying is banned after the turkey hut went up in flames."

"Yes! Luckily, Mason was on duty that day and got the fire out with minimal damage to the other huts. These are all minor mishaps, that's all. They could happen to anyone. Including whatever outside agency the town council thinks could do a better job."

"I'm sorry. That sucks."

"To add another Yule log to my fire, which is already burning out of control, Logan Crawford is back in town." I roll my eyes.

"Who's Logan Crawford?"

"Well, let me tell you about Logan Crawford. He is only the most annoying, condescending, know-it-all, arrogant jerk Mount Holly has ever produced. The cherry on top is he's the biggest pain in my ass."

"So there's history there. Did you date him? Wait! Did he dump you? You sound like a scorned ex-lover."

"No, and hell no. Why would I be the one getting dumped? Why can't I be the dumper and not the dumpee? Never mind, it doesn't matter. If he was the last person on this planet, I wouldn't want to date him. Like, if me and him were required to repopulate the earth, I'd send him a fruit basket wishing him the best of luck on the apocalypse and call it a day."

"Alright. What does him being in town have to do with anything?"

"So not only do I have to pull off the best festival this town has ever seen, but I also have to do it while he's organizing his own Christmas carnival."

"Okay. So, you'll have a little competition? You can handle it."

"But I don't want or need competition. I already have a lot riding on this without the added pressure of competition." When there's a first and second place involved, I always get the silver medal, and I can't afford to come in second. "He's not even in town for three hours, and he's already back to ruining my life."

"I've known you for eight years now, and you concede to no one. I know you'll put on the best festival this town has ever seen, and people will be like, 'What carnival?'"

My shoulders slump. I want to believe her. I don't doubt my abilities, but Logan Crawford has always been my kryptonite. If he and I are involved in anything that puts people on a podium, he's always at the top.

"You're Brie McKenna. You always rise from the ashes like a unicorn."

"Don't you mean phoenix?"

"Unicorns are more fun. They have a horn for spearing. Anyway, don't sweat it. Just do what you do best, and kick ass. It's like that time when Mrs. Peterson was choking on her donut at the diner, and you jumped to your feet and gave her the Heimlich and saved her life. Your quick thinking did that."

Well, Mrs. Peterson being the town's treasurer, I

needed her alive so she could write me a check for the 4th of July parade. I exhale a deep breath. "But seriously, this day has already turned into a flaming bag of dog shit, and fast. Like kerosene dumped on the bag. Explosion." The whooshing sound of a toilet flushing ricochets off the tile walls. With the phone still to my ear, I spin to where the sound originated, and I freeze like a baby deer. The far stall door opens, and Mrs. Peterson emerges. Maybe if I don't move, she won't see me. She strolls to the sink and washes her hands.

"Brie? Brie, are you still there?" Sloane says through the phone.

"I'm not alone," I whisper.

Mrs. Peterson dries her hands with a paper towel. When I think she's going to walk past me, she stops. Her floral perfume lingering in the air. "Don't forget about Margaret's phallic-shaped cookies she tried to pass off as lighthouses. We all know they weren't lighthouses."

I pinch my lips together and nod in a silent agreement.

She pats my forearm. "You go kick their ass," she whispers, then glides out like a benevolent gossip fairy.

"Brie? What's going on? Who are you talking to?" Sloane asks.

As soon as the door closes behind Mrs. Peterson, my heart thumps back to life. I sag against the tile wall. There's a good chance the entire town will know about my run-in with Logan by noon, and I'm not prepared for all the questions they'll have.

"Brie? Answer me or I'm calling 911."

"Yeah. I'm here."

Note to self: Always check the bathroom stalls.

Logan

Brie McKenna. For everyone else, she wears a sunshine smile, yet around me, she flips the setting to permafrost. Now, eighteen years later, nothing has changed—except she's somehow more beautiful. As she glared her ice queen daggers in my direction, there was still a little sparkle in her eye. Perhaps she's daydreaming that one of those daggers takes me out. But for a split second with her body pressed against mine, hands on my chest—her guard slipped. If I had to guess, it's because she didn't know whose arms she'd fallen into.

She always hated me. I'm not sure why. That's not entirely true. In elementary school, I might have saved all the open swings for my friends. And I would always get picked for the lead in the school play. Also, during the music class lip-sync battles, I always picked the song she wanted to perform. Nothing is more entertaining than three boys singing and dancing to "...Baby One More Time" by Britney Spears. The class enjoyed it; Brie not so much because everyone was over the song when it was her turn.

It seems, even after all these years apart, that hatred has never left. Sure, the population of Mount Holly has slightly increased since I left, but it's still not big enough for us to avoid each other. This will make for a very interesting holiday.

From the side of the road, I stare as her taillights vanish over the crest of the hill. If she plans on going back to town, she's driving in the wrong direction, but I'm sure she knows that.

"Hey boss!" Matt, a hired worker, yells. "Where do you want this?"

I twist to face him. He points to a large, enclosed trailer. "Put it in the far corner." I nod toward the northwest side of the field. Is it a wild idea to come to Mouth Holly and organize a Christmas carnival and have it up and running in three weeks? Yep. I've also been sitting on this for two years. It's now or never. A line of idling trucks sits on the freshly laid gravel, white exhaust curling into the cold like thought bubbles. I play conductor in a hard hat, sending crews to their marks. Thankfully, I've got a site diagram with placements for the big stuff—games, food row, and Santa's pavilion. On the south side of the field is my favorite add-on. The ice rink. As a professional hockey player from Minnesota, the "State of Hockey," it only made sense. Plus, what kind of holiday celebration would it be without a hockey tournament?

Several hours later, the sun dips below the horizon and

stars twinkle above us. With the back of my hand, I wipe the layer of sweat off my forehead. Day one is in the books. I'm exhausted, but there's more work to do tomorrow. I walk the perimeter to confirm everything is locked and secured. Mount Holly doesn't have a reputation for criminal activity. In fact, it's a community where most people leave their doors unlocked, but I've lived in the city for the past eighteen years, and I'm not taking any chances.

I pull my truck into the driveway of my parents' light-blue colonial-style house. Not much has changed over the years, only a bigger porch and new landscaping. I kill the engine and push open the door. My boots crunch over the thin crust of snow leading to the cement walkway. I jog up the few stairs until I reach the front door. I rap my knuckles against the wood before twisting the knob and stepping through. Before I can close the door behind me, a pair of arms wrap around me in a comforting hug. The scent of vanilla and sugar waft around me. My mom. If I had to guess, she's been in the kitchen baking all day.

"I'm so happy to see you." Her head rests against my chest.

"I saw you two days ago," I murmur, hugging her back.

"I know, but I never get to see you twice in one week, and now it's permanent."

Before the move, my mom and stepdad flew to Chicago to travel back to Mount Holly with Josie. They helped her tour her new school while I wrangled movers so I could make the drive to Northern Minnesota. While Josie is used to moving, the dynamic of a big city to a small town is a big change for an eleven-year-old, but it's one that will be best for both of us.

Mom pulls away and leads me into the living room. Josie's curled against the armrest of the couch next to my stepdad, John, who's in the recliner. When my mom told me about a house two streets over on the market, I immediately called the realtor. We did a video walkthrough, and with no hesitation, I bought it. Being close to my parents was a big selling point to move back to Mount Holly. Josie needs stability in her life, and my parents can help give her that. Plus, they adore their granddaughter, so they were more than willing to help.

Josie stops mid-page flip from the *Home for the Holidays* magazine. It's the same magazine she always looked through with her mom. They'd scour every page to find the most beautiful tree or the location with the best decorations. Every year, they have a "Favorite Hometown Christmas" competition. Josie's mom mentioned wanting to enter as soon as the carnival was up and running. But not the inaugural year—she wanted all the kinks ironed out first.

Josie glances up, and her eyes widen. "Daddy!"

The magazine tumbles to the floor as her big, bright hazel eyes meet mine. She launches herself at me. As far as looks go, it's the only thing she got from me. Everything else is all Brooke, including her sass and her big heart. All the same things that made me fall in love with her fourteen years ago.

Bending down, I hoist her into my arms.

"Hey Peanut."

"I missed you, Daddy." Her arms cling around my neck like a spider monkey.

"I missed you too. Did you get to see your new school?"

She nods. "I did. It's much smaller than my old one."

"Highland Park has a lot more people than Mount Holly." I press a kiss to the top of her head.

John stands from the armchair and wraps his arms around my shoulders and pats my back. "Good to see you,

Logan. I can't tell you how excited we are to have you permanently back in Mount Holly. Only seeing you and Josie a few times a year was never enough."

"Yeah." I try for a smile that doesn't quite make it. "I'm excited to be back."

"Your voice says otherwise," my mom says.

She could always read me. She calls it a mother's intuition. I call it creepy.

"Hey Josie," my mom turns to Josie, "why don't you get one of the cookies we baked earlier for your dad?"

"Okay!" I set Josie on her feet, and she skips into the kitchen, her blonde ponytail bouncing behind her.

When she's out of sight, my mom turns to me and rests a hand on my forearm. "I know it's hard. It'll always be hard. But we want to be here for you and Josie. For anything. With you only living five minutes away instead of an eight-hour drive, it makes it easier."

"It's kind of the reason I wanted to move back. Thanks for finding me a house."

"Luckily, Mr. Bernstein was selling. The sun was calling his name, but mostly, he was over the cold." Mom shrugs.

I nod. "And it appears most of the town doesn't know."

"We tried to keep it as hush-hush as we could, but you know Mount Holly. It doesn't take long for the Gigis to snatch a whisper out of the air, and once word is out, it's like head lice. Pretty soon, it's all over town. You'd think they'd find a new hobby."

"In a few years you'll be sitting at the same table as the Gigis." John nudges Mom with his elbow.

She laughs. "You're probably right, but good thing that day isn't today."

"Did you get things settled?" John asks.

"Almost. We made some good progress on the carnival. Also, thanks for finding that piece of land."

"Good. I thought something on the outskirts of town might be easier. Less red tape."

"It's perfect." I drag a hand over my jaw. "I had a nice, friendly run-in with Brie McKenna this morning. It wasn't the welcome party I was expecting." I fight the grin tugging at my lips as memories of her tangled in my arms rush back.

"Oh! How is Brie?" Mom's eyes light up. "I always liked her. She's such a sweet girl. And her parents live next door. I see her when she visits them. She's even helped me shovel the driveway a few times."

Shit. Looks like I'll be seeing her more than just around town. "Are we talking about the same Brie McKenna? Because she must have left her sweet at home." Or maybe she reserves that for people she doesn't hate.

"She's in charge of the Holly Jolly Festival this year," Mom says.

I nod. "So I've heard."

Josie reappears with a stack of cookies and passes one to each of us. "I made these all by myself! They're chocolate chip."

"You did?" I take the cookie from Josie.

"Yup!"

"Thanks, I'm starving." The cookie's halfway to my mouth before my mom plucks it out of my grasp. "Hey! I was gonna eat that."

"I'll make you a plate of hotdish. Then you can have your cookie."

"Or I can have the cookie to tide me over."

"Dinner first, then dessert." My mom disappears around the corner.

I glance at John, who takes a bite of his cookie and shrugs. I salivate as crumbs fall to the front of his shirt. "I'm a little envious of you right now."

"Grandma wouldn't let me have a cookie until after dinner," Josie says.

"Well, at least she's consistent." I stroll into the kitchen just as the microwave dings. Mom slides a steaming plate of tater tot hotdish across the kitchen island. When people talk about comfort food, tater tot hotdish is like a warm fire on a chilly night. Ground beef, cream of mushroom, onion, corn, cheese, and tater tots all baked together until the tots are golden brown. It reminds me exactly of home. My mom. It's something Brooke would never dream of making. Being a professional athlete, I always had to watch what I ate. Sure, I would indulge now and then, but nothing like this. Shoving a forkful into my mouth, I moan. "Thanks. I never realized how much I missed your hotdish until now."

"Now that you're back, we'll have a lot more dinners together." She spins around and puts the clean dishes from the strainer into the cupboard.

No complaints here. I clear the plate with the speed of a power play. When I'm finished, I glance down, half tempted to pick up my plate and lick it clean. It was that good. But I think otherwise, mostly to avoid the motherly glare she'd give me because she taught her son better manners than that. I set my fork down and push my plate away.

"Now you can have your dessert." She swaps the plate for the cookie.

Finally. I take a big bite. My teeth sink into the soft, delectable, and unapologetically perfect baked good. While I continue eating my dessert, Mom rinses off the plate before placing it in the bottom rack of the dishwasher.

"You know they make dishwashers where you don't have to do that," I say.

"I'm not convinced it would get it clean."

"You'd be surprised. They have jets that could strip paint."

"I like my dishwasher the way it is."

John enters the kitchen. "That's what I keep telling her as well." He wraps his arms around my mom.

"If it's not broken, it doesn't need replacing." While reaching behind her, he grabs another cookie from the counter. She spins around and spears him with a look. He shrugs.

I shove the last half of the cookie into my mouth.

Josie climbs onto the stool next to me. "Did you like it?"

"Mmm." I rub my belly as I chew. "There's no way you made these. Where's the cookie container?" I pretend to look around the kitchen.

"I did!" She giggles. "Grandma was my helper."

"In that case, I'm hiring you for the carnival bakery. You're on cookie duty for Christmas."

Her eyes go wide. "That's a lot of cookies." She tilts her head. "What's the Holly Jolly Festival?" She takes a bite of her cookie.

"It's Mount Holly's Christmas festival. There are games, food, and Santa," Mom answers.

Josie turns to me. "Like the carnival?"

"Similar," I say carefully.

"Who's Brie McKenna?"

Of course she overheard; she hears everything. "A girl I grew up with."

"She's your friend?"

I rub my neck. How do I translate *academic nemesis turned firecracker with a vendetta* to an eleven-year-old? "I wouldn't say friend. We... went to school together. Since Mount Holly is so small, we saw a lot of each other." Josie nods along. I hope she buys what I'm selling her. In case she doesn't, I change the subject. "Unfortunately, only half the things for the house showed up. Is it okay if Josie stays another night or two? Just until everything arrives, and she's not living out of boxes. I'm hoping to have the house together before Thanksgiving."

"Of course," my mom says. She'd never complain about spending more time with her granddaughter. I'm sure she feels as if she has years to make up for. A life of professional hockey didn't grant me too much free time.

"Thanks. Maybe we can have Thanksgiving at my house then."

"We can certainly host here as well." My mom leans against the counter.

I wrap an arm around Josie's shoulder and glance down. "Are you okay with staying with Grandma and Grandpa for a couple more days?"

She nods. "Yes!"

"There's a craft fair in Twin Falls we can go to," my mom adds.

Josie springs to attention. "Yay!" She rushes to my mom and wraps her arms around her.

"Alright, I'm going to head home." I walk to the entryway and slide my feet into my shoes.

My mom follows close behind. "Have you seen anyone else yet?"

"Only Brie. I've been a little busy." A humorless laugh escapes me. "Busy" is an understatement. Organizing a carnival in three weeks is crazy. But I started it, and I need to see this through now.

"I'm sure everyone will be excited to see you."

I give her a tight-lipped smile and nod. Seeing all my old friends will be great. Another run-in with Brie… that's still up for debate. I wrap my arms around her shoulders. "Thanks again for watching Josie."

"It's no trouble at all."

The cold air hits me as soon as I open the door. I jam my hands in my pockets as I stride to my truck. I let it idle for a few minutes before reversing out of the driveway. Rows and rows of houses pass by. Some already don decorations for Christmas while others remain naked. Surely after Thanksgiving, the rest of the neighborhood will hop on the holiday bandwagon. As I approach my house, instead of braking, I step on the gas. The night's still young. One drink at the Crooked Reindeer won't kill me. My old high school friend Simon owns the place, so it will be good to reminisce with some familiar faces. Also, perhaps it's better if I avoid falling asleep with Bric as my last thought.

Brie

The Crooked Reindeer—"the Deer" to the locals, is bustling tonight. But it always is when it's meat raffle night. The town could be under a blizzard warning, and no one would stay home for fear of missing a chance to win ten pounds of bratwurst. The chatter from the crowd overpowers the music playing on the jukebox. Luckily, everyone in town has been too preoccupied with tonight's festivities to gossip about the news of Logan's return. Unfortunately, it's still engrained in my brain.

Sloane snagged us a table before Willa and I got off work, which is the only reason we're not next to the bathrooms. I've known Willa since we were in diapers and eating dirt. Sloane's the adopted local. She didn't grow up in Mount Holly, but she moved here eight years ago and opened up her coffee shop. Instantly, we vibed well together, and she has joined our tight-knit group of friends. Plus, her coffee shop/bakery sells muffins to Willa's diner along with her freshly roasted coffee beans. And I pimp them both equally on the Mount Holly tourism board.

With an elbow on the table, I lean in and offer Sloane and Willa a brief recap of my run-in with Logan earlier today. I reiterated there was no kiss between us before I ramble on about his carnival.

"He has a prime location. Right next to Reindeer Ridge. All he needs to do is flash his dimpled smile and everyone in town will flock across the street. Granted, it's an empty field right now, but there were so many trucks." I tap my chin. "I wonder what he has planned. But being the week of Thanksgiving, he has a lot of work ahead of him to create something out of nothing."

"It's Logan," Willa says. "He'll get it done."

I glare at her. "Whose side are you on?"

"Yours, obviously. But remember senior year? He rallied our entire class in two days to stick googly eyes on everything for the senior prank. The school is probably still being watched by a thousand tiny plastic pupils."

I try not to smile and fail. "The googly eyes on the T-Rex poster in Mr. Schmitt's science class were pretty funny."

Willa giggles. "It was. Which proves when Logan gets an idea, he puts it into action."

Sadly, it wasn't the only time. During the state hockey tournament, he got the entire Mount Holly fan section to hold up a designated sign that spelled out Go Warriors. I hate how he makes all of it seem so effortless.

Sloane sips her drink. "My school banned pranks after

someone set off industrial fart spray. We evacuated. Twice."

"I'll take googly eyes over chemical warfare," Willa says.

"Pranks aside, with how much gossip spreads around here, why didn't anyone tell me Logan was moving back to Mount Holly? Surely someone knew." I glance around the full bar. The Gigis know everything, but they've been tight-lipped about his return.

"I believe I mentioned it." Willa raises a finger.

My gaze shoots to her. "I would remember if you told me Logan Crawford was coming back to town. That's not something one forgets."

"I mentioned Logan Crawford bought a house in town, and you glossed right over it. I assumed you didn't care." Willa shrugs. A second later, her eyes light up. "Oh! There's a good chance it was during margarita night."

"What the hell?" I scrub my hands down my face. The conversation is a blur, but the name Crawford is the only thing I can recall. "I just assumed it was his parents who were moving, not their son. This is why we can't share important information during margarita night."

"I assumed since you didn't dwell on it, you were over it," Willa says.

"You don't get over something like Logan fucking Crawford. What is he doing here, anyway? He could host a carnival anywhere. Why here? Mount Holly's been a much happier place since he's been gone." I point to the window. "See, it's cloudy and gloomy outside all because he's here."

"Um. No, that's weather," Willa says.

"And it's dark outside," Sloane adds. "Why are you so worked up about this?"

My molars grind together as a scream creeps up the

back of my throat. "Because Logan fucking Crawford is back in my little bubble, and he's ruining my happy place."

Sloane's brows pinch together. "Why do you hate this guy so much? Didn't all this happen years ago?"

"*Hate* is mild. I despise him. He makes me all stabby."

"But why?" Sloane crosses her arms, forearms resting on the table.

"I spent my entire life growing up with Logan fucking Crawford—"

"Do we need to refer to him as Logan fucking Crawford every single time?" Willa interrupts.

I shoot my stabby daggers at Willa.

Her hands raise in defense. "Just throwing it out there."

"Since we were kids, he thought his shit didn't stink, and it stunk. A lot. He always had to be the best at everything. Always had to be number one. On the playground, he always had to have the right swing because the left one squeaked, and no one wanted that one. Then, in middle school, he always got the lead part in the Christmas play. Even though everyone tried out, it didn't matter. It would automatically go to him."

"Maybe he was just good." Sloane shrugs.

"Or because he's Logan fucking Crawford, and he gets whatever he wants." I hold up my hand, lifting a finger with each point I make. "Spelling bee champion. Homecoming king. Valedictorian. Which cost me a full-ride college scholarship. Not to forget captain of the hockey team. Guys wanted to be him. All the girls flocked to him. And bile creeps up my throat at the sound of his name."

"That was eighteen years ago. Some people change," Willa says.

"Some people yes. Logan no," I deadpan.

Cara from the Mount Holly Community Club stops at

our table with a stack of tickets in her hand. "Hey ladies! A dollar a ticket. Are you in?"

A collective "yes" comes from all three of us. We exchange our dollars for a numbered white ticket before she moves on to the next table.

Sloane turns her attention back to me. "Maybe you're stuck in the past. He could have changed since then."

"You can't snap your fingers and magically turn into a good guy."

Sloane taps her chin. "I think you're just harboring a lot of deep feelings. Maybe you need to sit down and talk it out with him."

Willa brightens like a Christmas tree. "Oh yes! Lock them in a room together!"

I roll my eyes. "This is how true crime podcasts start."

"Fine," Willa concedes. "We'll lock you in a *nice* room. With snacks."

"Absolutely not." I cross my arms over my chest. I spent my entire life settling for second place. A collection of second-place trophies and silver medals doesn't feel the same. When it comes to the festival, it's first place or bust, and I can't afford a bust.

Willa's phone buzzes on the table. She glances at the screen but ignores the message. "I told him it was raffle night. He'll just have to wait."

"Who's *him*?" I ask.

"Clearly, it's not Mason. Otherwise, she would have answered." Sloane wiggles her brows, and I nod in agreement.

Willa side-eyes us. "If you must know, it was Ryan."

"The foot doctor? You're still dating him?" My nose crinkles.

"Podiatrist. And dating is a… stretch," Willa answers.

"More like seeing each other when we each have a spare minute. It's a mutually convenient agreement."

"Or in more simple terms, fuck buddy," I add.

"I certainly wouldn't *see* him if all he gave me was a minute, either," Sloane quips. I raise my hand, and from next to me, she slaps my palm with hers.

Willa rolls her eyes at us. "The 'doctor' in front of his name keeps my parents' scrutiny at bay. Social events with my family are slightly more bearable with him on my arm." She takes a sip of her drink. "I get fewer questions like when are you getting married? Your little sister has a lot going for her. Why didn't you finish medical school? You can't make a living running a diner."

Willa's parents own the local family medicine clinic. She was destined to follow in the family's medical field footsteps, but her passion to run a diner was greater than the eleven years of schooling and training that was in her future.

Willa takes a sip. "Suffering through the occasional toe fungus and bunion talk over dinner is better than having to answer all the questions from my family. Plus, both of us are way too busy to settle down. So the casual hookup works."

I grin. "Are you convincing us… or you?"

She points at me. "Don't knock it till you try it."

The music dies down as Cara rings a cowbell to get everyone's attention. In unison, the entire bar turns toward her as she stands behind a table in the bar's corner. "Who's ready for the first drawing?" she says into the microphone.

The entire bar erupts in hoots and cheers. All the noise dissipates as Cara spins a numbered wheel on the table. A low rumble fills the room as the needle connects with the pegs, slowing with each passing second until it comes to a stop.

"And the winner is… number eighteen!" Cara shouts.

I glance down at my ticket. Nineteen. Of course, just my luck. It's only one number away.

"I won!" Sloane's chair legs screech across the wood floor as she shoves away from the table and jumps to her feet, waving her ticket above her head. "I won!"

"Woohoo!" With a resounding clap, I celebrate my friend.

The bar booms in unison, "FIRST MEAT!"

It's a tradition that started years ago when George, and his pocket jerky, won his first meat raffle. He rose to his feet and pumped his fist in the air and declared, "first meat." It stuck, and now the entire bar joins in at the first raffle draw.

Sloane weaves through the crowd until she reaches the raffle table. With her meat prize in hand, she returns to her seat. "I got meat sticks!" She waves the package in the air before sitting down.

Cara does another round of tickets before starting the next raffle. With each passing round, my number doesn't get called, but Willa snags two pounds of bacon. Round after round, people win pork chops, jerky, steaks, ground beef, and even a whole chicken. Cara spins the wheel for the next prize as a hush falls over the crowd.

"If it isn't the hockey legend himself," Simon bellows from behind the bar.

My stomach drops like a bad amusement park ride. Before I turn around, a collection of "Hi, Logans" confirm my worst fears. Too bad there isn't another hockey legend in town. Meat raffle night ruined. The cacophony of the bar fades to muffled chatter as if I'm submerged five feet underwater. My gaze tracks Logan as he struts across the room to the bar. Cara's voice sounds over the microphone. Someone a couple tables away jumps to their feet.

"Holy shit!" Sloane backhands my bicep. "Do you know who that is?"

I turn my glare on her. "I know exactly who that is. We've only been talking about him for the past hour."

Her eyes widen. "Wait? Hockey legend Logan Crawford, the hat-trick king of Chicago, is the same Logan Crawford you've been talking about?" She points to Logan across the bar. "Can you introduce me? He's always been my favorite Chicago player."

I frown. "Um. How about not? When did you become such a hockey fan?"

"I had an ex-boyfriend who made me watch all the games with him. At first, I only did it to spend time with him, but I quickly found the appeal."

Cara stops at our table. "Are you in for the next round?"

Sloane and Willa both say yes.

I shake my head. "I think I'm going to head out. The bar suddenly got too crowded."

Willa rests a hand on my forearm. "You can't leave. There are still at least five more rounds."

"I'm getting tired." I cover my mouth with my hand and fake a yawn.

Willa slaps my hand away. "That's a lie. You've never left a meat raffle early, even when you had that terrible chest cold and were on the verge of dying. You want to leave because of Logan. Newsflash. It's Mount Holly. You're going to see a lot more of him. What are you going to do? Leave every time you see him?"

I hate that she's right. This town is too small to avoid each other. He hasn't been here for twenty-four hours, and I've already seen him twice. Granted, the first time was my doing. But either way, he doesn't get to strut into *my* favorite hangout and send me running. I've been here longer than he has. He should be the one to leave. Across the room, as if summoned, his head tips up. Our eyes lock. One beat. Two. Three. I don't blink. He doesn't either. My nostrils flare. The corner of his mouth ticks up into a smile. Of course, he would find this amusing. He always found joy in my misery.

"What are you staring at?" Sloane says to me. Without answering her, she follows my line of sight. "Oh."

"What's happening?" Willa twists, just as Logan rises from his seat. "Yes. Yes. Brie vs. Logan: Showdown, Part Two." She's practically vibrating with excitement.

Fantastic. Exactly how I wanted to end my night: beef, bacon, and a side of public confrontation.

Logan

I ease off the gas as the Crooked Reindeer draws nearer. Every spot in the parking lot is taken. Cars even line both sides of the street. I'm pretty sure all the residents in Mount Holly are here. As I roll past the front entrance, a sign out front reads, "Meat Raffle Tonight. Hosted by the Mount Holly Community Club." The MHCC is a non-profit charity organization that helps raise money for community members in need. Growing up, they helped when the Hendersons lost their house to a fire. When a portion of Mount Holly's high school hockey players needed help with expenses to travel to state for the championships, they donated funds. We might not have won those state championships if we didn't have all our best players.

Red taillights glow as a car pulls out onto the road. I speed forward to claim the spot. If anyone somehow missed the memo that I'm back, they won't after tonight. I turn off the truck and climb out. With each step, the snow crunches under my boots as I hurry toward the door. The wind knifes under my collar, and I hunch my shoulders. With my hands jammed in my coat pockets, I continue trudging toward the Crooked Reindeer.

At the entrance, I stop and peer up. A set of reindeer antlers hang above the door, crooked as its namesake. The legend goes: When Simon's grandfather bought the building, he hung the antlers over the door, and during the night, the right side dropped, so he straightened them out. The next night, they fell again, and the same thing happened. By the fourth night, he said to hell with it, and they've remained crooked ever since.

The cold, metal handle sends a shiver up my arm as I yank it open. I step inside and the noise dips just enough for a familiar voice to carry.

"If it isn't the hockey legend himself!" Simon booms from behind the bar.

Every single person in the bar turns in my direction, and I freeze. The bar erupts into a symphony of *hi* and *hey Logan*. Heat creeps up my neck. I give them all a tight-lipped smile and a small wave. Growing up, I loved the attention. But the last three years rewired me for the quiet.

Simon and I played hockey together from peewee through high school along with Mason, Henry, and Carson. We even managed to win a few state championships together. Over the years, we kept in touch, but not a lot. There were a few times I invited the guys to Chicago to watch a game. Of course, we'd party afterward. They even met Brooke a few times. Simon came out for her funeral. Out of all of us, I was the only one to go on to play professional hockey. A European league drafted Simon, but shortly after his grandfather died, he inherited the connected bar and laundromat. Instead of playing hockey, he took over the bar. He didn't keep the laundromat but instead turned it into a public sauna.

I approach the bar and shoulder into a gap between barstools.

"Someone buy this man a drink." Simon points to me from the other side of the bar.

I laugh. "Just one. I'm not staying long."

"If everyone here is buying you a drink, you aren't driving nowhere. But no worries, we'll get you home." Simon pops the cap off a beer bottle and places it on a cardboard coaster in front of me before rounding the end of the bar. We clasp hands in a handshake that turns into a hybrid hug and back pat. "It's good to see you, man. Word on the street is you're back for good."

"Something like that." We pull away from each other. "How's the bar?" I glance around at the wall-to-wall bodies. "Must be going well, since you have the entire town here."

"Meat raffle night is always popular. The ladies also go wild for purse bingo." Simon runs a hand through his thick black hair. "It's been a long time. How have you been?"

"You know, same old same old. Now I'm retired from hockey, I've found myself with some extra time on my hands, so I thought I would slow down a little and come back to familiar grounds. Get out of the city and away from everything." And hopefully stop feeling like I'm drowning, but he doesn't need to know that.

"What is this I hear about you coming back to town with a twenty-foot Christmas tree?"

I huff out a laugh. "I forgot gossip doesn't take long to spread around here."

"It's not gossip if it's true. So what's with the tree?"

"You know the empty lot across from Reindeer Ridge?"

His brows knit together. "Yeah."

"I bought it. That tree is part of a Christmas carnival I'm organizing."

"And you plan to do that in less than a month?"

"It's been in the works for six. I hired a crew that specializes in pop-up events to help with the execution."

"That definitely helps then." He rests his elbows on the bar and leans in. "You know Brie McKenna is in charge of the Holly Jolly Festival this year, right?"

"I do." I take a swig of my beer. Hearing her name brings back a flood of emotions, especially after my brief encounter with her earlier today. Her soft body pressed against mine. The way her fingers brushed against my chest. I harbored no hateful feelings toward Brie, but she certainly aimed truckloads at me. I never went out of my way to spite her, but also never went out of my way to befriend her either. She had her friends, and I had mine.

"And you ran into Brie."

"I did."

"And you were having sex on the side of the road. I guess that's one way to welcome home the hometown hockey hero."

My lips curve into a smile.

"The way you can't keep that smirk off your face must mean it's true."

I shake my head. "As great as that sounds, it's not even remotely true. More like I saved her from getting flattened by a truck on the side of the road, and afterward, she wanted to throw me in front of said truck."

"That sounds more like the welcome home party Brie would throw for you." Simon grins. "Remember, you're not in the city anymore. People will know everything about you, including what time of day you take a shit. If you don't want people in your business, you're in the wrong town."

It's a love/hate relationship with Mount Holly. Everyone will be sniffing down your neck whether you want them to or not, but at the same time, they are the first ones to rally behind you when you're in trouble. I knew my life would be under a microscope when I returned, but I've known these people all my life. Plus, it's comforting being surrounded by family and close friends again. For now, the pros outweigh the cons. I'll have to adjust to everyone being in my business.

On the TV behind the bar, highlights from last night's Minnesota versus Colorado hockey game play on the screen. Then an idea hits me. Just because I retired from professional hockey, doesn't mean I still can't play. "I'm thinking of putting a little holiday hockey tournament together to go along with my carnival. I'm already building a rink for free skating, might as well use it for a friendly tournament, maybe for charity."

"Nothing says Christmas like a little hockey."

"What do you say? Get the team back together."

Simon laughs. "It's probably been about ten years since I've laced up, but I'm in."

"Who else is in town? Henry. Mason. Carson."

"I'm sure it won't take much convincing."

A brunette with shoulder-length hair stops in front of me. The nametag on her shirt reads Cara. "Raffle ticket? They're only a dollar."

I glance from her to the stack of white tickets in her hand. "Sure. Why not?" I dig into my pocket and pull out a dollar bill. Her fingertips graze my palm as she deposits the ticket in my hand.

"Good luck." She winks before sashaying to the next customer.

Simon snorts. "Clearly, you won't have any issues making friends."

I claim an empty stool and face him. "Too bad I'm not here to make any friends."

"With the way Brie is trying to light you on fire with her heated glare, I'd say you're doing a pretty good job at that." He tilts his chin toward the far side of the bar.

I swivel around, and sure enough, Willa's on one side, a woman with auburn hair is on the other, and Brie is in the middle, glaring daggers at me. We lock eyes. A static hums between us. I might as well introduce myself. Rising from my stool, I grab my beer and stroll across the bar.

"Hey ladies." I stop at their pub-height table. "Couldn't help but notice you all were staring. So I thought I'd come over here and say hi."

Willa jumps up from her seat and wraps her arms around my neck in a hug. "It's good to see you, Logan." She lowers her tone. "Sorry to hear about your wife."

My arm around her waist stiffens, and I press my lips together. "Thanks." She pulls away. Her eyes are soft. I guess I'd better get used to the condolences from those I haven't seen in years.

The auburn-haired woman smacks Brie's bicep and stage-whispers, "Why didn't you tell me he's prettier in person?"

I bite back my laugh. "Thank you." I offer her my hand. She reaches across the table and grips it in a firm but gentle handshake.

"Hi. I'm Sloane. I own the hybrid coffee shop and bakery, Sip and Sleigh, in town. It's so nice to meet you.

I'm a huge fan. Stop by and you can have whatever you'd like on me. Not *on me*, but my treat. Unless you're into that kind of thing." Pink washes over her cheeks.

I laugh. "I understand what you meant. And thanks again." I release her hand and peer down at Brie. A moment ago she was watching me like a hawk. Now she's studying her drink like it's a science experiment. I return my attention to Sloane. "It's always great to meet a fan."

Glancing down at Brie again, I hold up my arms. "No hug?"

Finally, she peers up at me. Her bronze eyes darken to espresso as the soft, gold flecks from our earlier run-in are now sharp as broken glass. The soft curve of her brows draw together, creating a small furrow that somehow makes her even more beautiful. "I was already close enough to you once today."

The corner of my mouth curves upward. "That's right. You did have your arms wrapped around me earlier. If I remember correctly, you were reluctant to let go."

"Perhaps you need to get your memory checked." Her fingers curl into a fist on the table. "Now, I wish the truck had actually hit me," she mutters under her breath.

A small chuckle escapes me. The Ice Queen doing what she does best. She's gained more sass since high school. "I guess I should get going." I nod to Sloane. "It was nice to meet you. I'll be sure to stop by the coffee shop. Willa, it was nice to see you again."

"You too," Willa replies.

"Brie, it was good to see you as well." She lifts her brows in acknowledgment but doesn't say a word. "I'm sure we'll see each other again."

From the corner of the bar, Cara's voice comes over the microphone. "The winner is… number ten!"

I glance down at the white ticket in my hand. "Huh. Look at that, I won."

Willa and Sloane cheer while Brie drops her gaze back to the condensation on her glass. If she wants to play childish games, I have an eleven-year-old who's taught me the best. I stroll to the front, collect my package of steaks, and return to my spot at the bar. If day one back in Mount Holly has been this exciting, I'm looking forward to what the days leading up to Christmas will bring.

Brie

I stir awake and crack an eyelid. A sliver of blinding sunlight cuts through a narrow gap in the curtains. I groan and bury my face in the pillow. Sleep evaded me for most of the night. I was hoping the bottomless cocktails Willa and Sloane fed me after my second encounter with Logan would make me forget yesterday ever happened. Unfortunately, all it provided was a throbbing in my temples reminding me that yesterday happened, and Logan's back in town.

Since he was pretty adamant about the carnival, my chances of convincing him to leave Mount Holly altogether are slim. Avoiding him is not an option unless I lock myself in my house and never leave. Sadly, Mount

Holly is sorely lacking when it comes to keeping up with grocery delivery trends. Pretending Logan doesn't exist might be my only option, at least until after the holidays. The festival needs my full attention. Logan's only a distraction. Also, when did he get so attractive? If I threw a piece of duct tape over his mouth to keep him from talking, I could probably—nope. Abort. A flush creeps up my neck, prickling my skin with shame. What the hell is wrong with me? It's been way too long since I've had sex.

After a quick shower and mascara that promises to "conquer the world," I stroll into Sip and Sleigh. The fresh aroma of coffee beans and pastries already brighten my day. I queue behind an older couple and scroll my favorite Christmas blog. Emma St. Claire always offers the best tips and tricks for decorating for the holidays. She even travels to various Christmas festivals around the world. A vibrant warmth blossoms in my chest with each new pin on the map, charting her adventures. Her travels have included Vienna, France, Germany, and Toronto. She's even blogged about Oglebay's Winter Festival of Lights in Wheeling, West Virginia. Along with the blog, she also publishes a yearly magazine, *Home for the Holidays*. The magazine has a Best Hometown Christmas contest where Emma travels to the top three choices to pick the winner herself. Each year, I apply, describing the tradition and excitement of the Holly Jolly Festival, and every year I get the same thank-you-but-not-this-year response.

"Good morning, sunshine," Sloane greets me. It's nice to see you're alive and well. Your usual?"

"For good measure, make it a double."

"You got it."

As Sloane goes about making my drink order, I claim a small table near the window. I shrug out of my coat and set it over the back of the chair. I return to the counter just as she sets down my latte. Even though it's piping hot, I take a small sip anyway. The caramel, milk, and espresso dance over my tastebuds. "Instantly, my day is already better." I grip the cup with both hands and take another sip. "Have I told you I'm taking the high road regarding Logan? I can't do anything about him being here or his carnival, so I'm going to ignore him."

"That's great, but I'll warn you, maybe it's best you not be here right now."

"Why? Coming here every morning is my routine. Are you trying to ruin my routine?"

"No, but—"

"I bet it has something to do with me."

My stomach sours at the sound of *his* voice. Where's the duct tape when a girl needs it? He may be ruining my Christmas, but he will not fuck with my morning routine. I square my shoulders and spin around, ready to face my problem. Instead, my hand smacks against his bicep, sending my cup soaring through the air. The latte arcs like a caffeinated comet and splashes across the floor.

Logan drops his gaze to the mess and deadpans, "You spilled your coffee."

I glare at him. Which has become my permanent expression whenever he's nearby. Fuck nice. He doesn't deserve nice. He deserves a punch in the jugular. I'm not a violent person, but Logan certainly knows how to bring that to the surface. "I wanted to be nice—"

He huffs out a laugh. "Yeah, you've been very welcoming since I came to town."

"Um. Brie?" Sloane calls.

Without turning around, I hold up a finger. "Not now, Sloane."

"No, really—"

"It'll have to wait. I need to give Logan a piece of my mind."

"Fine. Do it while you clean up the mess before someone slips and falls." She slides a stack of napkins across the counter.

I snag them, but Logan plucks the napkins from my hands like a thief. "Hey! Those are mine." Heat pricks my cheeks.

"I'm not trying to steal your napkins. I'm just helping clean up the mess." With a frustrated huff, he squats and tosses a couple of the napkins onto the floor. The once-white napkins deepen to a brown hue as they soak up the liquid.

"I don't need your help." I reach for the napkins, but he puts them in his other hand and stretches it out of reach. "You are such a five-year-old."

With each passing second, the crowd in Sip and Sleigh grows more interested in our interaction like a live-stream fight night. I'm waiting for them to take bets.

"Thankfully, I have plenty of napkins for the both of you." I turn around, and Sloane tosses a stack of napkins over the counter that rain down on us like confetti. "Now you can both clean it up."

With a stack of napkins in hand, I crouch and blot furiously. "Pack up your carnival yet?"

"Nope." He continues to dab at the coffee spill.

"Mount Holly isn't big enough for two festivals."

"Yours is a festival and mine is a carnival. Two different things."

"It's a moot point. They both serve the same purpose —to entertain the townsfolk of Mount Holly. As the future head coordinator of the Holly Jolly Festival, I need this year to be the best festival anyone in Mount Holly has ever seen, and there can't be another festival ten minutes away."

He pauses, looks at me, and arches a brow. "What you're saying is you're afraid of a little competition."

"I am *not* afraid."

"Sounds like you're scared."

"I'm not scared of you."

"I think you are. Otherwise, you wouldn't be pushing so hard."

I inhale a sharp breath, my nostrils flaring. "You know what? Fine." I jump to my feet, and Logan does the same. "You continue with your little carnival, but I will give this town a Christmas festival they'll never forget."

"That's the spirit." He reaches up and plucks something off my shoulder. "Also… I believe these are yours."

My cheeks blaze the same exact shade of red as the cotton panties with lace side embellishments he's dangling in front of me. "So you've come here to steal not only the attention away from my festival but also my underwear." I rip them from his grasp and ball them into my fist.

The sexy dimple on his left cheek plays peek-a-boo. "No, I'm trying to help you so the rest of Mount Holly doesn't also see your underwear. You're welcome. I never expected someone as icy as you would wear something with lace. You seem like you'd take comfort over sexy."

"I'll have you know they're both stylish *and* comfortable." Fantastic. This morning's bingo card didn't include "discuss my panties with Logan Crawford." And yet the heat in his gaze says he'll be thinking about them— and, ugh, me—for the rest of the day. Do not picture what he'd do while thinking about them. Do not—

He slowly lifts his chin until his gaze drifts over my shoulder and points to the display case. "I'll have one of those red velvet cupcakes too. Suddenly, it's my new favorite color." He glances down at me and winks before sauntering to the counter.

All the words fail me. I shove the underwear into my pocket like this is my normal life and not a waking fever dream. A quarter of the town has now seen my underwear and by noon, the other three-quarters will have heard about my underwear. I'm rooted in place. What the fuck just happened? What was his comment about red being his favorite color and the wink? Or the dimpled smirk. My thighs press together without permission. The picture is permanently etched in my brain. Son of a bitch. I spent all of last night rehashing my confrontation with him on the side of the road. Now I have this encounter. Suddenly, my head and vagina are at war with each other. There can only be one winner. And it can't be the latter.

"Add another of whatever Brie's drinking to my tab," he tells Sloane. "She looks like she needs it. Also, can I hang a poster for my carnival?"

My ears perk up. Posters. Already? Yesterday, he had an empty field. How in the hell did he get posters made?

"Yeah, of course. There's a bulletin board by the front door. There should be some tacks over there as well."

"Thanks, Sloane." He grabs his coffee, the to-go bag and turns. "Good to see you again, Brie."

"I hope Santa brings you everything you deserve." I plaster a fake smile on my face.

He chuckles before brushing past me. Goosebumps sprint up my arm as his captivating, clean, manly scent wafts past me. He crouches at the bulletin board to set his coffee and bag on the floor. My traitorous gaze drops and lingers on the way his tight jeans perfectly mold to his ass and cling to his muscular thighs.

"Ahem." Sloane's cough snaps my eyes back where they belong.

A cold dread washes over me. I've been caught. A beaming smile covers her face. Instead of confessing my sins, I divert. "Why didn't you tell me about the underwear clinging to my sweater?"

"I believe I tried, but someone shushed me."

…Right. That happened.

"You know the entire town is going to know about their breakfast and a show in about five seconds." She nods to a group of Gigis ten feet away already vibrating with the thrill of public underthings.

My shoulders slump. "Yep, they sure will. Also—his poster?" I raise my brows.

She rests her hands on the counter. "Oh no, you don't get to be mad at me. This is business. I'm a business owner supporting another business. You're more than welcome to put yours next to his."

"You know what? I will do exactly that."

She holds out my coffee for me. "A gift. From Logan."

My lips curl as I glare at the cup in her hand. I hate the idea of taking it, but it's coffee that I desperately need right now. At least he didn't make it, so I know it's not poisoned.

After grabbing my breakfast sandwich from the Jolly Biscuit, I head to the town hall. Since I'm already behind on marketing, I spend the afternoon designing posters for the Holly Jolly Festival. Sadly, each design is worse than the last. By the end of the day, I was over it and added "hire a graphic designer" to my to-do list along with adjusting the budget to pay for said graphic designer. I'm better at planning events than creating marketing materials for them. In years past, we never had to do much print advertising, mostly because we were the only festival in town. Once again, Logan's return not only ruins my day but also throws my festival budget off kilter.

The next morning, I one-boot hop through the entryway, wrestling my peacoat and cursing the treacherous alliance between the Snooze and Off buttons. Someone really needs to rethink that design flaw. Now, if I want coffee *and* a breakfast sandwich, I'm going to be late-late. I yank open the door mid-button and kick something with a papery thwack. A red gift bag sits on my "Merry AF" mat, dusted with snow. My brows pinch together as I bend down and pick it up. I follow the large boot prints that trail off down the sidewalk. I glance up and down the street but it's empty. Cautiously, I peel back the white tissue paper and peek inside. I roll my eyes, but bite back my smile. Reaching in the bag, I pull out a reddish orange box. Dryer sheets. Taped to the top is a note with short, straight-line handwriting.

Thought these would come in handy.

I shove the box back into the bag and curl my fingers around the handle. Instantly, my mind goes to Logan. This has his name written all over it. As much as I want to be annoyed if it was him, it's oddly kind of sweet, and I hate I enjoy he was thinking about me.

Brie

This is my favorite weekend of the year, and after the week I had, I need it. Desperately. The Saturday after Thanksgiving is my day to start prepping for Christmas—I'll be hand selecting the perfect tree that will spread Christmas joy up until the New Year. I meander down row after row of pines on my quest for the perfect tree. Not too big, not too small, not too bushy, but not bare.

There's an art to this. Step one: freshness test—no mass needle loss, no brittle limbs, no flimsy "I gave up in July" vibes. Fresh trees will have flexible boughs and an abundance of crisp needles. I've spent years perfecting my tree-picking abilities, and every year, it pays off. I run my fingertips over the dark-green needles and shake my head.

Sorry, tree, you're staying here. Step two: sturdiness test—no bowed or crooked bases. I crouch down and peek underneath at the trunk. Slight lean to the left. That won't do. Rising, I move on to the next row, which features Canaan firs. They're rich in color with full branches that are great for displaying ornaments. But it's not my favorite tree, so I move on to the next row and inhale the woody scent of a balsam fir. The scent of Christmas fills the air. While an acceptable tree, the needle retention makes me twitchy, so I move on to the next. I run my hand over the soft, dark-green needles. Now this is Christmas tree perfection. The classic conical shape with compact upward-sloping branches makes for excellent support for all types of ornaments. Be still my tinsel heart. I continue to stroll around the Fraser fir. Step three: scent test—I inhale the crisp, woody pine fragrance as I inspect every branch to make sure it's flawless. Suddenly, a familiar voice piques my interest. Glancing up, Logan's wearing a red and white Santa hat while the little girl, who must be his daughter, is wearing a reindeer headband.

She runs past to a tree a few feet in front of me. "Daddy! Daddy! Let's get this one!"

That confirms my suspicion. Slinking back, I hide behind the dense branches of the Fraser fir. Between the needles, I fix my gaze on Logan as his head drops to the base and lifts up, and up, and up. It's almost twice his six-foot height.

"I don't think that one's going to fit in our living room. Let's keep looking." Logan rests his hand on his daughter's shoulders and guides her to a row of much shorter trees.

Spying on Logan is like gawking at a terrible car wreck. It's intrusive to stare but impossible to look away. I finally get to see him as Logan, single dad, and not Logan who annoys the hell out of me. Consider it research. Plus, hiding saves me from any potential unpleasant interaction, especially when he's with his daughter.

As they stroll from tree to tree, I ping-pong along, seeking refuge behind the needles of a white pine.

"Daddy, what about this one?" She points to a Canaan fir.

"Good choice," I whisper to myself.

"I don't know. Do you think you'll be able to put the star on top?" he asks.

"Yes!"

"Let's see." Logan picks up his daughter and hoists her above his shoulders. She pretends to place a fake star on top of the tree. "I think that one's going to be perfect."

"Me too!" She exclaims.

A tiny sliver of my Logan hate… thaws. Ugh.

He glances over his shoulder—toward *my* white pine and I duck. Unfortunately, the tree doesn't offer as much coverage as I'd like. Holding my breath, I send a prayer to the Christmas Gods he doesn't catch me spying on him.

"Hey Brie! I figured I'd see you here."

Willa. Shit. I pinch my eyes shut. My cover is blown. I whirl around and promptly hook my right foot behind my left, throwing off my balance. My arms windmill, but it's useless. Like a lumberjack chopping down a tree, I topple over. Willa lunges to help, but instead of saving me from falling, I grab her jacket sleeve and take her down with me in a tangle of limbs. I take the brunt of the fall. That's a lie —a white pine took the brunt while I came in a close second. Like dominoes, the entire row of trees crashes onto the snow. Willa cackles while heat flames up my neck.

Mason rushes to Willa's side. A rumble of laughter escapes his throat. "I can't take you anywhere." He stretches his hand out to her and hoists her to her feet.

"Not my fault," she retorts.

The sunlight disappears as a dark cloud passes above me. My gaze drifts up. Not a cloud—Logan. The corner of his lips tip up into a smile, causing his signature sexy dimple to peek through. He stretches his hand down to me, and I stare at it as if it's a venomous snake. I lift my hand to swat it away, but from the corner of my eye, I catch sight of his daughter, eyes glued to us, and I think better of it.

"I don't bite." His voice is low, almost seductive.

A montage of Logan's hands roaming my body, nipping at my heated skin, biting—nope. Not today brain. Instead, I reach up, placing my hand in his. As soon as my skin connects with his, an unfamiliar feeling races through my body. It's warm, almost comforting. Before I can think too much into it, he effortlessly hoists me to my feet.

"Are you okay?" The words are soft as they tumble off his lips. His fingers still wrap around my hand, our bodies inches from touching.

Physically, yes. Mentally, hell no. "Yeah. I think so," I squeak out. His gaze skims down my body, and I'm not sure if he's searching for wounds or checking me out, but as his lips part, I'm leaning toward the latter.

He brushes a hand down my arm and stalls at my hip. "I'll, uh… let you get that."

Glancing down, a smattering of snow and dirt cover my thigh and around to my butt. Why does a part of me wish he had brushed it off himself?

I wipe it off. "Thank you," I mumble.

He leans in a fraction, giving me a front row view of his dimple. "What was that?"

"Thank you," I grit through a fake smile.

"You're welcome." He steps back, and the air loosens its grip on my lungs.

"I guess the rumors are true," Mason says to Logan.

Ice slides into my stomach. What rumors? What has he

heard? My underwear? The coffee incident? Has Willa said anything to him?

Mason releases Willa and covers the distance to Logan in two easy strides. "It's good to see you again. I thought the rumor mill was drunk, but here you are. Nice hat." He flicks the pom on Logan's Santa hat.

Logan laughs. "It gets me into the holiday spirit."

The little girl from earlier barrels over and tugs his hand. "Daddy! I found the perfect tree!"

Logan wraps his arm around her shoulder and tugs her to his side. "And this one picked it out for me."

Willa crouches down. "And who is this cutie?"

"I'm Josie. This is my dad." She points to Logan.

"Hi Josie. I'm Willa."

Logan gestures between us. "These are my friends: Willa, Mason, and Brie. This is my daughter, Josie."

Friends is generous, but I let it slide. I squat beside Willa. "Josie, do you like candy canes?"

She bobs her head up and down. "Yes."

"Would you like one?" I pull a red and white striped candy cane from my pocket and hold it out to her. Surprisingly, it's still in one piece.

She glances up at Logan for a brief second, and then her hazel eyes, a spitting image of Logan's, meet mine. "My daddy says I can't take candy from strangers."

We all chuckle.

"Finally, something I tell her sticks," Logan says with a chuckle. "It's okay. You can take it."

Josie snatches the candy cane from my hands. "Thank you."

"You're welcome," I reply.

She peels the wrapper and pops the end in her mouth. "Daddy, can I look at the trees over there?" She points to a cluster of white pines.

"Yeah, but stay where I can see you," Logan says.

"Okay." She skips to a tall, full white pine.

"You have an adorable daughter," Willa says.

"Thanks. She gets everything from her mother."

"Except she has your eyes." Shit. Heat flames over my cheeks. I didn't mean to say that out loud.

Logan's gaze hooks mine; his mouth almost—*almost*—tips into a smile before he turns to Mason. "I hear you're a firefighter."

"Yep, protecting the fine folks of Mount Holly. He wraps an arm around Willa. "Especially this one."

While they talk, Logan flicks glances over Mason's shoulder to make sure he can still see Josie. My ovaries wave balloons and shoot off party poppers, wanting to invite the single dad standing in front of me to the party. Traitorous ovaries.

Willa lifts a finger. "That was only one time."

"Twice actually." Mason chuckles.

She winces. "Right. The flambé incident. But you were already at the diner, so I didn't *call* you."

"If I hadn't been there," he says, "the Jolly Biscuit might be a crispy biscuit."

"You're insufferable." Willa shakes her head but laughs.

"Are you free sometime this week?" Logan asks Mason. "I'm working on a few things and thought you might be interested in participating."

"Yeah. Call me," Mason says.

While Logan and Mason continue to talk, Willa nudges me with her elbow and whispers, "Did you thank him for your present?"

"No," I mouth. I regret telling Willa about the dryer sheets. Since yesterday, she's been hounding me about the meaning behind giving someone dryer sheets. I told her there is no meaning. They're dryer sheets, but she insisted you don't give just anyone dryer sheets. He was thinking of me or my underwear and brought them to my house. I reiterated Logan is cocky and probably did it for his own amusement. "There's no reason to—"

Willa blurts out, "Brie says thank you for the dryer sheets!"

Logan turns around, brows raised in amusement. "You're welcome."

I give him a tight-lipped smile with a shrug. "I'm static-free today."

"Glad to hear," he says.

Henry races over, hands raised in disbelief. A dark gray trapper cap with light tan, wool ear flaps sits on his head. It's kind of ridiculous but oddly fitting for Henry. It matches his black and gray flannel jacket, so he'd be stylish if he were to model for the *Great Northwoods* magazine.

"What the he—heck happened here?" Henry sensors himself when he spots Josie. His gaze follows the line of destruction.

"The trees wanted to play dominoes," I say, aiming for adorable and landing somewhere near guilty golden retriever.

Logan leans down and whispers, "While you were secretly spying on me."

I glare at him. Unfortunately, it's true. My gaze meets Henry's. "I'm so sorry. It was an accident. I lost my balance and took the trees and Willa with me. I'll help you pick them up. And if there are any damaged ones, I'll pay for them."

After we right the fallen trees, Josie leads Logan, followed by Henry, down the pathway to show them the perfect tree she found. Logan chases after her, and Josie's squeals of laughter fill the air. When she's within arm's reach, he scoops her up, a beaming smile covering his face.

Willa bumps my arm. "You're staring."

"No, I'm not. I'm—I'm assessing needle retention on that balsam fir to determine if it'll last until Christmas."

Willa mock coughs into her hand. "Liar."

Slowly, I turn toward her and glare. All she does is smirk. "We'll chat later." She waves as she saunters off with Mason to pay for her tree.

I'm now the proud new owner of three additional Christmas trees. Luckily, my SUV has plenty of roof rack storage, so transporting them wasn't difficult. Unloading them was a different story. If it were nighttime, I'm sure Vana, the county sheriff, would be knocking on my door, questioning me about the body bags my neighbors told her I was dragging through my front door. While I love Christmas and I'm enthusiastic about every aspect of the holiday, I never imagined I'd be the person with four trees in their house, but there's a first for everything. Maybe this will be the start of a new tradition. The silver lining: my home now smells like a high-end pine candle. After scouring through bin after bin of all my Christmas decorations, I find two extra stands, but I'll have to purchase a fourth one. In the meantime, I fill a five-gallon bucket with water and prop the tree against the wall in my spare room until I can place it in its proper home. In the kitchen, I fit the smallest tree. Another is set up in my bedroom, and the crème de la crème of trees is front and center of the picture window in the living room for all passersby to enjoy.

Unlocking my phone, I cue up my Christmas playlist. "Last Christmas" by Wham! floats through the air. I sashay from one side of the room to the other as I meticulously place boxes of ornaments by color on the floor. Every year,

I switch up the decorations. I've done scattered, random colors everywhere, and even candy cane stripes, but this year I want to try an ombre effect. Lifting a box of light pink ornaments off the floor, I hold them up to the tree. As I twirl to the opposite side, I contemplate whether I want to go light to dark or dark to light. With the box still in the air, I rest a hand on my hip. The smooth, rich voice of Dean Martin as he croons "Silver Bells" flows through the speaker, and I become one with the tree, letting the holiday music lead my way. As soon as he hits the chorus, I nod. "Yes. The perfect ombre effect with the dark ornaments starting at the bottom. Thanks, Dean. You always have the answer." I set forth to make my Pinterest-worthy Christmas tree.

When I finish the bottom half of the tree, I step back and admire my handiwork. All the pieces are falling together perfectly. The tree anyway. Everything else in my life is a clüsterfünke. Mariah Carey slides in with "All I Want for Christmas Is You," and like a traitor, all my thoughts drift to Logan and seeing him today. It's hard to deny that single dad Logan is hot. I pinch my eyes shut and scold myself for using "Logan" and "hot" in the same sentence, but it's true. Warmth skates up my spine. His daughter is adorable, though. The way he was so gentle and patient with her shows me he's not an asshole all the time, only to me.

Maybe Sloane and Willa were right, and I'm judging him too harshly. Maybe deep down, buried in the bowels of his soul, he has an ounce of friendliness in him. Or it was all for show because his daughter was there. That seems like the most logical answer. Either way, I need to stay focused on the Holly Jolly Festival and beating Logan's carnival and not on how I want to see him wearing nothing but the Santa hat.

Logan

For two straight days, sunrise to well past sunset, minus the couple of hours I went tree shopping with Josie today, I've been at the carnival. The original plan was a two-week run up to Christmas—finish on the twenty-fifth with skating, roasting marshmallows by the fire pits, and families spending the day together. It's what Brooke always wanted. Unfortunately, I underestimated what all goes into organizing a carnival, and the two weeks of holiday fun is now cut to one.

If there's a silver lining, work has been a good distraction from thinking about Brie and why she was secretly watching me at Reindeer Ridge. The way my body sparked to life when I pulled her up… yeah. Not helpful.

"What should we start with?" Josie's voice pulls me from my thoughts. She has been hounding me to decorate the tree since we picked it up, so I promised her we'd spend the afternoon fully immersed in decorations.

"Blue ornaments." I cue up a YouTube fireplace, playing a soft Christmas melody because our new place lacks the real thing. Ten out of ten for the ambiance. Zero on the heat, or lack thereof.

She pops the flaps on a box and hands me a blue and silver swirled ornament.

I hold it up in the air. "Where should this one go?"

Josie taps her chin as she contemplates the perfect spot. It's something her mom would always do. She would meticulously place every ornament in the best spot for optimal viewing pleasure.

"How about there?" She points to a spot on the top right side of the tree.

"Perfect." I secure the ornament to the end of the branch. We fall into a rhythm of passing and placing ornaments on the tree.

At the bottom of the next box, she pulls out one last ornament. A frosted white star edged in gold. "We have one more."

All the air is sucked from my lungs. I've avoided hanging that ornament on the tree for the past two Christmases, and I actually forgot about it, until now. "That was your mom's favorite," I say, my voice rough. "She said it reminded her of you— her brightest star." Every year, Brooke would buy a new ornament for Josie. The instant she saw the star, she knew it was perfect and refused to continue looking. "Where should we hang it?"

She holds up the ornament, tapping her finger against her lips. "I think it should go up there." She points toward the top of the six-foot tree.

"Alright, you're the boss." I hoist her up, and she slides the hook over one branch until it dangles in place. It's the exact same spot where her mom liked to hang it as well.

Once we're finished, we place the empty ornament boxes back in the plastic bins until it's time to take the tree down.

"I'm going to FaceTime Grandma so I can show her the tree!" Josie dashes out of the room, up the stairs, and toward her bedroom.

My gaze wanders over the tree. Brooke would be proud. God, I wish she could see it. Another year, and it still doesn't get easier.

Josie returns to the living room with her tablet in front of her. "See Grandma? This is the tree." She turns the screen around. "It's pretty."

"It's so beautiful," my mom says.

While they chat, I slip upstairs. When I reach my bedroom, I sit on the edge of the bed, resting my elbows on my knees and comb my fingers through my hair. They say time heals all wounds, but it's been three years, and my wounds are still gaping open. I thought moving from the house we shared and closer to my family would help, but so far, nothing. The grief counselor I saw after Brooke passed away told me everyone heals at their own pace. There's no set time limit, but right now I wish there was and that I'm nearing the end.

Sitting up, I slide open the nightstand drawer and pull out a picture of Brooke. I run my fingers over the smooth glass covering her bright, warm smile. I took the picture four years ago, right after Josie's seventh birthday party. We finished cleaning up, and Josie went to a friend's house for a sleepover, so we had the night to ourselves. I started a fire in the fire pit on the patio just as the sun dipped below the horizon. She had a glass of red wine in her hand. The reflection of the firelight across her face was the most beautiful thing I ever saw. It made her glow, so I snapped a picture. Something I did often. I joked that she never looked at me the way she does at a glass of wine. She said the wine is a quick burst of happiness, but I was her forever.

Moisture burns my eyes. Now, they're only memories. There'll never be a new picture. Not after that late summer day when meningococcal meningitis took her away from us. She fought hard, though. Just like everything she did, she gave two hundred percent.

"Daddy!"

I flinch and catch the picture frame before it crashes to the floor. Quickly, I shove it in the nightstand drawer and slam it closed.

"Yeah." I rub away the moisture in my eyes.

Josie hovers in the doorway, pink tablet clutched to her chest. "Grandma says I can come over and watch movies." She turns her tablet around, and my mom's face fills the screen.

"Yeah, okay." A night to myself will give me time alone to wallow in self-pity. "Pack a bag and I'll drop you off."

Josie turns the tablet around. "Yay! I'll be over soon, Grandma."

"Okay sweetheart. See you soon." My mom's voice sounds through the speakers.

She runs over to me, tosses her tablet on my bed, and wraps her arms around me. "Thank you."

"Of course, Peanut."

Josie pushes off me and scampers down the hallway. With my elbows on my knees, I scrub my palms over my face, trying to stitch my thoughts together. A big reason we moved to Mount Holly was so my parents could help me raise Josie. I tried to do it on my own for three years. Mostly because I was stubborn and didn't want the help or to burden anyone else. I thought I had something to prove. That I could do this on my own. Needing help doesn't make me a terrible father. In fact, asking for help was the best thing for Josie. She was grieving just as much as I was, so the support was not only for me, but for her as well. Plus, Brooke always dreamed of creating a big Christmas carnival. It wasn't my thing, but she loved it. And I loved her. It never fully developed because she got sick. So I want to do it for her. To make her dream come true.

I thought I was doing better at letting go of Brooke. Even my therapist said I was making great strides. I don't have to forget her, but I need to move on. I did that for a while, mostly because I had hockey to occupy my time. But retiring and moving back to Mount Holly to put this carnival together is opening old wounds. I just need a night. I'll be back to my normal self tomorrow.

A few minutes later, Josie barrels into my bedroom with a backpack slung over her shoulder. "I'm ready!"

"I think you're the fastest packer I know."

She latches onto my hand and tugs. "Hurry. I want to watch as many movies as I can before bedtime."

"Alright. I'm coming."

After dropping Josie off at my mom and John's, I drive back toward my house. But two blocks down the road, I think better of it and turn around in the next driveway to head in the opposite direction toward the Crooked Reindeer. Maybe it's best I'm around other people for a bit. It has to be better than sitting alone in misery.

Inside, the bar's relatively quiet. A few regulars all wave and say hello to me. At the far end of the bar, I claim a seat on an empty stool, hoping to have a little time to myself. Simon gives me a chin nod as he finishes with a customer.

A few seconds later, he greets me. "Hey, man. Want a spiked eggnog or Tom and Jerry?"

I grimace at my options.

He laughs. "Too festive for you? How about a beer?"

I eye the taps but know they won't cut it. "Give me a scotch on the rocks." Simon's brows raise. "Make it a double."

"Well, that's not a casual drink for six o'clock at night."

"It's been a day. And it's still not over."

Simon plants his hands on the bar and leans in. "Anything you want to talk about?"

"Not especially."

"Alright. Well just know I'm here if you need anything."

"Just make sure my glass isn't empty."

"Got it." He raps his knuckles against the bar as he pushes off and pours my drink. Once he's finished, he slides the lowball of scotch in front of me.

The first sip burns clean—like it might cauterize whatever's fraying inside. This carnival was a dumb idea. I don't know what the hell I'm doing. If I didn't have a crew of guys to help me get everything set up, I'd still be sitting in an empty field. This was Brooke's passion. Not mine. God, I miss her. Her smile. The way she wouldn't let me get away with anything. I wish I could have done something. I wish I had tried harder to convince her to go to the doctor sooner. Maybe she'd still be here. I just never expected it to happen so fast. In the blink of an eye, she was gone.

True to his word, Simon keeps the refills coming. Two rounds in, my glass never hits empty. I roll the glass on the round base, staring as the amber liquid swirls around. I came to Mount Holly for a change. Maybe I'll do something about it.

"Screw it," I say, rolling the glass between my palms. "Buy the bar a round on me. We're celebrating." I throw back the last drop of my drink and swallow it down.

The bar erupts in cheers.

Simon chuckles. "Celebrating what?"

"New beginnings." I push my empty glass toward him.

He pours three fingers of scotch into my glass before pouring himself water. He holds up his glass. "To new beginnings."

We tap our drinks on the bar top before I take a sip. Over the next hour, people send drinks back my way in thanks—beer here, a shot there. Now I'm anchored to the stool with my elbows propped on the bar, pretending it's the floor swaying and not me.

Her sweet laughter fills the bar before I see her. Slowly, I glance over my shoulder. With one eye closed, the silhouettes of Brie, Willa, and Sloane manifest as they stroll through the door. I track them as they land at a high-top table on the opposite side of the bar. As she sits, her gaze lifts in my direction. Our eyes meet. A tingle races through me. She looks away first—not away, but just past me, and the corner of her lips lift into a smile.

"If you crane your neck any farther, you're going to fall off that stool,"

Busted. So much for being discreet. I spin around, and Simon lifts his brows, a wide grin on his face.

Wait? Was she checking out Simon? No, that's not possible. Well, it is possible, but she's not his type. At least, not the type he liked in high school. He was more into leggy redheads, much like Sloane. I shove the thought of Simon and Brie together out of my head.

"You know what surprises me the most?" I take a sip of my scotch.

"What's that?"

"When did Brie become such a firecracker?" She's someone you can't forget, but somehow, I forgot her.

"You left," he says, chuckling. "She didn't. But she always had a little sass."

"Yeah, she certainly does like to sass me."

"The older we get, the less we care what other people think of us. We just do our thing."

"Was I a jerk to her in high school?"

He shrugs. "Shit. I don't know. Maybe a little. You mostly ignored her. Does it matter now? If you really want an answer, you could always ask her."

"She's better at giving me death glares than dialogue. I'm pretty sure she's hoping I spontaneously combust or something."

"She'd be first in line with marshmallows, passing out roasting sticks."

"Thanks for the vote of confidence." She hated me first, so it was only natural for me to hate her back. Then why do we always find ourselves running into each other? Sure, Mount Holly is small, but the next town isn't too far away. She could go to the bar there. The bar run-ins aside, the real question is why does my dick twitch every time she's near? And why do I want to feel her soft, pillowy lips against mine? Does she taste as sweet as she smells? Why can't I stop picturing what she looks like wearing that red lace underwear? Most importantly, why do I want to rip them off her body with my teeth? Some things are just unexplainable. Like Bigfoot. Damn. I hope she's not hairy like Bigfoot. I spare a glance her way again. Nah. Her skin looks silky smooth. No excess hair in sight. Her lips curve into a smile as she laughs at something Willa says. Images of her pink lips wrapped around the head of my dick flash before me. Fuck. I peel my gaze away. If I can't stop thinking about her on my own, I'll drink her out of my system. Said no one ever.

"Simon?" I tap the bar lightly. "Give me another."

Brie

Willa called for a girls' night, so we met at the Deer. After my embarrassing encounter with Logan, I could use a drink. Or two. Or five.

As we step inside, I'm giving Sloane the highlight reel—how I accidentally tackled a row of pines and now my house smells like a car freshener. From the corner of my eye, I immediately spot Logan. The Santa hat is traded for a chiseled jawline. My gaze lingers longer than what's considered appropriate. At our table, I shrug out of my coat and hang it over the back of my chair. I spare another glance at the bar, and Logan's still watching me. His eyes are gentle. This time I can't turn away. I don't know what he does to me, but it's so easy to get lost in his hazel irises.

Then I noticed Simon next to him, staring at me. I twist, pulling out my chair, and when Simon's gaze doesn't waver, I know he's not staring at me. His focus is firmly on Sloane. Happiness blooms in my stomach and a grin covers my face. I think someone has a crush.

"Maybe you should get the first round of drinks tonight," I say to Sloane as I take a seat.

"Or Willa can," Sloane replies.

"Su—" I kick Willa's shin under the table. She yelps before she shoots daggers at me. "Ouch! What was—"

I bore my gaze at her while winking and gently jerking my head toward the bar.

"What's with all the blinking? I don't understand Morse code?" she mutters, then glances up. Recognition dawns. "Right. Yes. Sloane, your turn. I'll take a beer."

"Same," I add.

"Ugh, fine." Her chair screeches across the floor as she pushes away from the table. She avoids Simon and goes to the opposite end of the bar. But naturally, he materializes right where she stops.

"There was a time they were friends, right?" Willa props her chin on her hand.

"There was, but then… something happened. They just stopped talking. Every time I asked Sloane, she always claimed that some friendships aren't meant to be. Then she wanted me to drop it."

"Yeah, I always got the same response, but she never argues about coming here."

Both of us turn to stare at Sloane as she gives Simon the cold shoulder while he pours her three beers. On her way back, she weaves between tables with the occasional not-so-discreet glance over her shoulder to Simon, who has been watching her intently. She sets the beers on the table and slides one toward Willa and one to me. Before taking a sip, she brushes her hair off her neck and over her shoulder. At the bar, Simon's mouth forms a half-smile before he turns to another customer. If hate flirting is a thing, these two have it in spades.

"It's been fun, but it's time for me to go home." I set my beer on the table.

"Stay for one more. We never get to chill out and have girls' night anymore," Willa whines.

"We did this like five nights ago."

"But it felt like forever." Willa pouts.

"If I stay any longer, I'll faceplant into the table, and I don't think Simon would appreciate that very much." I rise from my stool and throw my jacket over my shoulders.

"I should get going too," Sloane says. "I have bread that needs baking in the morning."

"Fine. If everyone is leaving, I'm not hanging out by myself." Willa rises from her stool.

"Bar tab is on me. We'll chat later," I say, hugging them. They head for the door, and I weave to the bar, flagging down Simon. When he's done serving a customer, he stops in front of me. "Can I get my tab?" I ask.

"Sure," he says, then drops his voice. "Or… do me a favor? Can you take Logan home?

At the end of the bar, a lump of a man is draped over the wood ledge. He's seconds away from using a coaster as a pillow while he swirls mostly water in the glass.

I shake my head. "One of his friends can take him home."

"But you're leaving now, and he needs to leave now."

"My car's full."

"Strap him to the roof."

"Seriously?"

"Please, just take him home?" he pleads. "I'll cover your tab."

"How much has he had to drink, anyway?"

"After his second scotch, I gave him mostly water. Whatever mission he was on tonight, I don't want him to regret anything tomorrow."

I exhale. I've been the person who needed a ride after too many drinks, but it's Logan in close quarters. "My tab *and* the rest of my tabs this year." I raise an eyebrow.

He doesn't blink. "Deal. He's at forty-six Yuletide."

Of course he lives in the house with my dream wraparound porch. I always pictured myself sitting on the porch swing, reading a book during the summer or decorating the railing with garland and lights for Christmas. Fine. Universe, I see your irony.

"Hey, Logan!" Simon calls. "Brie's your ride."

Logan squints my way. "My favorite person," he slurs.

"I'll need duct tape for his mouth," I mutter.

"Thanks, Brie. I appreciate it."

I roll my eyes and amble toward Logan as he rises on wobbly legs. "Alright, let's get you home. Less talking, the better."

"You don't enjoy talking to me?"

"It's not my favorite pastime." He sloppily throws his arm around my shoulder, and his fingers tangle in my hair. I wince.

"We'd have a better time if you hated me less."

"That's the entire backbone of our relationship." I flash him a tight-lipped smile. "Let's go. The sooner I get you home, the sooner I can be away from you."

We make it two steps before he comes to a screeching

halt. "Are you getting frisky with me?" He closes one eye. I'm not sure if it's a lazy wink or to reduce double vision.

"No! I'm taking you home."

"No. No." He enunciates each vowel. "You just touched my ass. You can just ask. I'll say yes."

"I did not touch your ass."

"Yes, you did. Your fingers grazed my right cheek."

"I assure you, they didn't."

He glances over his shoulder. "Oh, it was the stool."

"Want to ask if the stool wants to take you home?"

"Nah. It only wanted to cop a feel."

I shake my head but can't fight the smile that takes over. With his arm draped over my shoulder, the weight of a two-hundred pound retired hockey legend has me nearly doubled over as we exit. On our way through the parking lot, he rambles about Christmas ornaments and wanting to be a good dad. Most of my concentration is on not toppling over. When we reach my SUV, I shove him inside with moderate help from him. I really hope he's like a baby and the car ride lulls him to sleep, so I don't have to listen to him. Once I'm seated, I drop my keys into the cupholder and press the ignition button on the dashboard.

"Yuletide Drive. Forty-six," Logan mumbles.

"I know."

"Stalking me?"

"Nah. I only stalk people who can form complete sentences." He says nothing else. Wish come true? He passed out. As I pull out of the parking lot and onto the road, he remains silent. Glad I didn't need that duct tape after all, but that leaves my next challenge. How will I get him inside?

"Why do you hate me?"

So much for silence. I glance at the passenger seat as the passing streetlight briefly lights up the interior. The back of his head is against the headrest. His eyes are closed, and his chin is tilted toward the roof. "You're drunk. Do you really want to get into this?"

"I asked, didn't I?"

"Yeah. You did. I have a feeling if I tell you, you won't remember it tomorrow anyway. And I really don't want to repeat myself."

His head rolls toward me, though his eyes land on my cup holder. "I only hated you because you hated me."

I huff out a laugh. "I'm sure that's the reason."

"It is. You hated me so much." The tires hum over packed snow. For a moment, I think he finally passed out, but then he speaks. "Why are you giving me a ride home?"

"Because Simon asked, and I like him more than you."

His chin lifts as he faces the windshield. "I think you secretly like me."

"Hardly," I scoff. "If I liked you, I could also grow a unicorn horn out of my forehead."

"Really? You can do that?"

"Yeah." I lift my hand to my forehead and stick out my middle finger.

He barks out a laugh. "You've always been sassy, but I swear you hoard the extra sass for me."

"Only when it's warranted."

"So you didn't answer my question. Why do you hate me?" A silent pause passes between us. Before I can respond, he asks, "Is it because of my rugged good looks, and you don't know how to handle your intense attraction to me?"

A laugh shoots out of me. "Oh, that's the furthest thing from the truth." From the corner of my eye, he rolls his head toward me, his hazel eyes glossy under the streetlights. If I had to guess, he sees three of me right now.

"You know, I always thought I understood women. Females. Girls. Then I had to raise one on my own. Let me tell you, this shit is hard. I love my daughter. She's my whole heart. But I wish I could have someone to tag team in." He lifts his hand and gives himself a high five.

It's hard not to smile at his playfulness. "I'm sure you're a great dad."

"Sometimes I wonder, am I doing enough? Am I giving Josie the best life I can? Hell, I don't even know how many times we've moved to a new city." One at a time, he counts on each finger. "Four. She's had to move four times. Three different schools. You know how many times I had to move when I was a kid?"

I want to say none because I grew up with Logan in the same town since we were born.

"Zero. I never left Mount Holly until I turned eighteen." He blows out a deep breath. "She's only eleven and has already endured a lot. Sometimes I question whether I'm doing enough."

My voice softens, offering him a hint of kindness. "You lost your dad at a young age. I'm sure you can relate a little."

"You remember that?"

"Yeah. You were gone from class for like a week. Plus, it's Mount Holly. Practically the entire town was at his funeral."

He nods. "The only difference is I had my mom. For three years, Josie didn't have me."

Without thinking, I reach across the center console and rest my hand on his. A spark zips up my arm, and I yank my hand away. What the hell was that? A pinched nerve? I flex my fingers before clearing my throat. "You're here now."

He doesn't know how to deal with an emotional eleven-year-old, and I don't know how to deal with an emotional thirty-six-year-old Logan. He has been through a lot. We're older. Maybe we can push our differences aside. Even though I'm still going to kick his ass in the festival department.

As I turn into his driveway, snowflakes begin to dance from the sky. I leave the car running because I plan on tossing Logan through the doorway and leaving. Maybe not tossing—shoving? Before I reach the passenger side, Logan already has the door open, one boot on the ground. I loop an arm around his waist as he drapes himself over my shoulders. I slam the door behind us and guide him toward the sidewalk that leads up to his porch.

Halfway to the short set of stairs, his foot slips on a patch of ice. With physics doing what physics does, his body slams into mine and much like the trees at Reindeer Ridge, we topple over. Logan twists, taking the hit so I land on him. Snow blooms up around us like a slow-motion snow globe. Logan's eyes pinch shut as a deep groan rumbles from his chest.

My breath hitches as I scan his face, shoulders, and chest for any signs of injury. "Are you alright?"

"That's going to leave a bruise." He groans again.

Resting my hands on his chest, which is annoyingly warm even through layers, I can't help the giggle that bursts out of me. "If it's any consolation, thanks for taking one for the team."

His hands bracket my waist. "Why are you being nice to me? Driving me home. Hell, talking to me. I was such a prick to you, wasn't I? Or ignored you. I'm not really sure. Both are equally shitty."

I tuck a strand of hair behind my ear. "Apparently, I'm feeling generous today." Or I've lost my mind. "Plus, you took the brunt of a snowbank for me."

His fingers ghost across my face, brushing away stray hairs. My breath gets caught in my throat. "Snowflake," he whispers.

"Yeah, there's a lot of them around us."

His gaze steadies on me. "No. You. You're my snowflake."

I snort. "Someone has had too many drinks tonight."

"It's true."

Okay. I'll bite. "Is that because I'm one of a kind?" I bat my eyelashes, feigning innocence.

"No. Well, I mean, you are. But you're a new beginning." The crinkle in his forehead softens as the air grows heavy between us. "You have the prettiest eyes."

I bite my lips together, swallowing down the laugh that wants to escape.

"They're the most captivating brown."

Unable to hold it back any longer, a chuckle bursts out of me. "Brown eyes are not pretty."

"Yours are." His hand slides up my back. "They have little flecks of gold that shine brighter when you smile."

Well shit. That was kind of sweet. "Are those the types of compliments that get all the girls to swoon?"

"Honestly, I don't remember the last time I paid a girl a compliment."

His hand slides from my back to my shoulder. The tips of his fingers are cold against my cheek. A shiver skates through me that has nothing to do with the cold. His gaze flicks to my mouth; his tongue wets his bottom lip. He lifts his chin, eyes drifting closed. Oh shit, he's going to kiss me. His warm breath skates over my lips as he moves a fraction closer. If I dip my head just a centimeter, my lips will be on his. I'd be kissing Logan Crawford. My arch enemy. Abort! Abort!

"We should get you inside," I blurt out.

"You're my snowflake."

His head hits the snow, and a cloud forms as he exhales. "Yeah. That's probably best."

I scramble up, very careful to avoid any accidental snowbank dry-humping, then offer my hand. He almost takes me down again, but I wrangle him upright. We walk side by side until we reach the few steps leading to the porch.

His gaze drops to his feet as he takes the first step. "You don't have to walk me to my door."

"I want to make sure you get inside."

He doesn't protest any further. Instead, he grips the railing and climbs the steps until he reaches the door. He sways back and forth a few times before he fishes his keys out of his pocket. With the streetlight as his guide, he uses his other hand to select the correct one. He stabs the lock once, twice, finally, the third time's the charm. Visions of Logan trying to have sex right now flood my head, and I stifle a giggle. I dodged a bullet with the almost-kiss. Then I scold myself for thinking of Logan and sex right now.

Twisting the knob, he pushes the door open and stumbles through the doorway, abandoning his keys. I stand guard and brace for impact in case he falls over. Once he's inside, I grab his keys from the lock and follow him. He flips on a light switch, and a soft glow fills the expansive entryway as a wisp of pine fills the air. I've spent years imagining what the inside of this house looked like, but it's even more gorgeous than I thought. Beautiful exposed beams cover the ceiling to pair perfectly with the rustic wide-plank flooring. The open floor plan gives the house a spacious ambiance, yet it still feels warm and cozy.

While Logan leans against the wall, he toes off his boots. I do the same. "You can keep yours on." He points to my feet.

"Your floors look way too nice for my dirty, snowy boots."

"It's fine."

Logan ambles into the living room, and I follow close behind. He collapses onto a leather sectional and drapes his arm over his face. I place his keys on the kitchen island, hoping he won't have issues finding them in the morning. A colorful blanket is bunched up on a recliner a few feet away. Grabbing the edge, I unfurl it, exposing a narwhal swimming on a colorful background. It's much smaller than I expected, but it's better than nothing. I drape it over Logan's stomach and thighs since that's all it will cover.

Before leaving, I spare another glance around, without snooping… too much. It's actually a really nice place for a single dad. I stroll into the kitchen, and a half-empty case of water on the counter catches my eye. He must have some chilled. I open one side of the stainless-steel fridge, and my eyes widen. Granted, I didn't know what to expect, but this wasn't it. Fruits and vegetables pack the inside. Again, not something I'd expect from a guy, but he's an athlete and a dad, so he's trying to remain healthy. Based on the two times now that my hands have been on him, he's doing a good job. I spot bottled water in the bottom drawer, and I grab one. Back in the living room, Logan's fully sprawled out on the couch. His eyes are closed, and he softly breathes in and out. Leaning down, I place the bottle of water on the end table next to his head. My gaze wanders over the soft features of his face. The light brown eyelashes that fan over his cheeks. The gentle slope of his nose. The light stubble that covers his sculpted jawline. I like this Logan the best. Mostly because he's quiet.

"Thanks for the ride," he mumbles, eyes still closed.

I recoil, my back snapping upright. Guess he's not sleeping. "Yeah, no problem. Have a good night."

He lifts his hand in a half-assed wave, saying nothing. At the door, I slip into my boots and exit. Inside my SUV, my fingers tight on the wheel, I replay the last ten minutes on a loop: ice, snowbank, almost-kiss I'm eighty-seven percent certain I didn't want—except for the thirteen percent that absolutely did. But not tonight. Not like that. But maybe… he isn't the villain I assigned him to be. Maybe—*maybe*—we could be something resembling friends.

I crank the heat, pull away, and try very hard to think about literally anything besides how close his mouth came to mine.

Brie

Mmm… right there. I rock my hips. My fingers sliding over soft, cool cotton. That feels so good. More. I need more. Yes. Logan.

My eyes snap open. As the room comes into focus, a wave of disappointment crashes over me, and I fling the pillow aside. Who let Logan into my dream? Maybe it wasn't really him. I think it was only him because he was who I was with last night—dirty blond hair, hazel eyes you could get lost in for weeks on end. Son of a bitch. Why the hell am I having sex dreams about Logan Crawford? Clearly, the lack of non-self-induced orgasms in my life is making me delusional. There's no way that the way he runs his fingers through his strands is sexy. I blame my pebbled nipples on a cold breeze and not his dimple that could launch a thousand bad decisions or his dark gray Henley that clings to his chest like a second skin. Not sexy one bit. I will not fantasize about any of that any longer. Who am I kidding? I'm totally going to fantasize about it.

If I had almost kissed anyone else in Mount Holly, I'd be on the phone with Willa and Sloane giving them a play-by-play, but it was Logan. They'd ask a bunch of questions I can't answer. The most logical answer is he was drunk, and I refuse to be the girl who only gets kissed when he's drunk. Hard pass. All I know is the almost-kiss keeps looping like a never-ending Ferris wheel. Maybe we can do the adult thing and leave high school where it belongs— behind us along with my hot pink, Juicy Couture tracksuit and his hockey hair.

Since we're in the thick of the Holly Jolly Festival, I trudge into the office on a Sunday to work. Apparently, Mrs. Kingsley had the same idea. Maybe this will help me score some brownie points. I power up the computer, open the vendor spreadsheet… and, um, a second tab. For research. Market research. I type "Logan Crawford" into the search, and his profile appears at the top. I never stalked his social media after he left town. My mission was to forget him, not keep tabs on him. Now he's here, ignoring him is going to be slightly more difficult.

Starting at the bottom, I scroll through row after row of photos. Logan's always been an attractive guy, and somehow age made him even more attractive. In high school, he was always the cute jock with the hockey hair that would flare out from underneath his beanie. All the girls would follow him around like lost puppies. They couldn't see his cockiness and arrogance like I could. He had to win at everything. Case in point, I stare at a picture of him holding the championship cup he won when he played for Chicago. I scroll past various pictures of him on the ice, playing in various games. There's a couple with his daughter when she was a baby, maybe only a couple of months old. I continue scrolling past several pictures with his wife. I never knew her, but based on her wearing his Boston College jersey, they must have met in college. The feed gets quieter over the last three years.

Mid-scroll, I stop on a black-and-white photo of Logan holding his daughter, their backs facing the camera. Josie rests her head on Logan's shoulder. I glance at the date and see he posted it three days after his wife had passed away. The caption reads, "Forever in our hearts. Never forgotten. Always loved." The comments are a tide of condolences. Tears sting my eyes, blurring my vision. I can't imagine losing someone so close to me. My heart cracks a little. Through the gossip mill, I heard about his wife passing, but we were never close, so it felt out of place to reach out.

As I continue scrolling, there are a couple of pictures of Logan on a beach. He's shirtless. His swim trunks ride low on his hips, and water slicks back his hair, as if he had just finished swimming. Why are the attractive ones always assholes?

"Brie!" Mrs. Kingsley's voice ricochets down the hall. "I need you in my office."

My heart leaps to my throat, almost choking me. Before anyone catches me, I quickly minimize the tab. "Yes! Coming." Shoving away from my desk, I rise and stroll down the hallway. My heels echo off the walls to the thumping of my heart. When I reach Mrs. Kingsley's door, I pause and run my hands down my blouse, smoothing the imaginary wrinkles, and I peek around the door frame. "You wanted to see me?"

"Come in. Take a seat." She motions to the chair in front of her desk.

I swallow down the lump in my throat and do what she says.

"How are the event contracts coming?"

That's what I was supposed to be doing instead of stalking Logan on the internet. One seemed more fun than the other. "Good. They're going great." I sit up, straightening my shoulders. Fake it till you make it, right?

"You've made all the necessary phone calls?" She raises a perfectly sculpted brow.

"Yes, that's next on my list."

"You'll need to confirm all the vendors comply with town laws, and they have the appropriate permits."

"Yes, it's all under control." I lie through my smile. Shit. Well, guess who's working all night?

"I want the paperwork on my desk by the end of the week."

Double fuck. "No problem. I'm already halfway done."

"Good. That's what I like to hear. Also, next week I'll have an assistant for you, much like you've been to me over the years. I'll let you get back to it."

"Great." I flash her a fake smile. The second I clear her door my smile slides off like a cheap press-on nail. How in the hell am I going to get all this done by the end of the week? Why couldn't the assistant start like yesterday? When I reach my desk, I plop down in my chair and faceplant into my palm. Once again, Logan Crawford is nothing but a distraction that threatens to ruin everything without even being here. The small rectangle at the bottom of my screen glares back at me. I slide the mouse over and click the *X* button, making it disappear. Out of sight, Logan out of my mind.

By noon, my head is pounding, and my stomach is ready to eat itself. I ditch the paperwork for lunch and stroll into the Jolly Biscuit, the aroma of warm maple syrup causes me to salivate. "How was tree decorating?" I ask Willa who's behind the counter.

"It was going great until Mason decided traditional is boring and instead arranged all the ornaments and lights into the shape of a giant middle finger." She tries to keep a straight face and fails.

I snort laugh. "At least there was an attempt to be festive."

"It wouldn't be so bad if the decorated side didn't face the window."

"So all his neighbors get to enjoy a Christmas salute?"

"No. Because the window is shorter, from the outside you only see two knuckles and a finger, which in turn looks like—"

I nod. "Oh! Got it." Another laugh bursts out of me.

Willa shakes her head, grinning. "Your lunch will be right out. Grab a seat and I'll bring it to you."

"Okay, great." She abandons the counter and heads toward the kitchen. I spin around and run face-first into the one man I'm trying not to think about.

"Whoa." Logan's hands close around my biceps. "We need to stop running into each other, literally. But… I'm glad to see you."

This is news. My eyebrows rise. He drops his hands and takes a step back. That's not the reaction of someone happy to see me.

"Can we talk for a minute?" he asks.

"Yeah. Sure."

Willa reappears with my plate. "Brie, I've got your— oh. Hey, Logan."

"Hi Willa." Logan lifts his hand in a wave. "Can you give us a minute?"

"Oh yeah. Go ahead." She sets my food on the counter and props her chin on her hands like she's front row at the theater. Her eyes quickly shift between us. Both of us lock our gazes on hers. "Just ignore me. Carry on." She rolls her hand in front of her.

"Maybe… somewhere private?" he murmurs to me.

"Yeah." I head toward a small table in the corner. Logan's large frame trails behind me. I can't see him, but it's hard not to feel his presence. It's all-consuming, even when it's unwarranted. As I take a seat, Logan sits in the chair across from me. Three tables over, the Gigis have synchronized their bifocals. Fantastic.

He rubs the back of his neck. "Um. Thanks for the ride home last night."

"Yeah. No problem. I got a free bar tab out of it." I shrug.

"That's a bonus." A tint of pink covers his cheeks. "I'm glad I could make that happen for you. I didn't… say or do anything too embarrassing, did I?"

Do I mention the kiss? He doesn't seem keen on bringing it up. Do I want him to bring it up? Does he want me to bring it up? It was a kiss, well an almost-kiss, but we've never been the almost kissing type of people. More so the if you try to kiss me, I'll punch you in the face kind of people. But oddly, the almost-kiss felt right. And it especially shocked the hell out of me when I woke up dry-humping my pillow. That was a first.

Screw it. I'm not playing chicken with the elephant in the room. "About last night," I lean in, keeping my voice low, "you tried to kiss me."

His gaze ricochets off mine. Leaning away, he tugs at the collar of his charcoal-colored jacket. "Did I? Huh. Weird. I, uh… don't know why I'd do that. Maybe I was… stretching my neck?" He lowers his shoulders and lifts his head like an ostrich.

"Yeah, maybe that was it." I nod solemnly. Eyes closed,

lips puckered. Classic neck stretch. From the corner of my eye, I sense the heavy weight of the entire diner on us as they enjoy their lunch, including a couple of the Gigis. Great. By dinner, I'll be pregnant with Logan's love child.

"Are you sure I tried to kiss you?" he asks.

I cross my arms over my chest. "Are you sure you want to pretend you don't remember?"

"No!" He shoves his hands into his pockets. "I just can't imagine I'd… do that with you."

"Because I'm unkissable?" I arch a brow. This man doesn't need a shovel. He's doing a pretty good job of digging his own grave.

"I mean—someone probably wants to kiss you." His shoulders drop. "Maybe I thought you were someone else. It was dark."

"Right." I roll my eyes. "That must be it. I mean, I would have punched you in the face if you had done it anyway, so it's probably better you didn't. Otherwise, you'd be sporting a black eye today."

He nods. "Great. We can pretend it never happened. Nothing really happened anyway."

What an asshole. He totally remembers the almost-kiss. He wouldn't have rambled on for so long about *nothing* happening. I thought maybe Logan was a different person, more grown up, but I was wrong. So fucking wrong.

Ever so conveniently, his phone rings. He glances at the screen. "Sorry, I need to take this—construction worker for the carnival. It's almost set up."

I purse my lips together and give him a tight nod.

"I'll see you around." He turns and presses his phone to his ear as he exits the diner.

"Hopefully not," I mumble. His carnival. I lost sight of his carnival that's trying to ruin my festival. Eye on the prize, Brie. Don't let yourself get distracted by a guy.

Especially one who's as big of an asshole as Logan fucking Crawford.

Four hours later, I'm sitting on my floor, cross-legged with half a dozen open binders surrounding me, the whooshing sound of paper flipping fills the quiet room. A sharp knock on my door slices through the silence, startling me. Climbing to my feet, I peer out the closed curtain, and Willa's standing on my doorstep. I twist the knob and pull the door open.

She barrels in with a hug. "Oh good, you're not dead."

"Not yet, anyway." Turning around, I take my place back on the floor.

"I tried calling you like twenty times. I never got an answer, so I thought I'd do a wellness check."

I wave my hand over the scattered binders around me. "I've been drowning in town bylaws."

Her gaze wanders over my living room floor. "Are you supposed to take those from the town hall?"

"Probably not, but I'll return them when I'm done."

"So what's all this research for?" She takes a seat on the couch to my left.

I flip through pages without glancing at Willa. "His carnival can't be legal. I've scoured all the town's records, and there's nothing that shows he pulled any permits, got any required licensing, nothing. There's no way he can have a carnival in Mount Holly, and I'm going to prove it."

"Good luck with that, Nancy Drew."

"A girl's gotta do what a girl's gotta do to save her festival."

"Is it bad to have a little competition?" she asks.

Mid-page flip, I pause to glare at her. She shrugs. "It's not that I don't want competition. I'm fine with competition. I just don't want it to be Logan. It's ingrained in his DNA. He sees a line and sprints through the ribbon. I'm simply sprinting too."

Willa tilts her head. "If it were anyone else, I doubt you'd be this frothy. Instead of working against each other, don't you think you would gain more success working together?"

"Is that what you said when Breakfast To Go tried to open right off the freeway?" I quirk an eyebrow.

"Big difference. That's a franchise. No one wants a chain restaurant in a small town. People want local charm and ambiance, not rubbery egg patties on barely toasted, unseasoned English muffins. My food is fresh." She shakes her head. "It's completely different. Logan's not franchising a carnival."

"At this rate, anything is possible. Either way, I need to stop it before it even starts."

"Alright, well good luck with that. I have to go meet Mason. He needs my help with paint schemes for his bedroom."

I bite back a grin. "Or it's just an excuse to hang out with you in his bedroom."

"We're not sixteen. No excuses necessary. Either way, we're best friends. We hang out. Help each other when needed."

I raise a questioning eyebrow. "I didn't know best friends also spoon each other while lying down on the couch."

Pink washes over her cheeks. "We were watching a movie. It got late. I was tired. I got cold, and his body is a natural radiator. Are you jealous? Do you want to cuddle?"

She hoists her legs onto the couch, lies down, and pats the cushion in front of her.

A laugh bursts out of me. "Rain check."

"Don't say I never offered." She drops her feet to the floor and sits up. "Now I regret ever mentioning it to you."

"I'm only pointing out the obvious." Now I feel like a jerk for not telling her about the almost-kiss. But is it really that important? Logan wants to pretend as if nothing happened anyway, so it's irrelevant. I drop my gaze to the papers in front of me and continue scanning. "Ah! Found it! Sections forty-five to forty-seven. Special events. City limits allow only one similar event at a time unless permission and a specialty permit were previously acquired. Time for him to pack up his carnival and hightail it out of Mount Holly." My lips curve into a wide smile. "He's done none of this."

Willa laughs. "You're going to have fun telling him that, aren't you?"

"Oh, I'm making it this year's Christmas card." I tried to be nice for a whole five seconds. Well, you know what? That's five seconds longer than he actually deserves. If he wants a Christmas war, he's getting a Christmas war.

Logan

Fuck. What did I do last night? Oh, that's right, I tried to kiss Brie McKenna. In that moment, with her bright brown eyes staring back at mine, I wanted nothing more. I wanted her. Kissing random women wasn't my goal when I arrived in Mount Holly. But Brie isn't random. We have decades of... whatever this is. The sharp pain in my temples increases, and I pinch my eyes closed against the throbbing, and, through the fog, I catch a flicker of words —*Mostly Nice. Sometimes Naughty.* Her keychain. Fuck. Now I'm wondering exactly how much is "sometimes." Focus, Crawford. I lift my head and wince as pain shoots up my neck. At roughly five a.m., I migrated from the couch to my bed like a wounded moose. Now I'm lying in bed, not feeling any better.

"Daddy!" The patter of feet thump down the hall. Josie bursts through the doorway and jumps onto the end of the bed.

"Hey Peanut." I inch upright and lean against the headboard, doing my best to keep my hangover under wraps. "Have fun with Grandma?"

"Yes! We went to a craft fair this morning and I got you this." She holds up a little wood ornament with hockey sticks.

"Wow, that's pretty cool. Did you unpack your bag?"

"No."

"How about you do that, and when you're done, we'll find the perfect spot to hang it on the tree?"

"Okay." She crawls up the bed and wraps her arms around my neck. I hug her to my chest. Best. Kid. Ever. She scampers off the bed, dragging her backpack behind her.

A few seconds later, my mom appears in the doorway. "Have fun last night?"

"Something like that." I scrub both hands over my face.

"I heard you didn't leave the bar alone." She lifts a brow.

Fuck. It hasn't even been twelve hours, and the gossip mill is already turning. Do they ever take a break?

"And judging by the body print in the snowbank, you didn't *arrive* home alone." She flattens me with an unimpressed look. "You know, you should really keep your escapades indoors."

"There were no escapades." I sigh. "But duly noted for next time."

"How is Brie McKenna doing?" She wanders into the

room, doing a not-so subtle sweep of the floor beside my bed.

"If you're looking for someone, you won't find them."

As she sits at the end of the bed, a frown etches her face. "Did you kick her out already?"

I roll my eyes. She's relentless this morning. But it's also not the first time I've tried to hide a girl in my room. There may have been a time or two in high school when I had to get clever with my hiding spots because under the bed and in the closet weren't cutting it. But now I'm an adult, I shouldn't have to hide anyone anywhere. "No one got kicked out."

"But she's the one you left the bar with?"

Suffocating myself with a pillow sounds more fun than this conversation. I scrub my hands over my scruff-covered cheeks and groan. "She gave me a ride. That's it."

Her brows furrow. "Then how did you two end up in the snowbank together? You two always seemed like an unlikely pair. You spent most of your childhood bickering. However, I could see how the connection would grow." She nods as if she's agreeing with herself.

I'm sure she's seconds away from making wedding plans. "Look, Mom," I sit up, squaring my shoulders, "there is no connection."

"Is that why your eyes lit up brighter than the town Christmas tree as soon as I mentioned her name?"

Damn her for being so intuitive. Can I blame the glossy eyes on the hangover?

She squeezes my leg through the blanket; her soft smile turning serious. "It's okay to find love again, honey. It's been three years."

Me and Brie? There's no chance. Even though part of me is curious about the possibility. Then there's Brooke. My dead wife, who I spent fourteen years with.

"You don't have to forget," Mom adds. "But there's nothing wrong with moving on."

I press my lips together. "Thanks, Mom. I'll consider that."

"Alright." She pushes off the bed. "I'll talk to you later."

"Hey Mom?" She stops and spins around. "Thanks for watching Josie."

"Anytime. I'm glad you're back in town so I can spend more time with her. Also, John called me. He's already at the carnival helping with the finishing touches on the ice rink."

"Thanks."

After Josie and I hung the ornament on the tree, I popped some ibuprofen, guzzled down a bottle of water, and drove to the carnival. When not in school, Josie likes to help when she can. It makes her feel important. Josie helps John with some decorations, well, more like bossing him around about garland symmetry. Brooke would've loved that—both the garland and the bossing.

By lunchtime, I leave Josie with John and head to town to grab lunch for everyone. It's mostly a skeleton crew on weekends, but a few of them have nothing better to do, so they'd rather collect overtime, and I'll gladly take the help. I park my truck outside the Jolly Biscuit and climb out as an icy gust of wind blows past me. For a brief moment, it eases the pounding in my head and keeps all thoughts of Brie at bay.

As I approach the large front window of the diner, I peer inside and freeze. Her hair is a dark ribbon down her back, resting on a cream-colored sweater that falls off her shoulder. It's exactly like the sweater from our coffee shop run-in. Except this time, she's missing the red underwear. My lips twitch into a smile. Then everything from last night slams into me. Fuck. Her weight on top of me in the snowbank. Inches away from a kiss I shouldn't want. Through the window, I see her throw her head back in laughter. I can almost hear it. Sweet. Infectious. As if she doesn't have a care in the world. And for a second, I hate that I'm the reason her laughter usually comes with an eye roll. It's Mount Holly. Unless I become a hermit, we'll always run into each other. Might as well get the awkwardness out of the way.

"Logan, it's so nice to see you." Mrs. Whitman rests a soft, wrinkled hand on my forearm, interrupting my thoughts.

I shift my gaze from the window to the older woman, catching a subtle scent of baby powder. "Good afternoon, Doris. How are you?"

"I'm just dandy. I'm meeting the gals for an afternoon lunch and chat."

Which really means it's time to unleash all the juicy gossip.

"Are you going to come in, or are you going to wait till you turn into a popsicle?" My gaze drifts from Doris to Brie. She reaches for the door handle, but I step behind her and pull it open.

"Let me get that for you."

"Always such a gentleman." She winks and breezes by me, heading straight to her waiting table.

The aroma of butter and maple syrup wafts around me, replacing the powdery accords. For half a second, I forget the part where I almost kissed Brie last night. It was nothing. It meant nothing. I got caught up in the moment. That's all. Maybe if I say it enough times, I'll convince myself it's true.

I fall in line behind her, working up the confidence to speak. I'm not the nervous type, but something about Brie turns my palms into slip-n-slides. She spins and—whump—walks right into my chest.

"Whoa." My hands grip her biceps. "We need to stop running into each other, literally. But… I'm glad to see you." Her face is like a poker table, devoid of any expression. Does she still hate me? Hate me extra? Or have we graduated to tolerate with caution? With standing so close to her, my brain votes *kiss her*, which is exactly why I release her like she's a hot stovetop. "Can we talk for a minute?"

That went… spectacularly not to plan. Probably because there was no plan. Instead, I used Josie's call as a fake emergency and bolted like a coward. Brie discombobulates all my coherent thoughts. If she didn't hate me before that conversation, she certainly does now. It's for the best. I'm not here to fall in love. I'm here to give Josie a better life and leave a lasting legacy in Brooke's honor.

Leaning forward over the steering wheel, I rake my hands through my hair. Locking myself away and becoming a recluse isn't looking so bad. A knock rattles my window. Glancing to my left, Willa stands on the other side holding two plastic bags full of takeout. Shit. Lunch. I roll down the window.

"In your hasty getaway, you forgot these. I didn't make a bunch of food just for you to order and dash."

"Sorry." I grab the bags from her and set them on my passenger seat. Digging in my pocket, I pull out some cash and pass it to her. "This should cover it. And keep the change for the delivery service."

Her shoulders hunch as she runs her hands up and

down her arms. "I don't know exactly what's going on between you and Brie, but whatever it is, don't hurt my best friend. It hasn't been easy for her to get where she is, and then the added stress of the festival is keeping her on edge."

I give her a tight-lipped nod. "I can say with full certainty that my being in town isn't creating a stress-free holiday."

She smiles at me. "Just play nice, okay?"

"Got it. Thanks again for always taking my lunch orders for my crew."

"Thanks for the business. I'm going to get back in. I'm sure I'll see you around."

"Bye, Willa."

The next morning, I'm up before the sun, mostly because I couldn't sleep, which is becoming a more common occurrence as of late. The common denominator: Brie. By the time I pull into the carnival grounds, the sun has barely breached the horizon. Luckily, my mom's an early riser, so she came over early to see Josie off to school. A couple hours to myself while I add the finishing touches to the s'mores house Josie wanted is exactly what I need. No interruptions. Just a man with his thoughts. Which might not be the best thing, either. I clip the battery onto the drill. The hum of the power tool mixing with the crisp, dead air of winter is meditative, until tires crunching over gravel ruins my zen. I set down the electric drill and step out from the s'mores hut. Bright headlights shine directly at me like an interrogation. Shielding my eyes, a black figure steps out of the SUV and moves in front of the headlights. Slowly, my eyes adjust to the new light. Brie. Did I just manifest her?

She comes to a halt only a few feet away from me. She crosses her arms over her chest, papers clutched in her hand. "You need to shut down your carnival."

Not the good morning I was hoping for. I sigh. "Not this again," I mutter under my breath. "What did I do now?"

"I'm already in charge of the Holly Jolly Festival in Mount Holly—"

I mimic her stance. "So you're saying you have a monopoly on the Christmas festivities that happen in Mount Holly?"

"No. I'm saying according to the bylaws—sections forty-five to forty-seven to be exact—there can only be one holiday event within Mount Holly city limits. And I already have all the permits for mine." She uncrosses her arms and waves a stack of papers in my face. "So I'm sorry, actually, not sorry—but you will just have to take your carnival elsewhere."

I rip the papers out of her hand and skim them. She's wearing a smug like it's custom-tailored. When I'm finished, I hand the papers back to her and chuckle.

Her jaw ticks. "Are you laughing at the bylaws of Mount Holly? You can take it up with the mayor, but it'll take weeks, if not months, to get anything settled, and Christmas will be long gone by then."

"You see that fence post?" I point to my right, about fifty yards away. Her gaze follows the imaginary line. "That is the town boundary line. And if you can't tell, my carnival is just north of that line, which means I am not within Mount Holly's city limits."

She frowns.

"Sorry, actually, not sorry to burst your holiday

bubble." I give her a smile that used to drive opposing defensemen nuts. "The carnival is staying."

A vein throbs in her forehead, which is slightly adorable, but more so if it wasn't directed at me. She pivots and stomps back to her SUV. I lift my hand in a little wave as she backs up and returns to the road. The taillights disappear over the crest of a hill. Maybe she's a little mad I pretended not to remember the almost-kiss or she really wants the carnival gone. Either way, I don't think that will be the last I see of her, and I can't pretend I'm disappointed.

Brie

Of course his field is on the other side of the town's limits. I have never hated a fence post before, but congratulations to that splintered little jerk across from Reindeer Ridge— you're my villain origin story. When I'm back at town hall, I triple-check the town's boundary line and, sure enough, a fence post is the marker. Now I've shown Logan all my cards. This was supposed to be my surefire way to stop his carnival. Nope, Logan Crawford thought of everything. Because why wouldn't he? Mr. Perfect. He already knew I have no jurisdiction to end his carnival, so Plan A is out of the question. Now it's time for Plan B. Which would be so much easier if I had one. Another thing Logan ruined is my morning routine. My bottom lip juts out. I never got my coffee this morning.

Instead of finalizing contracts, I tap a pen against the keyboard, willing carnival demise ideas to come to me, but nothing worthwhile comes to mind. After fifteen minutes ticked by all I got were:

Burn it to the ground. But some people consider that arson. Even though it would certainly get rid of my problem.

A Road Closed sign placed on both ends of the road so people can't get there. Unfortunately, with Reindeer Ridge across the street that would also impact Henry.

Start rumors about tainted hot chocolate?

Or unleash all of Henry's farm on the carnival grounds?

"Brie, come to my office!" Mrs. Kingsley calls from down the hall.

We have an intercom. I don't know why she doesn't use it. I step into Mrs. Kingsley's office. A young woman in a blazer bright enough to guide ships to shore sits across from her, vibrating with enthusiasm.

"Brie, come in. Take a seat." Mrs. Kingsley waves me in. I smile at the young woman as I sit down next to her. "This is Lauren. She'll be your assistant for the rest of the year while you finish planning and executing the Holly Jolly Festival."

Lauren bounces in her seat. "I'm so excited to get started. I love planning and organizing."

She's certainly bright-eyed and bushy tailed. Just like me when I first started. Not a care in the world. Thinking you'll turn the job into a career. She doesn't know it yet, but they'll dangle that promotion in front of you like a carrot and threaten to offer it to an outside agency.

"Great." I smile. "Much of the planning is already done. We're just working on the execution phase."

"Fantastic," she beams. "I love executing."

At least she's enthusiastic. "Awesome."

"Why don't you show Lauren around and fill her in on everything that's happening at the moment?" Mrs. Kingsley adds.

"Yes. Of course." I rise from the chair, and Lauren follows suit.

"Also, Brie?" Mrs. Kingsley nails tick on the desk as she taps her fingers. "Where are we with booking the reindeer?"

I nod. Reindeer. Oh. Oh! What if Logan doesn't have any reindeer for his carnival? "I'll call Henry right now to confirm."

"Fantastic. Carry on." Mrs. Kingsley turns her attention to her computer screen, dismissing us.

It'll be hard to run a successful carnival when there are no Christmas things for the townspeople to enjoy like reindeer. I hightail it out of Mrs. Kingsley's office and throw myself into my desk chair. Lauren trails behind me. Immediately, I pick up the phone and dial.

"Reindeer Ridge. How can I help you?"

"Hi Henry, it's Brie."

"Hey Brie, I was just about to get in touch with you about the reindeer for this year. I have you down for nine reindeer. Is that correct?"

I press my lips together and tap my chin. "How many reindeer do you have?"

"Eighteen. Why?"

"I'll take them all."

"You want all eighteen reindeer?"

"Yes, we're being extra reindeer-y this year."

"You know Santa only had nine."

If I take all the reindeer, that leaves Logan with none. I can't chance it. "I know, but I expect to be so busy I'll need two sets."

"Are you sure that's the reason? And not to freeze Logan out?"

"No," I spit. "That's not the reason at all."

Henry chuckles. "I doubt that. Do you know that eighteen reindeer will be twice your budget?"

"Don't worry about my budget. I have it all under control."

"I won't say no to the extra cash."

"Perfect. Thank you, Henry."

I hang up. From across my desk, Lauren flips through a folder of papers. "Do you have a restructured budget to accommodate the extra reindeer?"

No, Lauren. I needed to beat Logan to the punch, so I did this on the fly. "I'll figure it out." I wave her off. "Plus, the entire town will love the extra reindeer. They're always a big attraction at the festival." And Logan gets none. I rest my elbows on the desk and steeple my fingers together. An evil laugh sits on the tip of my tongue, but it might scare Lauren.

On our way to the Holly Jolly Festival grounds, Lauren and I stop at Sip and Sleigh. I need to reassemble my morning routine because Logan threw it off kilter with his fence post.

From behind the counter, Sloane takes one look at me and smirks. "I heard it was an epic failure shutting Logan's carnival down."

Seriously, do people have microphones and cameras covering every inch of this town? How did she find out so fast? "It didn't go as planned."

"Logan? What carnival?" Lauren asks.

"Oh, this is my assistant, Lauren." I point to Lauren

and then Sloane. "This is my friend Sloane. She also owns the coffee shop."

"Oh my god! Oh my god! Oh my god!" Lauren bounces on the balls of her feet, her gaze directed over my shoulder. "Is that?"

We said his name too many times, just like Beetlejuice. My nightmare before Christmas strolls through the door. I sigh. "Logan Crawford. Mount Holly's very own hockey legend," I say, my voice as monotone as a robocall.

Lauren's gaze jumps from me to Logan and back to me. "I've been a huge fan since he got traded to Chicago. Do you know him personally? Oh gosh, can you get me an introduction?"

"No," I deadpan.

"Hi Sloane." Logan greets her with a wave.

"Hi Logan," Sloane replies.

"Hi Brie." He flashes me a dimpled half smile. One that can still turn my insides to goo. I hit him with my iciest glare. He leans down so only I can hear. "If you want to shut down my carnival, you'll have to try harder than that." He straightens and offers his hand to Lauren. "Hi, I'm Logan."

"I—Lauren—hi!" she squeaks. Her cheeks turn redder than Santa's suit as she latches on to his hand.

"Nice to meet you, Lauren." He tries to pull his hand away, but she refuses to release her grip. His eyes widen, the whites taking over his irises.

Maybe Lauren can kidnap Logan, and problem solved. My brows raise at the idea. Images of him tied up in her basement flit through my mind. On second thought, I don't have time for police questioning. I nudge Lauren with my elbow, and finally, she retracts her claws.

Logan backpedals a full step. "I'll see you later." He

hits me with a wink before retreating to the opposite side of Sip and Sleigh.

"Oh my god. It's Logan Crawford." She's practically levitating with happiness. "We should invite him to the Holly Jolly Festival. He'd draw a crowd the size of Minnesota."

Sloane stifles a laugh.

I clear my throat. "No, Lauren. Logan is the enemy."

She blinks. "The… enemy?"

"He's organizing a Christmas carnival to sabotage the Holly Jolly Festival."

"Well," Sloane interrupts, "it's not sabotage per se, but it has put a burnt-out bulb in Brie's string of Christmas lights."

"That's putting it mildly." I direct my attention back to Lauren. "He and his carnival are the enemy, and we will not fraternize with the enemy."

I had a lapse of judgment for a moment. I don't know what I was thinking. Clearly, I wasn't. It won't happen again. After we finish the festival tour, we make plans to meet at the office tomorrow morning and part ways.

The bell above the door chimes as I push my way into Holly Hammer Hardware, my parents' store, after work. "Hey Mom."

She looks up from a Christmas magazine. "Oh, hey Brie."

"Where's Dad?" I come to a stop at the counter across from her.

"He's tinkering with the snow shovel display. Trying to determine the optimal position to encourage snow shovel sales."

I nod along. "That sounds like Dad."

"Precisely." Mom turns to the next page.

"Hi Brie! I thought I heard your voice." My dad

appears from around the corner. "Here, come check this out. Let me know what you think."

"Is this about your snow shovel display?"

"It needs a woman's touch."

"Mom's right there." I hike my thumb behind me.

"Apparently, I'm not the target market for snow shovels," Mom says.

I shrug. "Doesn't everyone need a snow shovel?"

"That's what I said," Mom replies.

I follow him past a row of shelves to a pyramid display of six different shovels. He puffs out his chest. "What do you think? I have them tiered from good—they'll get the job done but maybe not to your satisfaction. Better—it'll clear the snow with minimal back pain afterward. And best —your neighbors will weep with envy."

"Oh wow. You can't go wrong with that type of marketing. I think it looks great, Dad."

He beams at his handiwork. "Thanks. These babies will fly off the display in no time." He turns his focus to me. "So what brings you in today?"

"I need a Christmas tree stand."

"Didn't you just buy a new one last year?"

"I did. But I've gained three additional trees."

He squints. "So instead of a cat lady, you're a tree lady now?"

I bite my lips together. "It's a long story."

From behind the counter, Mom calls, "Does this have anything to do with Logan Crawford?"

I whirl around. "Why do you say that?"

"I just heard you had a run-in with him at Reindeer Ridge. Something about you two being awfully close. A lot of sexual tension."

My nose scrunches. "Mom, don't say sexual tension."

"Well, when you stare longingly into someone's eyes—"

"There were no long stares."

"That's not what I heard."

"He just caught me off guard. I tripped and took some trees with me. Because they were damaged, I told Henry I'd buy them."

"That was nice of you," Mom adds.

My dad plucks a stand from the shelf and hands it over. "Here you go, dear."

"Thanks." We wander to the counter.

"So how is the festival planning coming?" he asks.

My shoulders tense. Do I give him the truth or how I wish it was going? I plaster on my best Christmas cheer smile. "It's going great!" Minus the giant roadblock named Logan Crawford. "I got an assistant today, so hopefully we can double the fun activities we have planned. I think this will be the best festival yet."

Mom shoves the magazine to the side. "We have all the faith you will do an amazing job and get the promotion. You haven't been this motivated since your class-president campaign."

"Yeah, and all I got was treasurer." While the golden boy himself got the crown. All hail President Logan Crawford.

"If you don't, you know there's always a job waiting for you at the hardware store," Mom adds. Dad clears his throat and shakes his head.

I laugh. "Well, I really hope that won't be necessary. We all know how the first time went, but thanks for the offer."

My dad's been Mount Holly's resident handyman since before I was born. He can fix anything, from broken fences to cursed snowblowers. I, on the other hand, can barely operate a tape measure. After losing my last job, I came home to work at my parents' hardware store with a one-year plan but it somehow turned into four. Honestly, I think they kept me on payroll out of pity. Luckily, when the Mount Holly assistant coordinator job opened up, they finally got to fire me with slightly less guilt.

"Bring a flyer when you have them," Dad says. "We'll put it on the corkboard."

"Will do." I slide my card into the reader, turn toward the exit, and freeze. The corkboard boasts exactly one flyer. Logan's carnival. Center stage. Of course. Dammit. Number one item on the to-do list tomorrow. Flyers. So I can staple them over Logan's.

I pull out my phone and dial Lauren's number. "I have my first task for you."

"Yes, I'm eager to get started."

"How are your design skills?"

"I love design. Fonts, color palettes, the whole thing—sometimes I do mock posters for fun—"

"Perfect. We need the best flyers Mount Holly has ever seen. Bright, bold, candy-cane gorgeous. I want Logan's posters to look like reindeer poo in comparison."

"On it!"

"Text me drafts tonight," I say sweetly, end the call, and glance back at the board. My parents are across the store debating a giant inflatable snowman. I casually pluck Logan's poster from the corkboard. It rips satisfyingly down the middle, the tack staying put like a tiny, triumphant flag. I crumple the paper, drop it in the trash, and smile.

Game on, Logan fucking Crawford. Game on.

Logan

With the flip of a switch, Brie hates me again. Truthfully, I don't know if she ever stopped, but for twelve hours, she hated me less. Is she mad I dodged the almost-kiss conversation? Probably. But the truth—*I was drowning from missing my deceased wife and you were right there*—didn't exactly scream "healthy boundaries." My original answer sounds less asshole-ish. Now, not only does she hate me again, but she's actively trying to destroy my carnival. Fuck with me. Fine. Fuck with the carnival. Not going to happen. Prior to moving back, I had a lawyer friend scour the Mount Holly bylaws line by line, and because of sections forty-five to forty-seven, I made sure the carnival was just on the other side of the town's boundary.

Now, it's nine at night and SportsCenter is murmuring in the background while I pretend to read contracts. I'm a paragraph in when my phone rings, glancing at the screen *Jason Clarkson*, a former teammate, flashes across the top. I press the talk button. "Hey Clarkson, how are you doing?"

"I'm not so bad. How about yourself?"

"Good, good. Of course, you know, the holidays are always tough." When I played in Chicago, he lost his girlfriend in a car accident. We've gotten close because of it.

"Yeah, they definitely are. So how is the change from big-city life to country boy treating you?"

If he only knew what the last few days have been like, he'd shit himself. "Well, actually not so bad. I kind of like it. It's much slower paced."

"I couldn't do it. Too cold for me."

"You played in Chicago with me for four years."

"It still doesn't change the fact that I hate the cold."

"You played hockey."

"Playing hockey in the cold differs from lounging around in a snowbank. You're moving. Working up a sweat. I don't want to be wearing ten layers of clothes just to stay warm. If I can walk around with my hockey gear on all the time, sure. Anyway, how's the carnival life treating you? Did you find yourself some clowns? A magician? A Ferris wheel?"

I bark out a laugh. "Definitely no Ferris wheels."

"Oh that's right. You refused to come with us when we rode up to the top of the Willis Tower."

"I value my life more than standing on top of a glass floor, one hundred and three stories in the air, with nothing but pavement below me. Hard pass." Now it's Jason's turn to laugh. "Anyway, wrong kind of carnival. This is more Christmas themed with games, vendors, and an ice rink.

I've been busting my ass to get it up and running, and I even found myself in a Christmas war with a girl named Brie McKenna. She's in charge of the Christmas festival the town puts on."

"Well, you've always thrived on competition."

"Oddly, it's been the best distraction."

"Perhaps a war in the streets and then later you can get freaky between the sheets."

A laugh escapes me. I won't lie, the thought has crossed my mind. "No. Nothing like that. Just when I see her, everything else disappears. She makes me feel."

"I understand that."

"Let me guess, once you get those feelings out, you move on to the next."

"I did the settling down thing once. See how well that worked out for me? I'm trying a different approach now. It's something you should try," he suggests.

"I've never been the type of person to jump from bed to bed."

"Jumping beds is pretty fun."

"Plus, I don't want Josie to see me with a different woman every week."

"Yeah. That's true. Alright, well, I just wanted to call and see how things are going. It sounds like you've got your hands full."

"It'll keep me busy for sure."

"Talk to ya."

"Later."

After hanging up, I kill the TV and stare at the ceiling. Tomorrow will be better. Or Brie will find a new way to sabotage it, unless she's given up. But if I know her, she doesn't give up easily.

The next morning, after dropping Josie off at school, I drive to Reindeer Ridge. Once parked, I kill the ignition and climb out. My boots sink into the fresh powder from last night's snowfall. Next to the barn, Henry's muscling hay bales onto a trailer.

"Hey Henry!"

He straightens and pulls off his gloves. "Hey Logan." We meet halfway and he greets me with a handshake.

"I wanted to stop by and arrange reindeer for the carnival."

"About that…" He studies the snow like it holds answers. "They're all booked."

"*All* eighteen?" My stomach drops. Reindeer are a pivotal component of the carnival. What Santa doesn't have reindeer? Henry rubs the back of his neck. I arch a brow. "Brie?" His gaze drifts up to meet mine, lips pressing into a thin line. His silence confirms my answer. I grit my teeth. "If she wants a Christmas war, she'll get a Christmas war." I called it. I had a feeling it wouldn't stop at the town's boundary line. I have to hand it to her; she's grown a backbone since high school. If she thinks a lack of reindeer at the carnival's going to stop me, she'd better prepare for a little tit for tat.

Henry lifts his hands, palms out. "Leave me out of this. I still have a business to run."

"Of course. I'll be sure to add some extra signage for Reindeer Ridge around the carnival. By the way, what's the tallest Christmas tree you have this year?"

"I have a fifteen-footer."

"I'll take it!"

He winces. "I usually save that for Brie."

"I'll pay you double." Henry twists around, rubbing the back of his neck as his eyes tick over the fields. "Triple."

"Shit," he mutters, then sighs. "That's a really good price. Are you sure you're not doing this to get back at Brie?"

Obviously, I am, but I also don't want this to interfere with their friendship. "It's business." I lift a brow.

"Yeah." He nods, dropping his gaze to the snow. "And I can definitely use it." He drums his fingers on his thigh. "Alright. I can't turn down the money." I hold out my hand, and he grips it with his, shaking on it.

"What's the second tallest tree?"

"I have three twelve-footers."

"I'll take those too."

"Jesus," he mutters.

"It's business," I reassure him, which is technically true, but also includes a side of revenge.

After moving my newly gained trees across the street, I spend the rest of the afternoon adding the finishing touches to the s'mores hut and lacing up my skates to test out the rink. The second the blades cut into the ice, my brain quiets. My mom likes to say I came into this world wearing ice skates. It's where I feel most comfortable. Most relaxed. Plus, a winter carnival in Minnesota is like Santa without cookies—possible, but why? Minutes turn to hours as the sky transforms to vibrant hues of red, orange, pink, and purple. My fingers are numb, and my legs are pleasantly dead. I glide toward one of several benches surrounding the rink and exchange my skates for my boots. On my way home, I stop at the Crooked Reindeer.

As I step inside, the usual chorus of *hi Logan* and *hey man,* rolls through the bar followed by a couple of chin lifts and a few back slaps. At the end of the bar, I claim an empty stool.

Before I'm fully seated Simon slides a beer to me. "I found some of my old hockey equipment to donate for the junior league tournament if you want to pick it up, or I can drop it off?"

"Great. Thanks. I can pick it up. I tested the ice today, and it's perfect." I take a swig of beer.

"That didn't take you long to lace up." He tilts his head. "How's the rest coming?"

"Good. I have everything set up and I have a wide variety of vendors. Everything's coming along smoothly."

"How many teams do you have for the hockey tournament?"

"Surprisingly, I have ten adult teams and six junior teams, which will make for a nice, long weekend of hockey."

He goes quiet, eyes on mine. "Question for you. Are you doing the carnival because you want to? Or is there another reason?"

Organizing a Christmas carnival wasn't on my bucket list. It's not remotely close to anything on any list of mine, but it was on Brooke's. Over the years leading up to what was supposed to be the inaugural year, she'd often ask for my input on activities or my advice on what type of vendors to have, but otherwise she did the rest. She was only months away from making it happen. Then she was gone.

"Your silence is my answer." He nods. "I'm going to be real with you. And you might hate me for it and won't want to hear it, but it's been three years. I think it's time for you to live your life for yourself. And not someone else."

A spark of heat shoots up my neck. "You're right about one thing—I don't want to hear it."

He raises both hands and backs off a step. "Alright. As

your friend, I want to be honest with you. I've known you for a long time. I only want to see you happy."

I lift the beer to my lips, letting the cool liquid settle my jumbled thoughts. When was the last time I was *happy*? Certainly not anytime in the last three years. Sure, there were brief moments of joy, like when Josie nailed her part in the school play. She was very excited. Or when she brought home her report card with all As. Proud dad moment. Or the year she wanted ice skates for Christmas because she wanted to be like her dad, so we spent the afternoon skating at the park. The first time I felt *less alone* was lying in the snowbank with Brie's body pressed on top of mine.

I down another gulp of beer and scan the room, mostly to change the subject—and there she is. Brie throws her head back at something Willa says, laugh lines fanning at the corners of her eyes. Even when she hates me, she lights up a room. And she's still beautiful when she does it.

"Brie's looking good these days, huh?" Simon murmurs.

I tear my gaze away, hoping I didn't stare too long. "Yeah." Stunning would be more accurate.

"I was thinking of asking her out." He shrugs.

My muscles tense. Simon likes Brie? No way. Not possible. "Why would you do that?"

He chuckles. "Well, we've been friends for a while. She's single, and I'm single. Perhaps something will develop between us." He throws the bar towel over his shoulder and rests his palms on the smooth wood surface in front of me.

The words "the fuck you will" get lodged in my throat. I have no claim on her. Then why do I want to reach across the bar and wrap my hands around his throat and tell him she's mine?

"Unless you're planning on asking her out?" He lifts his brow.

Oh shit. This is a test. We're playing chicken. I make my mouth form the words. "You go right ahead."

"Alright." He straightens to his full height; eyebrow cocked like a challenge. "I'll do that right now."

"You do that." My foot bounces on the ring of the barstool. My grip tightens on the bottle of beer, and I'm surprised I don't crush it into a thousand shards.

He pivots on his heel and struts toward Brie. He's not going to ask her out. He's probably just going to ask if she needs another drink. Discreetly as possible, I glance over my shoulder to witness their interaction. As soon as he reaches their table, all three of their heads turn to him. His mouth moves, but I don't know what he's saying. A second later, Brie jumps up from her stool and wraps her arms around his neck. Their embrace lasts entirely too long for my liking. Fuck. He just asked her out, didn't he? They break apart, and he nods at the other two girls.

Simon returns wearing a smug little half-smile. "It's done."

"Congratulations." I grit through my teeth.

Pain knifes through me—clean, sharp, just below the ribs. Tipping back the last of my beer, I slam the bottle a little harder than necessary. The stool screeches as I stand. "I forgot I have some things to take care of at home," I mutter. Reaching into my pocket, I pull out some cash and toss it onto the bar before stomping my way toward the exit. I punch through the door, the dark, cold, crisp night air smacking into me like a brick—a stark mirror to my current mood.

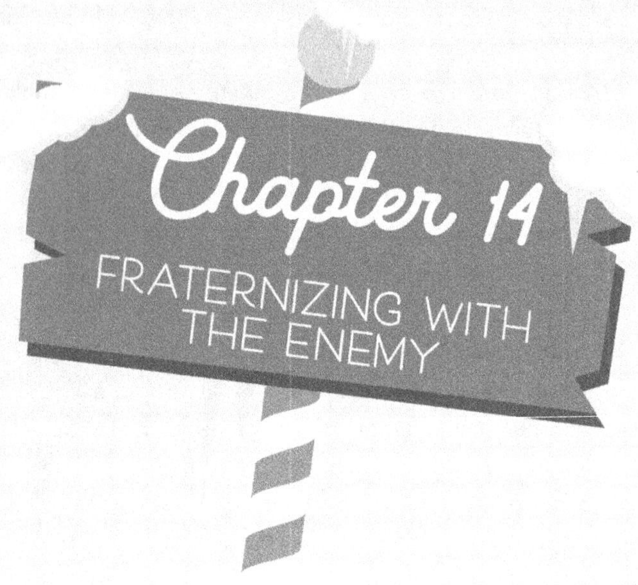

Brie

I swing into Reindeer Ridge just in time to catch the end of Henry's latest episode of *Brad's Great Escape*. He's half-dragging, half-sweet-talking the escape artist toward the open barn, a bucket of feed in one hand and patience hanging by a thread in the other. Tilly, his speckled Australian shepherd, did the real negotiating—one authoritative bark and Brad gave in and clomped inside. After he secures the gate, Henry rounds the corner, mumbling to himself.

"Morning," I call, wiggling my fingers. "Did Brad make it far this time?"

His head shoots up. "Oh. Hey Brie. He made it to the

Ericksons' farm." He pulls off his knit cap and runs his hand through his dark-brown hair. "If I had to guess, he's planning a multi-farm jailbreak."

I laugh. "Why can I picture that happening?"

Henry smiles and jams his beanie back on. "You laugh now but just wait. We'll be living on our own *Animal Farm* in a few years. What can I help you with today?"

"I'm here to pick up my tree for the festival. How tall is it this year? Fifteen feet? Seventeen?" I rub my mitten-covered hands together, leaning in, as I wait for his answer. Maybe it's even bigger than I expected?

"About that." He winces. "The tallest one I have is ten."

My hands go limp, falling at my sides. "As in ten feet? Not ten times two?" I blink. Once. Twice. My skin prickles like I've stepped into a freezer. "What the hell? Did you have a bad growing season? Stunted growth?"

"Look, I'm not going to lie to you, but I also don't want to get in the middle of this war you two have—"

"Logan," I say flatly.

"Yeah."

"What the hell, Henry?" I shake my head. My stomach seizes into one giant, hard mass. I always got first pick from the big trees. "Whose team are you on?"

"I'm on Team Henry. He offered to pay me triple the price. I couldn't turn that down. You know we've been struggling for the past couple of years." He waves his hand over his field. "I had to take what I could."

My mouth hangs open for a beat, then I shut it, because honestly? If I were in his position, I'd do the same. But this is certainly one big, swift kick to the candy cane. "I understand. Maybe I can put the tree on a riser or something, so it doesn't look so sad."

"Sorry, Brie."

I wave him off. "I'll make it work."

After arranging delivery of my tree, I drive back into town as if the posted speed limit is only a suggestion. The bell over the Jolly Biscuit door jingles cheerfully, the opposite of my current mood.

"Someone's spicy," Willa greets me from behind the counter.

"Do you know what he did?" I plant my hands on the counter.

"'He' being Logan?" Her brows rise.

"He bought the tall trees, Willa. *All* the tall trees. I get the runt." My voice goes a little wild at the end. "The tree lighting kicks off the entire Holly Jolly Festival. I can't debut a tree that screams 'meh'."

"No one will think it's 'meh'. They'll think 'ooo, lights!'" She leaned in, lowering her voice. "Did he do it because you… commandeered all the reindeer?"

Of course she's right, but I don't want to admit it. At least not out loud. "It's just another layer of stress added to this holiday season."

"You've worked your ass off for too long to let Logan dampen your spirit."

This won't be high school all over again. I will not stand in Logan's shadow. "You're right. My Christmas spirit tank needs to be overflowing." I lift my chin and square my shoulders. "And I need everyone in Mount Holly to know it."

Willa thrusts her fists into the air. "That's my girl!"

The bell jingles again followed by clacking of heels on the linoleum floor. A woman in a navy peacoat, with black hair that shimmers like silk, strolls toward the counter. My heart cartwheels. "Oh my God." I grab at Willa's sleeve. "Do you know who that is?"

She shakes her head. "Should I?"

"Yes! That's *Emma St. Claire*, world renowned Christmas blogger turned editor and chief of her own magazine. She spends her life flying around the world to cover holiday festivals—like a real-life Mrs. Claus with a first-class boarding pass." My eyes widen. "What if the Holly Jolly Festival finally won the Best Hometown Christmas contest?"

"Go talk to her." She shoos me away.

"What do I say?"

"Introduce yourself."

"Right." I inhale a deep breath. Oxygen to the brain is crucial right now. I wipe my palms on my pants because no one likes a clammy handshake and cross the diner. "Excuse me." Emma whirls around. "Hi." I give her a small wave. "I'm Brie McKenna." I extend my hand for her to shake. Her soft fingers, and most adorable snowman-painted fingernails, grip mine. "I'm a huge fan. I've been following your blog since it started. And I subscribe to your magazine. Are you here for the Holly Jolly Festival?"

"Hi, Brie," she says warmly. "In fact, I am."

In my head, fireworks, a marching band, and me on a float wearing a sash that reads *Not Today, Logan* rolls by. A world-famous blogger showcasing the Holly Jolly Festival is exactly what we need. This will surely not only boost my chances at the promotion but will also make Logan's carnival eat my dust.

"The Holly Jolly Festival is the one on the outskirts of town, isn't it?"

"No." I frown. Who gave her the wrong details? She's new in town, I'll forgive her. "The Holly Jolly Festival is right here in the center of Mount Holly, and I am the event coordinator."

She taps a finger against her lips. "No. I was told it's in a field outside of Mount Holly."

I wave her off. "There's a stupid carnival taking place, but it's not important."

"Two holiday events," she muses, eyes sparkling. "How festive."

"Not quite. Mine's a festival. The other one's just a teeny, tiny, silly carnival."

She nods. "I look forward to checking out your festival."

"Oh gosh, we have so many amazing things planned. I can't wait to show them all to you. Actually, I have some free time. If you want, we can start right now." If all goes as planned, she'll be writing her blog post about the festival tonight with publication the following week. It'll be perfect timing for the kick-off. Finally, I'm getting a little tinsel thrown my way.

She tugs the cuff of her coat up and glances at her watch. "I have a few hours until I can check in, but I want to grab a coffee and," she leans around me, "one of those cinnamon rolls."

"Oh my gosh, we're almost the same person. That's my order too." Emma smiles at me.

"No, it's not," Willa says, appearing with a to-go bag. "You get the breakfast sandwich. Which is right here."

I glare at Willa, giving her my best *just go with it* look before directing my attention to Emma. "Yes, but the cinnamon roll is my second choice. I'll grab both. On me."

I lean over the counter toward Willa. "Write 'Paid for by Brie McKenna, Holly Jolly Festival Coordinator' on the receipt."

"You never told me you liked my cinnamon rolls."

"Play along. I'm trying to connect with Emma."

"By lying about your breakfast order? Just be yourself."

I sigh. "Just write it."

Willa's mouth twitches. "Should I add your phone number? Email? Blood type? Maybe a lock of hair?"

"Phone number is good, but the rest might be a bit much."

"This whole thing might be a bit much. Especially the cinnamon roll." Willa rings me up, and I pay for our orders before she turns around and collects a cinnamon roll from the display case.

I turn to Emma. "It might be weird to ask, but can we take a selfie together?"

"Sure." She smiles.

I pull out my phone, tuck in close to Emma, and snap a picture. This is going on my social media. I already know the caption: *Me + Christmas Royalty = Holly Jolly Destiny.* It's not every day you meet a celebrity, especially in Mount Holly. "Thanks. I have to ask, what is your favorite type of Christmas—"

The diner erupts into a collection of *hi* and *hey Logan*s.

I roll my eyes as Emma swivels around. "Is that Logan Crawford?"

"No. I don't know who that is. Must be some guy passing through town. Oh! Maybe he's the Northwoods Killer. You know they never caught him."

"They caught him twenty years ago," Willa says, sliding a coffee and cinnamon roll to Emma.

I cut Willa a death glare and steer Emma gently away from the human magnet in the doorway. "Now that you've got your items—want a private tour of the festival grounds?"

Emma spins away from me. "No. I think that's Logan Crawford."

"Logan Crawford! Can I get your autograph?" A little boy runs up to Logan with a hockey puck and a marker.

"That is Logan. I need to introduce myself." She abandons our plans and beelines it to Logan.

"But what about the festi—" she's already shaking his hand, probably memorizing his jawline while she's at it. "—val." My shoulders sag. "Meet you there? No, I'll be busy drowning myself in the Winterberry Creek," I mutter to myself.

"The creek's frozen." Willa bumps my shoulder. "But with that glare you're giving Logan, you'll thaw it by noon."

"Does he have telepathy or something? It's like the moment he knows something good's about to happen to me—poof—he shows up and ruins it."

"He's here for me," Willa says lightly.

My head snaps to her so fast I give myself whiplash. Logan's here to see Willa? Why?

"Oh my god!" Willa doubles over in laughter. "Not to see me. But your face certainly gave you away." She laughs again as heat creeps up my neck. "He comes in every morning, and almost every afternoon, to get food for his crew. I'm going to have my best fourth quarter because of him."

"First Henry and now you. You can't be fraternizing with the enemy. Where's the line in the sand?"

"We're not ten. There are no sandboxes. I don't have to pick sides."

"This is a war. A Christmas war. And I can't have you passing secrets across enemy lines. He can't know all my marketing tactics on drawing a crowd and keeping everyone entertained."

She waves a hand at Logan. "He's a hockey legend. I'm sure he can draw a crowd on his own."

"Which is precisely why he can't know any of my surprises."

"You have a surprise?"

"Maybe? Okay, no. I don't. Not yet. But I will. I will give him the best damn surprise he's ever seen." From across the room, Emma laughs at something Logan says and touches his arm. I shake my head. "I've lost her."

Logan's gaze skims the diner and lands on me. For a heartbeat, the hostility between us dissipates. He almost looks defeated—something I've never seen from him. Then Emma says something, his mouth tips up, and I staple my heart back to my ribs. Now is not the time to get soft.

All afternoon, I conjure up ideas for the demise of Logan—I mean his carnival. But mostly, I avoid Mrs. Kingsley because I don't want to mention Emma being in town until I nail down a meeting with her. She'll only be disappointed I didn't tie her up, throw her in my SUV, and drive her to the festival myself. If there weren't so many witnesses, it could have been a possibility.

After work, I swing by my parents' house to drop off some chocolate chip banana bread for my dad since it's his favorite. He always tells me my bread is the best. At least I'm number one in someone's eyes.

I pull into my parents' freshly shoveled driveway and step out.

"Hi Brie!" a voice yells from next door.

I peer over my shoulder, and Josie's standing next to a snowman that looks like he's about to rappel off a casino roof. Wide-brim hat. Black mask. Serious swagger. "Hi Josie!" I wave. "I like your snowman. That's a really pretty scarf."

"Thank you. It was my mom's." Her fingers smooth over the fringe.

My throat tightens. What do I say to that? I don't know how Logan has described death to his daughter, and I don't want to be the one to ruin whatever her idea is.

"She's an angel now. My dad says she's my guardian angel. Did you know my mom?"

I shake my head. "No, I didn't. But I heard she was a really great mom."

"I miss her." Her head droops toward the snow.

This was not a conversation I was expecting to have today. "I'm sorry. It's always hard to lose a loved one, especially your mom."

"Did you lose your mom too?"

"No, my parents actually live here." I hike my thumb toward my parents' house.

"Oh, your mom brought cookies over for me and my grandma."

"My mom does like to bake."

"I used to bake with my mom. She'd let me stir the batter or add the chocolate chips."

"When I was your age, that's what my mom would let me do too."

"I overheard my dad on the phone talking about you."

My ears perk up.

"I was supposed to be sleeping, but I wasn't tired. I overheard him talking about how it's been a long time since he's felt happy."

That can't be right. Surely, she was mistaken. I shove the thought away. "Are you practicing for the snowman competition?"

"What competition?"

"At the Holly Jolly Festival. Every year, we hold a snowman building contest."

"That sounds really fun!"

"It's a blast. You should enter. Your snowman would definitely be in the running for first place." My gaze wanders over her unconventional snowman. "Why's the snowman wearing a mask? Is he in hiding?"

"He's a secret agent snowman." She beams.

"Oh, that's fun! I've never seen one of those before."

As Josie turns back to adjust her snowman's hat, an idea snaps into place. During wartime, one often crosses enemy lines to gather intelligence. It's time to go secret agent, gather intel, and out-holly that carnival till it jingles surrender.

Brie

My pulse hammers like a snare drum, and with every ring through the speaker my bravery dwindles. I've never done anything like this. I tend to stay on the right side of the law —parking within the lines, stopping for pedestrians, returning library books only fashionably late, but desperate times and all that. The call clicks. Before Willa can say hello, I blurt, "Meet me at my place—and wear a disguise."

"What's the disguise for?"

"A real best friend wouldn't ask. They would just do."

Willa laughs. "Alright, alright. Disguise, check. I'll be there in twenty."

"Twenty? You only live ten minutes away."

"I'm at Mason's. He had the night off."

"Okay. But hurry."

Twenty-five minutes later, my front door opens, Jason Voorhees steps into my entryway… in tan MUK LUKS. "Sorry I'm late," Willa says through the white hockey mask. "It sounded urgent, so I didn't want to stop at home. Luckily, Mason had this in his closet."

"Really? A Jason mask?"

"You told me a disguise." Willa rips the mask off her head. "You didn't give me any direction. So I interpreted this as a disguise." She waves the mask in front of me. "Are you going to tell me what we're doing now?"

"I'll tell you what we're not going to do. That is taking a trip to Camp Crystal Lake and partaking in a murderous rampage."

"But I have the perfect mask for it," Willa whines.

"Maybe next time, but tonight we're going on a little recon mission."

"Oh, shit," Willa mutters.

"I heard that."

She sighs and tosses the mask onto the entry table; it skitters into a glass bowl with a clink. "Well, I wasn't trying to be discreet about it. Either way, the trip to Camp Crystal Lake and murderous rampage sounds more fun than whatever this is."

"Hear me out." I clap my hands together. "Recon. We're going across enemy lines to peek at his arsenal. Since Logan bought all the good trees like the Christmas cartel, we're going to scout his carnival to see what he's working with. I need to know his game plan so I can be a step ahead of him. That's the only way I'm going to win."

Willa plants a hand on her hip. "So we're not going there to steal trees?"

Tilting my head, I press a finger to my lips. That's a

really good idea. I hadn't considered that. "I do have a sled. And rope."

"We're not stealing any trees. You know what happens to people who go across enemy lines? They don't get served charcuterie in a penthouse. You know this is trespassing, right?"

"Don't think of it as trespassing, but as recon."

"I highly doubt Vana will think like that when she captures us and throws us in jail." Willa crosses her arms over her chest.

"Perhaps we can bribe her." I shrug.

"Let's add bribing a police officer to our list of felonies tonight. Sounds like an excellent idea. Much like this trespassing one."

"Fine." I blow out a breath. "I need to see what he's working with, so I can one-up him."

"Sounds more like an in-the-bedroom situation than a carnival one."

"I'm much less concerned about the bedroom and more concerned about the carnival."

"By the way, are we talking about the same Logan?" She lifts a brow. "I don't think that man has ever been one-upped in his life."

"Maybe it's time someone," I point to myself, "brings him down a peg or two."

Willa sighs and tugs the mask back on, the elastic snapping around her head. "Okay. I'm here. In disguise. Ready to commit medium crimes. What's the plan?" She plops down on the couch, crossing her arms over her chest and leg over her knee. Her foot bounces as she waits for instructions. If this weren't important, I'd laugh at how ridiculous she looks.

"Jump in my SUV, and I'll fill you in."

She groans. "But I just sat down." Her foot thumps to

the floor, and she peels herself off the cushion. "What's your disguise, anyway?"

Reaching behind the armchair, I grab a mask and tug it on. "This." I vogue pose as the mask flops around on my face.

"Betty White! Our *Golden Girls* party was so much fun!"

"I never thought I'd get to wear it again, but here we are." I pull open the front door, and Willa passes through.

"Betty and Jason. The dynamic duo," she says over her shoulder.

Down the road from Logan's carnival, I park my SUV in a partially plowed field entrance. I turn off the engine, and we both step out into the dark, snowy night. We creep down the desolate road with nothing but the moon reflecting off the snow to light our path. Willa comes to a halt when we reach the chained entrance.

"Follow me. We'll go along the ditch until we reach the tree line, there's a gap near the fence line we can crawl through."

"Great plan, but you know they'll be able to see our footprints in the snow."

"I'm going to start the path. You follow in my footprints. Then on our way out, we'll take the same path and brush snow into the holes." I wave a hand in a come-here motion. "Follow me." On my first step, my boot sinks down to my ankle. With all my weight, the snowy ground gives, and I sink to my shin. Well, this is deeper than I was expecting. With another step, I sink past my knee. After a few more high steps, I glance over my shoulder, and Willa has disappeared. Jason Vorhees is a terrible wingman.

"Or," Willa says cheerfully, standing in the wide-open gate, "we could use this thing called an entrance. It wasn't even locked."

On wobbly legs, I backtrack my steps while stopping to

shovel snow into the hole with my mitten-covered hand. Once I reach clear ground, I brush the snow off my pants, boots, and mittens. Rising to my full height, I stroll past Willa. "Gate it is. Let's do some recon."

We tiptoe along rows of vendor huts in various states of almost finished. We pass a trio of firepits circled with log stools.

"He has a s'mores lodge," I hiss. "With log seating."

Willa squints. "And logs are bad because…?"

"Because they're charming," I snap, and dammit, why didn't I think to use logs? They're so much more rustic than my benches.

In the distance, moonlight ricochets off a display of Christmas decorations. I quicken my steps to a trot. When the shapes take form, it hits me. They're like the Rolls Royce of light-up decorations. I gasp. "How in the hell did he get those? They've been back-ordered for the last four years."

Willa comes to a stop next to me. "I don't know what you're talking about."

I rip off my Betty White mask and pass it to Willa. "Those reindeer." I point to the patch of snow a few feet from the path. "They're all animatronic with top-of-the-line LEDs that work in any condition, even underwater."

"You're orgasming over Christmas lights, aren't you?"

"A little. I need a closer look." I hurdle the snowbank, and my boots press into the freshly fallen snow.

"Sure," she mutters. "Leave an obvious boot trail directly to the crime scene."

"I'll be sure to cover my tracks on my way out."

"That won't be any better."

Up close, the lead reindeer gleams like a frosted dream. I stroke its neck with reverent fingers. "It's beautiful," I whisper, "and so much bigger in person." I circle around while admiring the front. The toe of my boot catches on a jagged rock, and I tumble forward. My arms flail wildly, smack into something hard, and a sickening snap crackles through the air. Snow puffs up as I crash into the powder. Seconds later, it sprinkles down on me. I blink, shake the snow off, and look up just in time to watch the reindeer's head fall delicately onto my lap.

"Shit. Shit. Shit." I sit up and hoist the decapitated head in the air. A vise locks around my chest. In my hands is a four-thousand-dollar light-up reindeer head. Technically, since it's only the head, it would be worth only one thousand, three hundred and thirty-three dollars. Either way, it's expensive.

"That would be a lot scarier if it were a real deer's head," Willa says from the pathway.

I scramble to my feet with the broken deer's head in my trembling hands. I jerk my gaze to Willa. "You wouldn't happen to have any tape or glue with you?"

She shoves her hands in her pockets. "I have some gum." She holds a paper package in the air.

Chew a bunch of gum and use it as an adhesive? My lips press together. Unfortunately, I'm not MacGyver so that's out. I hoist the deer's head in place, but it's too dark to see anything. Dodging shards of metal and plastic, I search for a spot to join the two pieces. At the base of the neck, I wedge a few stray plastic tabs into place. Once secure, I remove my hands with the tenderness of a bomb tech and hold my breath. Any slight breeze could cause the head to drop. After a few seconds, it holds. I exhale a deep breath. The right-side dips before it plops into the snow. "Dammit." I retrieve it from the ground and, instead of trying to fasten it to the body again, I tuck it under my arm.

"Are you taking a souvenir?" Willa holds out her hand and helps me through the snow and onto the path.

"It won't stay. Maybe he won't notice."

"He won't notice a deer is missing its head?"

"He has five others. I don't know how observant he is. At this moment, I'm reacting first and thinking later. I'll figure it out." We continue to sneak down the path that leads toward the back of the carnival.

"I get to add breaking and entering *and* stealing to my resume," Willa says.

"If you want to get technical, you're only an accomplice in the stealing."

"Oh, even better."

The path curls toward the far corner of the grounds where something smooth and pale gleams in front of the tree line.

I stop dead in my tracks. "What's that?"

Willa continues past me until she realizes she's alone. She spins to face me and turns to where I'm pointing. "Is it some sort of building?"

I rush forward, and Willa's hot on my heels. We round the last corner and an oval of ice stretches before us with bleachers flanking two sides

"Son of a bitch. He has an ice rink." My shoulders drop. "Why didn't I think of an ice rink? What is a Christmas festival without an ice rink?"

Not only do I have a decapitated reindeer head tucked under my arm that I need to contend with, but now I have to compete with an ice rink. Bah humbug.

Logan

With my elbow resting on the kitchen counter, I take a sip of my second cup of coffee for the morning and drum my fingers on the newspaper like a metronome with anxiety. Every time I closed my eyes, an army of fir trees chased after me. A spruce brigade seeking revenge. While balsams wave garland like nunchucks. Maybe buying four trees was a bit excessive. Then again, Brie had hoarded every reindeer in a tri-county radius. If she could corner the market on antlers, I could corner the market on needles. What if I donate a tree to her festival? That way, it won't seem like I'm just giving it to her. *Tree courtesy of Logan Crawford's carnival.* She'd love that—if love meant I want to strangle you with my bare hands. Then again, she's dating my friend, or at least I think so. Their hug lasted three Mississippis too long to be considered friendly.

"Daddy! Daddy!" Josie barrels into the kitchen like a stampede.

"Whoa! Slow down, Peanut. Get yourself a bowl of cereal and take a seat." I pat the empty stool next to me.

She darts around the kitchen and collects everything to pour herself a mountain of Rice Krispies. An avalanche of puffed rice cereal spill over the sides as she drops a spoon into the bowl. She races around to the other side and climbs onto the stool. Even more Rice Krispies spill over the sides as she pulls her spoon out for a big bite. "Can I join the—" she says around a mouth full of food.

"Finish chewing. Then talk."

Her jaw moves a mile a minute until she swallows. "Can I join the snowman building contest?"

"What contest? Is this for school or something?"

"No, it's at the Holly Jolly Festival. Brie told me about it. She thinks my snowman could win." Her hazel eyes sparkle.

My brows pinch together. "When did you see Brie?"

"At Grandma and Grandpa's. I was building a snowman in their front yard, and she saw me. Her parents live next door. She told me about the contest. Can I join?" She intertwines her fingers. "Please? Please?"

I set my coffee mug down and rake my fingers through my hair. How will it look? Rival carnival owner hanging out at the festival? When did the Holly Jolly Festival start holding contests? It has to be new. They never did that while I was growing up.

"Please, Dad."

Saying no to Josie is like refusing a puppy a treat—it hurts your soul. Plus, it's only a snowman contest. At the festival Brie's hosting. At least she's not asking for a brand-new iPhone. "Sure, Peanut."

"Thank you!" she shrieks. Bending over, she wraps her arms around my waist and squeezes.

I'd do anything for her, even if it includes crossing enemy lines.

After dropping Josie off at school, I head to the carnival grounds. Surprisingly, we're ahead of schedule, and a soft opening the weekend before Christmas looks promising.

My boots kick up the newly fallen snow as I meander down the path toward Santa's hut. Brooke always wanted me to play Santa at her carnival. I already have the suit since she bought it for me for putting presents under the tree for Josie. Brooke wanted authenticity in case Josie snuck out of her room. The best thing about being dad and playing Santa: I convinced her Santa likes English toffee cookies, not chocolate chip.

My gaze glosses over the reindeer, and I freeze. One of these things is not like the others. Why doesn't Rudolph have a head? I frown and scan the ground. It wasn't windy last night, so if it broke, it wouldn't have blown too far. No head in sight, but faint prints emerge from the newly fallen powder. I step into the snow, pull away, and compare the two prints. If I had to guess, it's about a size seven. Beside the boot prints, something catches the light. I crouch and pluck out a silver keychain. *Mostly Nice. Sometimes Naughty.* The corners of my lips twitch into a smile. It's the same key chain from the night Brie drove me home from the bar. My thumb brushes over the sharp metal of a bent end. It must have fallen off. Most people would be mad having someone trespassing on their property, but not me. It only means revenge. I casually do a couple of laps around the festival grounds, planning my attack and confirming no one is around.

This isn't the same Brie from high school. She's braver, fiercer, and fuck, I like it. Our back-and-forth Christmas pranks may be childish, but it's keeping my head occupied with things that aren't Brooke.

I roll my truck to a stop near the front entrance of the Holly Jolly Festival. A snowman for a reindeer head seems appropriate, and I spot the perfect victim. Leaving the truck running, I jump out and stand in front of a plastic snowman holding a Welcome to the Holly Jolly Festival sign. "You're coming with me Frosty." I bear-hug the snowman around the torso and lift. The black top hat slides off the head and lands in the snow. I bend over, pick it up, and place the snowman in the cab of my truck. Once in place, I jump back inside and set the top hat on my passenger seat. I peel away, the tires kicking up snow on my exit.

My phone rings through my truck speakers with an incoming phone call. *Mason* flashes at the top of the dashboard screen.

"Hey, man," I answer. "What's up?"

"Are you close to the fire station?"

"Yeah. I'm only a few blocks away."

"Can you pick me up and give me a ride to Willa's?"

"Sure. I'll be there in a few."

At the fire station, Mason pulls open the door and lifts the hat before climbing in. He holds it out to me, brows pinched together. "Why do you have a top hat in your truck?"

"It belongs to the snowman." I take the hat from him and toss it behind me.

He glances over his shoulder. "Next question. Why is Frosty hanging out in your back seat?"

Frosty's black, beady eyes stare back at me in the rearview mirror. "Collateral."

"Do I want to know?"

"She not only decapitated my reindeer but also stole the head."

"When you say she, I'm guessing Brie?"

"Yep. So I stole her snowman." I merge onto Frostpine Road. Frosty wobbles and grins at me in the rearview mirror, unbothered by the morality of it all.

A throaty chuckle escapes him. "And you're going to chauffeur it around?"

"For now," I deadpan. Mostly because my plan doesn't extend past stealing her snowman.

"Don't you think this is getting a bit much?"

My grip tightens on the steering wheel. "She started it. I'm just putting an end to it."

"I doubt stealing her snowman is putting an end to it. This sounds more like some weird foreplay you two enjoy."

"Have you ever been in a Christmas war before?"

He shakes his head. "I can't say I have."

"Then if I want your advice, I'll ask for it."

Another deep laugh comes from next to me. "Alright. I'll just sit back and enjoy the entertainment."

I don't back down from a challenge. I never did while on the ice, and I certainly won't do it against the Ice Queen herself.

Brie

Before I have both feet inside the door of Sip and Sleigh, Sloane greets me with a smirk. "What is this I hear about you decapitating deer now?"

"Shhh." I scan the shop for eavesdroppers. I lean in and whisper, "Willa told you?"

"Yeah, she stopped in here earlier for her morning supply of muffins and spilled the tea."

"I'll have you know it wasn't a real reindeer! Just a light-up one. And it was an accident that blossomed into the perfect opportunity for revenge."

She folds her arms and pops her hip. "So you stole the reindeer head. It seems a little passive-aggressive instead of talking it out."

"Stop being the voice of reason," I whine. I cross my arms over my chest and pout like a five-year-old. "He started it."

"How?"

I drop my hands to my sides. "By showing up in town, thinking he's the king of Christmas because he's Logan Crawford, who gets everything handed to him on a silver platter." I flutter my hands. "Oh, look, I'm a famous hockey player who's not only charming and charismatic but who's defied Father Time. And somehow, he's only managed to become more attractive." Shit. Did I just say that out loud? Spew some more words to cover it up! "It's not happening while I'm here. The Christmas crown is mine, and he doesn't get that title. Not this time." If people weren't eavesdropping before, they certainly heard me now.

"You think about him a lot for someone you don't like," she sings.

I glare at her. "Whose side are you on?"

"Yours. Always yours." She passes me a coffee and a cranberry lemonade muffin on a plate.

"Thank you. I'm going to take a seat and wait for Lauren."

Half a muffin later, Lauren breezes in, cheeks pink from the cold. "Sorry! Brad was blocking Mistletoe Street. Just… vibing without a care in the world."

"He's very unapologetic about wasting people's time," I say, pushing an open folder between us. The Holly Jolly budget stares back at me. Mocking me. I will show them. When Brie McKenna wants something, she gets it.

"One thing the Holly Jolly Festival is missing is an ice-skating rink. Now I figure if we—"

"An ice-skating rink?" she squeaks. "Is that even in the budget, let alone reasonable to get it done in time?"

"I've crunched a few numbers, and it's totally doable." Mostly, I said to hell with the budget; we have to make it happen for the future of the Holly Jolly Festival and for my future event coordinator position. "If we eliminate a few of the inflatables. And the Santa bounce house. Do kids even like those anymore? I think they'd enjoy an ice rink much more. Only one tree is necessary. We can shave a few minutes off the firework display. That'll surely save us a little money."

"But I don't think it'll be enough for an ice rink."

Dammit. "Maybe I could offer my services for extra money for an ice rink?"

Sloane appears with a coffee for Lauren. "You're going to prostitute yourself out for an ice rink?" She shrugs. "Well, I've seen people do a lot more for a lot less."

"No! Not sexual services, though I bet that would get me the money faster." My brows raise at the idea. But this would also require me to shave my legs. "Business services. Advice. Plans. Strategy."

"Right," Sloane says. "Because nothing says fiscal responsibility like 'Pay me so I can blow up my budget.'"

"Ugh. Stop throwing snow on my sunshine." I deflate. "Fine. Cross that off the list."

Lauren flips through a few pages. "Even with the suggested cuts, the budget is still nearing the cap. The ice rink might have to wait another year."

"Where is your *where there's a will, there's a way*?" I slap the manila folder closed. "Who cares about the budget? Budgets are just meant to be broken, anyway."

"I don't think that's what the saying means," Lauren adds. She taps her finger against her lips as seconds pass. "I got it!"

My brows raise with optimism. "*You're* going to prostitute yourself out for the festival."

She shakes her head, her blonde ponytail swishing behind her. "Um. No. But this is better! My friend Eli works as a conservation officer for the Department of Natural Resources, and he told me about a new trail by Winterberry Creek. It would make the perfect place to organize a sleigh ride. It would give the DNR an opportunity to showcase the new trail, along with some educational programming to the community. I'm sure it could all be done with a minimal budget."

I nod along. This could work. I bet Logan doesn't have a sleigh ride. "Yes! I love it! It will be an amazing addition to the festival along with an ice rink." I stare off into the distance. "I can picture it now. Skaters could leave the rink and take a winter wonderland sleigh ride. The townsfolk will love it."

"No. This is in lieu of the ice rink. To save the budget."

Resting my elbows on the table, I lean in. "My job and promotion are hanging on by a strand of tinsel, which in turn, also means your job is on the line. Budgets are currently out of the equation. We need this year's Holly Jolly Festival to be the best festival the state, no, the country has ever seen. And that's not going to be possible if we follow a budget. We're competing against Logan Crawford. If he has an ice rink, we have an ice rink." Lauren's eyes widen to the size of giant Christmas ornaments as she slinks back in her chair, afraid to fight me anymore on the budget, and that's okay with me. The less resistance, the better. "But I do love your sleigh ride idea. Can you talk to your friend and make that happen?"

Her head jerks up and down. "Yes. I'll get right on it."

My phone chimes with an incoming message. Willa's name pops up in preview mode.

WILLA

Have you been to the festival grounds yet?

I unlock my phone and read the message again.

BRIE

No, I haven't. Going there right after we leave the coffee shop. Why? Is there something I should be concerned about?

Three dots dance on the screen. And then stop. And start again.

WILLA

Mason told me that Logan paid a brief visit to the festival last night and took a snowman hostage.

My phone tumbles out of my hand and crashes onto the table with a loud bang. I snatch it up. My simmering rage turns into a blistering wave. My thumbs slam against the keys.

BRIE

He STOLE my snowman?

WILLA

Yeah. The one out front. A deer head for a snowman.

A collection of *hi* and *hey Logan*s fills the coffee shop. This guy gets a welcoming party every time he enters a room. He's about to get a party from me, and his party favor will be my fist to his face. My chair scrapes harshly against the floor as I shove away from the table. As I near the counter, the coffee mugs next to the coffee machine rattle with the force of my frustration. Logan's gaze drifts to mine. Damn him for looking so hot. When I'm only a foot away, his clean, manly scent wafts around me. And damn him for smelling so good too. *Focus.* I come to a halt, the toes of my boots inches from his.

"I want my snowman back, Logan. You have it, I know. Mason told Willa, and she told me."

He leans in a fraction, all calm dimples. "I only took it because you took my reindeer."

"False. I didn't take the whole reindeer, only the head."

"You know, those reindeer aren't cheap."

"Yes, I'm quite aware of their cost." And super jealous that you have them.

"Would you have preferred if I had only taken the head of your snowman?" He raises a perfectly sculpted brow.

Stop admiring his eyebrows or getting lost in the brown flecks that swirl in his green irises. "No. But you can't just go around stealing things."

"Oh, you're one to talk." His mouth twitches. "By the way, how was your date with Simon?"

I rear my head back. "Date with Simon? What are you talking about?" Why is he so concerned about who I date? And why does he think I'm dating Simon.

He shoves his hands into his pockets. "The other night. He asked you out. You hugged." His casual tone isn't fooling anybody.

A giggle bubbles up, threatening to escape. Me and Simon? Hell no. Plus, I'm not his type. But Logan asking about it is more telling than anything. Clearly, the idea of me and Simon dating gets under his skin, so I'm going to play into the ruse. I press a hand to my chest like a soap-opera heroine. "Oh. That night." I give him my sweetest smile. "Yes. Simon and I are dating."

His dimple falters.

Sloane slides a white pastry box between us like a referee tossing in a puck. "Here's your taste-test cookies."

After a several-beat stare off, Logan breaks first. I win! Take that!

He rests a hand on the box. "Thanks," he says, voice a little gruffer than usual. "Based on the smell, I already know it's going to be a tough choice of which ones to pick for the carnival." He pats his jacket pocket and then his jeans. "I forgot my wallet in my truck. I'll go grab it so I can pay you."

Sloane waves him off. "Don't worry about it. Next time."

"No. I can't do that. I'll be two seconds." Logan spins on his heels and strolls out of the coffee shop.

The bell jingles as he leaves. I'm two parts irritated, one part… appreciating the view. Focus. I narrow my gaze at Sloane. "What the hell? You're providing cookies for his carnival? Can't you see he's trying to drive a wedge between me and my friends? He wants your business, so you're obligated to take his side."

"No one is taking sides. If you had seen the number of zeros on the contract he gave me, you wouldn't have turned it down either. I'm only providing the cookies." She holds up her hands. "I drew the line at running the booth. Everyone loves my cookies. Not only is it great exposure for the coffee shop but the extra money will help me buy a new espresso machine." When I don't release my glare, she continues to soothe my concerns. "Don't worry, I'm still providing cookies for your festival like I do every year."

As much as I want to be mad at her, I can't because, like Willa, I'm sure she's going to have her best year yet because of Logan. I'm thrilled that this is all working out for her. For me, on the other hand, everything is crumbling to the ground. "It's business now, until he steals you all away. Like my snowman."

"The only wedge is the one you're creating with this ridiculous feud. In fact, this Christmas war needs to stop. You're tearing the town apart, forcing us to choose sides."

"No, we're not. Stop being dramatic."

"Okay, fine." She throws her hands up in the air. "I'm just sick of the gossip. You're the will-they-won't-they couple of the century with all the sexual tension that radiates from you. Maybe you need to bang it out."

I shake my head. "No one said that." Even though after the almost-kiss, it's crossed my mind a time or two. Hate sex is a thing, right? If not, we could make it a thing. Shove a paper bag over his head and go to pound town. Goosebumps prickle my skin at the thought.

"I'm saying it now. Plus, I need new gossip. I'm over this."

The bell jingles on Logan's return. Rays of sunshine illuminate behind him like a halo. He slides his hand through his hair, straightening the strands at the top of his head. Why can't I tear my gaze away?

When he reaches the counter, he hands a check to Sloane. "I got it."

"Thanks." Sloane smiles at him. "One more request."

"Sure, anything," Logan replies.

"This war you two have," she points between Logan and me, "needs to end for the sanity of everyone in Mount Holly. You two need to apologize to each other and arrange an exchange of stolen goods." Neither of us says anything. In fact, we avoid eye contact. "Okay. If you two don't apologize, I'll rip up this check and you don't get any cookies." She glares at Logan.

I lift my chin. Yes! I beam. My best friend going all benevolent tyrant on his ass. *Go Sloane.*

Her gaze swings to me. "Oh, you're apologizing as well. Otherwise, same deal."

I deflate. No more benevolent.

"Logan," Sloane says, "you need to apologize for stealing her snowman."

"Fine." Logan sighs before shifting his gaze to me. "Brie, I'm sorry for stealing your snowman."

"Apology accepted," I say primly.

The three of us stand in silence until Logan clears his throat. Sloane glares at me and nods toward Logan.

"I really shouldn't have to apologize. I did it in retaliation. He started it." Sloane crosses her arms over her chest and glares at me like she's scolding a five-year-old. "Fine.　　　　I'm-sorry-for-decapitating-your-reindeer-and-stealing-its-head," I mumble.

"No. A genuine apology. Now you have to look him in the eye." When I say nothing, she adds, "Go on."

My jaw clenches and I lift my chin to meet Logan's eyes. "I'm sorry for decapitating your reindeer and stealing its head."

"Great!" Sloane claps her hands together. "Now that's settled. We'll arrange a drop-off and pickup of the stolen goods here at 8 p.m."

"Uh. I can't do tonight," Logan says. "I have a movie night with Josie."

"Okay. Tomorrow night," Sloane replies.

"I've got the parade committee till… who knows," I say.

Sloane huffs. "Fine. The next night. Anyone have plans?"

Logan and I shake our heads.

"Nah. I think I'm good," Logan says.

"Me too," I add.

"Then it's settled. Thursday at eight o'clock." With the

flip of a switch, a wide grin takes over Sloane's face. "I'm glad we got that settled. Now, to seal the deal, buy each other a drink. Mostly because I want the money."

"We can finally call a truce." Logan extends his hand toward me.

I eye his palm and my nose wrinkles as if a steaming pile of reindeer poo is sitting in the middle. I'm deep in the trenches of this holiday war for the long haul. A handshake will not make me surrender. "Never." Meeting his gaze, my lips pull into a wide grin. "But I will enjoy the extra-large, double shot, vanilla latte you're buying me." At least Sloane's making the drink, so I know Logan can't poison it.

For the rest of the morning, I sip my coffee, which tastes like victory and vengeance. I'm sure he's thrilled about getting an apology from me. It's just one more thing to inflate his oversized ego. Even though I begrudgingly agreed to buy him a coffee, he still refused. Instead, he had me buy the coffee for the person standing in line behind us, which—annoyingly—I admire.

"Brie, can I see you in my office?" "Mrs. Kingsley's voice booms from down the hall.

"I'll be right there!" I rise from my chair and smooth my blouse. At this rate, I'm terrified of what requests Mrs. Kingsley will have for me next. Go to the North Pole, find the actual Santa, and bring him back to Mount Holly?

I poke my head through the doorway. "Yes, Mrs. Kingsley?"

She peers up from her computer monitor. "The word through town is there is a famous Christmas blogger in town."

"I heard that," I say, very cool, as if I didn't fangirl over her already.

"I want you to arrange a meeting with her. See if we can get the Holly Jolly Festival on her blog. And potentially her magazine. I think it'll do wonders for exposure for the festival."

I nod. "I completely agree." Again, I tried, but my efforts were fruitless.

"I trust you can do this."

Shit. "Yes, absolutely. I will get it done as soon as possible."

She nods, fingers flying across the keyboard. "Time is running out—for the festival and the position."

She doesn't need to remind me. "I'll get right on it." I step into the hallway and inhale. Oh, great. All I need to do is woo a celebrity, out festival a hockey legend, and reclaim a kidnapped snowman. Going to the North Pole to find Santa might be easier than this. Merry freaking Christmas.

Logan

The last few days have been eerily quiet. No run-ins with Brie at the coffee shop. No accidental encounters at the diner. Not even a showdown at the bar. No more stealing Christmas decorations or booking all the Christmas props for herself. And the worst part? I kind of miss it. Most sane people would celebrate not seeing the one person they argue with more than they breathe, but apparently, I'm not most people. The bickering, the banter, the sparks—it's like some twisted addiction. And I need my fix. My pulse kicks into overdrive just thinking about catching a glimpse of her tonight. Even if it's only a quick exchange of holiday contraband. The warmth that shoots through my chest says it's not the arguing I miss most. It's her. She's been the most unexpected thing to happen to me in the last few years, along with the fluttering in my stomach. Of course, then there's Simon. It can't be serious. Right? One date doesn't qualify as serious.

I tug open the coffee shop door, bracing myself. It's only Sloane inside, the giant reindeer head perched on the counter.

"Sorry, I'm late." I come to a halt in front of her. "Where's Brie?"

"She couldn't make it." Sloane nudges the reindeer head toward me. "She left this for you."

"Oh." My chest tightens, and my chin drops. "That's probably better, anyway. Otherwise, we'll spend the next twenty minutes arguing over the nonexistent scuff on her snowman."

Sloane's gaze softens. "Yeah. Probably for the best. Plus, I need to finish closing duties."

"Okay. So here you go." I set the snowman on the floor, exchanging it for the reindeer head. "Oh. Also I have this." I pull out the *Mostly Nice. Sometimes Naughty.* keychain and set it on the counter. "This belongs to her. Alright, I'll see you later."

"Bye, Logan. I'll let Brie know I have her things."

I press my lips into a tight smile and nod. Before I reach the door, I spin around. "Can I ask you something?"

"Um. Sure."

"Is it serious between Brie and Simon?"

Her brows shoot up. "Serious?"

"They're dating, right?"

Sloane's laugh cuts through the silence. "You're funny. Brie and Simon are not dating. Trust me, I'd know."

Well shit. Fucking Simon. "Um. Thanks." A wide smile covers Sloane's face. Before I completely expose myself, I bolt. Back in my truck, I chuck the reindeer head in the cab. If they're not dating, then why the hell did Brie say they were? Just to mess with me? And why didn't she show tonight? I grip the steering wheel, torn between pounding on her door and demanding answers—or pretending none of this matters. Spoiler alert: It matters way too much.

I drum my fingers on the coffee shop table, checking my watch for the fifth time in two minutes. Emma, a Christmas blogger, has been hounding me for an interview. I've been putting it off mostly because I've been busy, but partly because interviews make me itchy. When I played hockey, reporters only wanted to know how I handled the pressure of a power play or if the other team really brought the heat. Easy stuff. Now? They want the messy, personal details I'd rather keep locked up tight. But this could be good exposure for the carnival, and that's what's really important here.

The bell over the door jingles. Emma sweeps inside like she's on a runway. Her lips curve into a wide grin as she sashays toward me, unbuttoning her coat as if she wants to give me a private lap dance.

"Thank you so much for meeting with me," she purrs.

"Of course," I say, rising from my chair. "Though let's be real—you weren't leaving Mount Holly without this interview."

She giggles. "That is true." She shrugs out of her coat, and I help her take it the rest of the way off.

"You're such a gentleman," she says, giving me a sultry once-over as I drape her coat over the chair.

I fight the urge to roll my eyes. "How'd you even hear about the carnival?"

"Actually, your carnival was nominated for the Best Hometown Christmas contest, and it's in the finals as one of the top three events."

My first thought is somehow Brooke entered the contest from beyond the grave since it's what she always wanted, but I quickly shake that thought away. I glance around the coffee shop on the lookout for any guilty faces who could have outed me. It could be anyone here. Hell, anyone in this town. Maybe my mom? She subscribes to the magazine.

My brows pinch together. "Who submitted it?"

"It was anonymous. But when I heard hockey legend Logan Crawford was running a small-town Christmas carnival, I had to see for myself."

I nod. "So you came here because of who I am?"

"Not every day do I get the opportunity to meet a hockey star." Emma reaches across the table and rests her hand on mine. "Let me say, I'm sorry to hear about the passing of your wife."

My eyes drop to the stark contrast of her red snowman nails against my skin. It twists something in my gut like eggnog left out overnight. "Thanks," I mutter before pulling my arm away.

A frown twitches on her lips before she recovers. "So tell me, how does a hockey star trade slapshots for sleigh bells? And why Mount Holly?"

My foot taps under the table. I can talk penalty kills all day long. But this? This is Brooke's story. "I grew up here. The town has always been about tradition. And now, with my daughter… I wanted her to feel the same Christmas magic I did."

"And the carnival?"

I huff out a laugh and lean against the chair. "That wasn't my idea. It was something my wife had always aspired to do. She loved Christmas. All aspects of it. She wanted to create something fun and magical for families to enjoy during the holidays. She planned every detail— layout, buildings, even the decor in the hot cocoa stand. My voice goes tight, and I drop my gaze to the table. "The year she passed was supposed to be the carnival's inaugural year. Obviously, it didn't pan out. But I wanted her dream to live on."

Emma's smile softens, her pen pausing. "That's really beautiful. How has the carnival planning been so far?"

"Challenging?" I chuckle. "But I've always been up for a challenge. It's the competitor in me. But now that things are coming to fruition, it's exciting to see the finished product."

She jots notes in her notepad. "What has been the biggest challenge so far?"

I want to say Brie, not because of the competition but, because I can't get her out of my head. "The execution. Making sure it's perfect. The way Brooke wanted it."

"And the town has been supportive of the carnival?"

I grin. "Oh, yeah. Everyone's excited. Well… most people."

Her brows lift. "Why most people?"

"There's a tradition in Mount Holly called the Holly Jolly Festival. Another similar Christmas festival." I rest my elbows on the table.

She nods along. "So, dueling festivals."

"Something like that. The organizer is Brie McKenna. We grew up together."

"You two are friends?"

I bark out a laugh. "Friends might be a stretch. More like lifelong enemies." This time she laughs. "We didn't necessarily get along growing up. A lot of competition."

She perks up, scribbling furiously. "So it's personal?"

My chest tightens. "The purpose isn't competition. But it's there. Mount Holly loves Christmas, and there'll be support for both events from the entire town. For me, the most important part is honoring Brooke's dream."

"Of course," she says, but the gleam in her eyes says she's already writing the headline: *Hockey Legend vs. Hometown Heroine: Dueling Festivals in Mount Holly.* "Tell me more about Brie?"

I fight the urge to smile hearing her name. "She's so strong-willed, fierce, and determined. She works her ass off. Shit, can I say ass?"

"I'll edit it out." She chuckles.

"She has such an icy exterior, but once you break through, she's an incredible woman." Shit. Word vomit. I snap my mouth shut, but Emma's smirk says it's too late. "I need to get back to the carnival. I have some more work to do."

"Oh yes. Thank you so much for sitting down with me."

"No problem." I rise, and she does the same. "I hope the article brings a lot of exposure to the carnival in Mount Holly."

"I'm certain it will."

I shrug into my jacket, keeping my eyes fixed on the door. By the time I'm back in my truck, I'm kicking myself. I came to Mount Holly for Josie. For Brooke's dream. Nothing more. And definitely not to let one stubborn, infuriating, beautiful woman hijack my every thought.

The drive to my parents' house goes by in a blur of regret. I don't know what she's going to publish, but I went rogue. I should never have even mentioned Brie. Once I opened my mouth, it was nothing but diarrhea of words, and I couldn't stop. I should have never agreed to the interview.

At my parents' house, I shove through the front door, stomping snow off my boots. "Josie, are you ready? Josie?" Muffled chatter echoes through the house, followed by the clatter of pots and pans. "Hello? Anyone home?" Just as I pass through the foyer and toward the kitchen, my mom turns the corner. "Hey Mom, where's Josie?"

With a wooden spoon in hand, she says, "She's next door with Brie and her mom baking cookies." She casually walks to the stove and stirs a simmering pot.

My jaw clenches. "Excuse me? You sent my daughter away with a stranger?"

Mom arches a brow. "Brie is far from a stranger. You've known her since elementary."

"But Josie hasn't."

"She's fine. They spent the afternoon building snowmen in the backyard. I was with her when we first went over there, but I had to come home to make dinner. She was having so much fun baking cookies and begged me to let her stay."

What the fuck? "That's when you tell her no! Or at least call me and ask. That's how kids get kidnapped."

"There hasn't been a single kidnapping in Mount Holly since the town was founded."

"And I don't want my daughter to be the first. It's the principle of it. You just don't send someone else's kid off to a stranger's house."

She rolls her eyes. "We used to send you off all the time as a kid. Half the time we didn't even know where you were, but you always came home as soon as it got dark. You were just fine. Mount Holly isn't like a big city. I don't think you've been gone that long. Anyway, dinner will be ready in about ten minutes, if you're hungry."

My stomach growls, but I ignore it. "No thanks. I'm getting my daughter."

"Be nice!" my mom yells as I storm out.

Nice? Right. My teeth grind together. What the hell was she thinking? Leaving Josie alone with Brie. You don't dump someone's kid with someone else. Who does that? My mom apparently. Once outside, I hurdle the snowbank separating the two driveways and jog up the pathway to the front door. I jab the doorbell, taking my anger out on the button. Several seconds pass before the door opens.

Mrs. McKenna greets me with a warm smile. She has the same dark hair as Brie, but it's laced with silver. "Logan! Come in. Josie's in the kitchen."

I don't waste time. I stride past her, following the sound of giggles. And then I stop dead in my tracks.

Brie stands at the counter, her ponytail swinging while her red sweater is dusted in flour. A smear streaks across her cheek, and all I want is to wipe it away with my thumb. Feel her soft skin under mine. Next to her, Josie's perched on a chair in an apron so big it nearly swallows her. Flour also covers her cheeks along with a wide grin. The sight punches me in the throat. Josie used to do this with Brooke. And now she can't. Instead it's Brie.

I clear my throat. "Josie. Time to go."

"But Dad," Josie protests, "the cookies are still baking."

"I'm sure Brie can finish them." My tone is sharper than intended.

Brie shoots me a glare hotter than the oven behind her. Then, with the kind of composure I clearly lack, she tells Josie, "I'll pack up some of the ones we already made for you."

"Okay, thank you." Josie jumps off the chair and tugs

off the apron. "Thanks for inviting me over to bake cookies. I had so much fun."

"Josie. Put on your coat and boots," I say, my eyes locked on Brie.

As soon as Josie's out of the room, I lower my voice. "What the hell are you doing?"

Brie rears her head back. "Excuse me?"

"Do you think you can take charge and do whatever you want with my daughter?"

"I'm sorry for crossing any boundaries. Your mom was with us but had to leave. Josie wanted to stay. What was I supposed to do? Break her heart and tell her no?"

"Yes, that's exactly what you do." I cross my arms over my chest.

"If you want to deny your daughter an afternoon of fun, go for it. But I think you are directing your anger at the wrong person right now." Her voice sharpens, matching mine. We're locked in a stare-down, two gunslingers at high noon. And damn it, she doesn't flinch.

"Dad, I'm ready." Josie comes back into the kitchen with her winter gear on.

Brie stacks several cookies into a container and passes it to Josie. "Thanks for helping me bake today," she says, her tone soft as if she wasn't annoyed with me a second earlier.

"I hope we can do it again," Josie replies.

I tear my gaze from Brie and take Josie's hand, leading her out of the house and back to my parents' driveway without another word.

At the truck, I help Josie in before rounding the front. Once in the driver's seat, I slam the door, my head pounding.

"I had so much fun today. I wish I didn't have to leave." Josie kicks her feet as she stares down at the container of decorated cookies in her lap like it's treasure.

Fuck. Josie always loved baking cookies. I'm a shit baker, so it's something I never did with her. And Brie—damn her—gave Josie one of the best afternoons she's had in years, and I ruined it.

"I'm glad you had a good day." I flash her a small smile.

"You seemed a little mad." Her voice cuts through me like a knife.

"No, Peanut. It's just been a long day."

"I made a cookie especially for you." Opening the lid of the container, she reveals a sugar cookie decorated with red and green icing that spells out *Best Dad*.

My chest squeezes. "That's almost too pretty to eat."

She giggles. "But you have to eat it. It's a cookie."

"Alright, when we get home, we'll share it."

"We were going to make chocolate chip cookies, but I told Brie your favorite was English toffee, so we switched to those."

Best damn cookie ever invented. Brooke's recipe always held the number one spot. Soft but slightly crisp from the toffee. "Let me try one of those." She digs out one of the English toffee cookies, and I take a bite—and nearly moan. Instantly, I'm hit with an overload of delicious buttery caramelized flavor. The cookie is soft and chewy in the center but chocked full of sweet and salty toffee bits. Did my dick just twitch from a cookie? Quite possibly. Once I'm done chewing the first bite, I stuff my mouth with the second half.

"Do you like it?" Josie asks.

I nod. "This might be the best cookie ever created."

Josie giggles. "Even better than moms?"

"Your mom's toffee cookies are hard to beat, but these are good. Really good."

"I thought so too." She kicks her feet as her smile fades to the window.

Guilt gnaws at me. Brie didn't deserve my fury. She gave Josie a piece of her mom back. And me? I stormed in like the Grinch, hell-bent on stealing it. I don't deserve Best Dad. Asshole Dad is more like it.

Logan

Through the grapevine, I learned purse bingo is on Tuesday nights at the Crooked Reindeer, and it's best to stay away until after eight. Since I'm not in need of a purse, I heed the warning. By a quarter after, I stroll in, desperate for a distraction. Skating didn't cut it, the walls of my house are closing in, and stewing in my thoughts is about as fun as listening to carolers sing off-key in January. Another lesson I learned, even when purse bingo is over, the crowd lingers. I search for an empty barstool, but most were still occupied except for a few near the middle. My fingers curl over the back, when a hand on mine stops me.

"Sorry, Logan, the seat's taken."

I blink. "Uh… sure. No problem." I move to the next one. "Hey, Frank, this one free?"

He flicks his gaze to the bartenders, then to the far end of the bar, then back to me. "Nope. The missus is in the bathroom."

My brows pinch together. "Alright." I continue down the row of stools. Every empty stool has suddenly been "claimed," like there's a secret no-Logan rule I didn't get the memo about. By the time I reach the end, there's only one spot left—next to Brie. I clear my throat. "Let me guess, this seat's taken as well?"

She peers up at me through her dark lashes. "If I say yes, are you going to stand there until another seat opens up?"

"Probably."

She motions to the empty stool. "It's all yours. I'm about finished anyway."

"Wait." I take a seat. "Before you go, I owe you an apology. I was kind of a jerk the other day."

She rolls the bottom of the beer bottle on the bar top. "More like asshole."

"Kind of an asshole."

She lifts a brow. "Kind of?"

I laugh. "Okay. A lot of an asshole. You didn't deserve that. Especially being so nice to Josie."

Her face softens. "She's a great kid. Super smart. She even knew the conversions when we doubled the recipe. I was impressed."

"She gets that from her mom."

Brie playfully elbows me. "Give yourself more credit than that, Mr. Valedictorian."

A smile pulls at the corners of my lips. She has no reason to be nice to me, but here she is cracking jokes.

"Yeah, well. I haven't been feeling very smart as of late. Anyway, I just want to say I'm sorry."

She nods slowly. "Apology accepted. And… I'm sorry too. I should've asked before baking with Josie. If I were in your shoes, I'd be upset if a stranger was baking cookies with my kid."

I shake my head. "You're not a stranger. You're forgiven." I exhale a deep breath. "What ever happened to Minnesota Nice?"

This time it's her turn to laugh. "Minnesota Nice is alive and well. But screw with the wrong person, and it turns into Minnesota Vindictive. You haven't been gone that long."

"It feels like a lifetime. Either way, you didn't deserve my wrath. The holidays are… stressful."

"You can say that again. This year especially." She takes a sip of beer, her pink lips wrapping around the bottle. I force my gaze away before my imagination goes R rated. There's one question that's been on the tip of my tongue. Now that I know the truth, I want to know what her answer is. "How was your date with Simon?"

She chokes on her beer. "Oh! Uh… grrreat."

I smirk. "So great it didn't happen?" Her head snaps up. "Sloane told me the truth."

"She would. Always the responsible one." She takes another sip.

"Why lie?"

"Why do you care so much?" She arches a brow.

Clearly, these are questions neither of us want to answer. So I take a new approach. "Then why didn't you show up to exchange the Christmas decorations?"

Something flickers across her face before she exhales. "Something came up."

I nod, not buying it, but an interrogation doesn't seem appropriate.

"Alright." She swallows the last gulp of her drink. "I should get going."

The thought of her leaving twists something in my gut. "Let me buy you another one. It's the least I can do for being an asshole."

She side-eyes me. "Are you trying to get me drunk so I'll spill all my Christmas festival secrets?"

I laugh. "No. But if you want to share your secret of how you keep your hot chocolate piping hot, I'm all ears."

Her lips curve into a small, genuine smile. "I knew it. You're here for recon."

"Josie scolded me for my lukewarm hot chocolate. Plus," I point between her and me, "this is kind of nice."

"Conversation?"

"Yeah." I shrug. "No sabotages. Plans of infiltration. Decapitating reindeer."

She bursts into laughter. "I barely touched it, and its head fell off. You need to secure your reindeer heads better."

"Fair." I wave Sydney over for another round, and I glance at Brie for confirmation.

She sighs, but her smile lingers. "Fine. One more."

While Sydney gets our drinks, I turn to Brie and ask, "What have you been up to? Did you stay in Mount Holly after graduation?"

She twists a napkin between her fingers, a wry chuckle escaping. "No. I went to college. In my senior year, I started an internship which later led to landing my dream job. I was the marketing director for the nation's most sought-after Christmas treat."

"Wow, sounds impressive. Congratulations." I lean

toward her and whisper, "So what is the nation's most sought-after Christmas treat? The Yule log?"

"Nope. A fruitcake. It gets a bad rap, but come December, everyone is lining up for blocks to get their hands on one. They're closet fruitcake enthusiasts. They go feral for the moist, dark cake that's loaded with yummy, dried fruits. We could hardly keep up with the demand."

I take a swig of beer.

"Huh. Who would have thought? Clearly, this job isn't in Mount Holly, so what happened between the fruitcake and now?"

Her smile dims. "After three years with the company, I lost my job. To meet the demand, they moved production out of the country."

"Damn. So they fired their marketing director?"

She huffs out a humorless laugh. "Technically, *assistant* marketing director. But it was my campaigns that went viral. The real kicker? I went home to tell my fiancé I'd been laid off—"

My gaze drifts to her left hand, which is thankfully empty.

"—only for him to tell me he's calling off the wedding and dumping me. Apparently, Tiffany across the hallway was much better at keeping him satisfied."

"Shit," I mutter. "I'm sorry."

She lifts her chin. "It stung. But honestly? It was for the best. I wasn't about to fight for a man who didn't put me first. Since the apartment was his, I tucked my tail between my legs and came back to Mount Holly. I did what all the cool kids do and moved in with my parents and worked at my dad's hardware shop for four years until I got the job as Mount Holly's assistant event coordinator."

"Don't be so hard on yourself. It's a tough world out there."

She smirks and elbows me. "Says the guy who played in the NHL and got a bajillion sponsorship deals with five houses scattered across the US."

I laugh. "I only had two. One in Boston and one in Chicago. But now it's just the one in Mount Holly. Either way, it's still tough." My voice drops as I pick at the label on the bottle, little flakes of paper falling to the bar top. "I never imagined I'd be a widower at thirty-three."

Brie's hand lands on my forearm, warm and grounding. Her voice softens. "I'm sorry about your wife. I can't imagine what that's been like. Especially with Josie."

Slowly, I lift my gaze. Her eyes hold mine, steady and kind, and for one dizzying second, I want to lean into her. "Thanks. Every time I think I'm over it, I question whether I really am."

"Is it something you can ever get over?" She yanks her hand away when she realizes her hand is still on my arm. I immediately miss her touch, but sitting here with her, it hurts a little less. "Now, I should probably get going."

"Can I walk you to your car?" Asking her to stay for another might be a bit much. It makes me feel desperate for attention. Maybe I am. Hers, anyway.

"Are you leaving? You just got here."

"No. But it's dark out."

"You don't have to."

"I insist."

"I—I can't say no to that." She spins on her stool toward me. Her knees brush against my thigh, and my pulse skitters. The dim lighting causes a twinkle to dance within her brown irises. "Sorry," she murmurs before sliding off the stool.

We shrug into our coats. I toss a coaster over my beer, calling out to Sydney, "Be right back!" She smirks and nudges the other bartender, and I swear they're both in on some kind of bet.

As I pass Frank, the stool next to him is still empty. "Hey Frank, I thought the missus was in the bathroom." I nod to the empty stool next to him.

He shifts guiltily. "Oh. Um. She must have snuck out the bathroom window."

I can't fight the smile. "Not the first time, I'm guessing." Jogging to catch up, I lean down so only Brie hears. "I think the whole bar's conspiring against us."

Her brows knit together. "Why do you say that?"

I shake my head. Maybe I'm imagining it. "It's nothing." I hold the door open for her, my arm brushing hers as the cold air slaps me awake. "Did you know there's a reporter in town doing a story about Christmas festivals?"

"Yes!" Her eyes light up. "She's only the editor of one of the largest Christmas magazines in the nation. I've been subscribing to it for years. If I can land an interview, it'll seal the deal for the Mount Holly coordinator position." When we reach her SUV, she unlocks it with the key fob.

"You're applying for the job?"

She nods, back pressed against the door. "It's what I've been working toward for eight years."

"You'd be amazing at it." She smiles at the compliment, and for one reckless second, I'm ready to close the distance between us—this time no snowbank, no interruptions. Just my lips on hers.

Instead, she whispers, "Thanks for walking me out." She slips into her seat, starting the engine. With a look that's equal parts warning and tease, she adds, "Just because we're civil tonight doesn't mean anything. I still hate you."

A smile flirts on my lips. "I wouldn't want it any other way."

"Good. Then we're on the same page." She pauses, eyes catching mine again. "Oh—and that hug with Simon? Strictly festival business. He's making me a custom drink."

I'm such an idiot. "Good night, Brie."

"Night, Logan."

Her lavender scent lingers long after I close the door and the taillights disappear down the street. Somehow, one great night erases all the shit-tastic ones. Now with the Simon shit put to rest, perhaps we're headed in the right direction of at least not hating each other. She says she still does, but I think that's bullshit. And I'm going to prove it.

Brie

"Brie! Come to my office."

I groan, wanting to slam my forehead against my desk. What ridiculous task does she want today? Find a reindeer with an actual glowing red nose? I plaster on my fakest smile and step into her office. "Yes, Mrs. Kingsley?"

She taps her pen against her desk with all the subtlety of a ticking bomb. "I think we need a refresh in the Santa this year."

My jaw drops. "You want to fire Mr. Bernstein? He's been Santa for decades. He *is* the Holly Jolly Festival."

"Exactly. Which is why we need something new."

My chest constricts. "Okay, but don't you think it's a bit late? We kick off the Holly Jolly Festival in two days. Santa makes his first appearance in four. And you want a replacement now?"

"If you can't manage it, I'll certainly do it myself. But it won't bode well for your initiative to become the Mount Holly event coordinator."

Shit. Shit. Shit. I square my shoulders. "No. I got it. New Santa. Check."

"Mr. Wilkins's son plays an excellent Santa in the Chester Creek parade," she adds. "Poach him."

I choke. "You want me to *steal* Chester Creek's Santa?" How do I find myself in these situations?

"Make him an offer he can't refuse."

I'm assuming "make him an offer" doesn't mean sexual favors. Sure, I joked about exchanging sexual favors for services earlier, but she must be kidding. Right? But it's Mrs. Kingsley; she's a do-whatever-it-takes kind of person. From the gleam in her eye, I'm not entirely convinced.

"I assume you will make this happen. I'd hate for this to be your last opportunity to make something great of the Holly Jolly Festival."

"Yes. Absolutely. I got this." Or it will be an epic fail, and I'll be searching for a new job by New Year's.

Stalking Santas in a twenty mile radius wasn't on my holiday to-do list, but if I want this promotion, I need to stalk like my life depends on it—because it does. My first phone call was to Nathan Wilkins. He informed me he's not playing Santa this year, as he's going on vacation. Even if sexual favors were on the table, they'd be useless. I dial a number and cross it off my list when they decline. Unfortunately, bribes of free tickets to the Holly Jolly

Festival don't make a good exchange when the festival is already free. I even offered free coffee and cookies for the duration of the festival, but they all pass up the amazing opportunity to play Santa in the best Christmas festival in the state, if not the entire nation.

By my twentieth phone call, my voice is raspy from leaving so many messages. I sip tea to soothe it as I scan over my dwindling list of potential Santas. Suddenly the room goes dark. Setting my pen down, I rise to my feet and glance out the kitchen window. The streetlight in the alley is out as well. Checking all the windows, the entire street is dark. By the time I stumble back into the kitchen to grab my phone to make sure I have cell service, the lights flicker to life. At least it didn't last for days like two years ago. I'm the proud owner of a generator that I've only used once because of it. But my dad insisted I get it.

One hour and ten more calls later, I'm no closer to finding a Santa. Then my phone rings. All my muscles tense. This could be the future Holly Jolly Festival Santa. Without glancing at the screen, my fingers fumble to answer. "Hi, Brie speaking."

"Brie, we need your help."

"Simon?" Did I accidentally ask Simon to play Santa? My brows raise. He wouldn't be a bad Santa. It's workable.

"Yes. Bring every cooler you have. And ice to the diner."

I pause. "Look, I know we're good friends and all, and we have each other's backs no matter what, but I don't want to be interviewed by the police later."

"What are you talking about?"

"Coolers. Ice in the middle of winter. Next, you'll ask me to bring a chainsaw, which, by the way, I don't have."

"I don't know what you're referring to, but no. All of Willa's freezers went out. The power outage must have caused a surge or something. We need to get all of her food into coolers."

"Oh!" I jump to my feet. "Yeah. I'm on my way."

The diner is pure chaos when I arrive. People rushing from one side of the kitchen to the next. "Hey Willa! I have coolers."

Her usually perfect hair is frizzed as much as she is. "Thank you so much." She exhales a deep breath.

"How long were they out?"

"An hour tops. When I came in to work on menu planning, I noticed the freezers weren't running. We tried the breaker, but nothing. I can't lose thousands of dollars of food." Her voice trembles.

"Don't worry. We've got you." I spin around and crash into a wall of muscle. "Oh, sorry." A wall that smells like fresh laundry and manliness. Logan. Of course, he would be here. Why wouldn't he be here? If the day needs saving, he's not far away.

I offer him the world's tightest smile before darting away. We're in limbo—somewhere between enemies and not-quite-friends—and this is neither the time nor place to analyze why he makes my heart stutter.

We form an assembly line, hustling containers out of the dead freezers and into coolers. Then Mrs. Peterson's voice booms over the clatter.

"I'm so glad you could come help, Logan. It's nice to see strapping young men who are ready to lend a hand."

"Happy to help." Logan smiles, the dimple on his cheek making an appearance.

Fuck me.

"Why don't you go near the front of the line to help there?" She grabs his hand and leads him toward me. "Here, this is a good spot." She pats his arm before walking away.

Perfect. Because what I really needed tonight was to save a diner full of food while standing shoulder-to-shoulder with the man I'm supposed to hate but can't stop noticing smells way too good.

I shoot him a tight smile, determined not to stare. Logan inches closer to me as more people shuffle into the line. His shoulder brushes against mine. The touch is nothing—barely there—but my body reacts like he just plugged me into a socket. Exciting. Unwelcome. Totally traitorous. I am supposed to hate him. Not imagine pushing him against the walk-in freezer, climbing him like a tree, and dry-humping his stupidly muscular thighs.

"Brie? Brie?"

I jerk my gaze up. Cara's holding a frozen ham, brows raised.

"Right, sorry." My voice comes out squeaky. I grab the ham and pass it down the line to Logan, whose fingertips graze mine deliberately—or maybe that's just my overactive imagination. Either way, every accidental brush is a chemical explosion, and by the fifteenth exchange, I'm buzzing on some cocktail of dopamine and lust. And of course, he knows it. Each time, he sneaks me a sidelong glance, dimple flashing like he's cashing in on my weakness. By the time we slam the last cooler shut, I'm practically floating.

"Thank you, everyone," Willa breathes, sagging against the empty freezer.

"Of course," I say, swiping sweat from my forehead. "Fingers crossed it all stays good."

"Me too. It should be good." When everyone else scatters, Willa steps up next to me. "I was a little nervous about you and Logan working next to each other, but not a single insult was hurled in either direction."

"We can be around each other without bickering."

"Have you not seen you two? Especially in the past three weeks?"

"Tonight, we came together for a common cause."

"Well, glad I could bring you two together. But there's no other reason there were no expletives thrown at each other?"

"Nope. Nothing that I can think of," I spit out entirely too fast to be casual. I can't tell her I want to drag him outside and kiss him in the snowbank like it almost happened before.

"Uh-huh." She smirks knowingly.

Before I can dig myself deeper, Mason calls for Willa. "I got my truck loaded up to head over to Sip and Sleigh. Sloane's going to meet us there."

"Thank you again." She wraps her arms around me, and I hug her back.

"Of course." When I turn around, Logan's gone. Just… gone. My heart dips. I don't know why. Was I actually going to say anything to him, anyway? What would I even say? *Every time you touched me tonight, you lit my body on fire. I can't stop thinking about you, even though I want to strangle you. I had a sex dream about you, but now I want the real thing.* Yup. I'm sure that would go over well.

On the drive home, my phone chimes with a message. Glancing at the screen, it's from Scott, Santa number eight from my list. He tells me he's available for this year's festival. I guess it's better than nothing. As I pass the festival grounds headlights catch my attention. I ease off the gas pedal, keeping my eyes focused on the other vehicle. What are they doing? The vehicle crawls to a stop, and I continue to move toward them. As I get closer, I squint my eyes, trying to focus. My shoulders sag once recognition hits.

I park my SUV behind the white truck and jump out,

leaving the vehicle running. "What are you doing here? Looking for something else to steal?" I cross my arms over my chest.

Logan spins around. "No. I was checking to make sure the power surge didn't spark any fires."

"Oh." I blink. That's unexpectedly thoughtful. "Thanks."

"No problem. I better check on the carnival. I don't want it to burn to the ground if there's a fire. But I'm sure you'd be excited about that," he teases.

"I may have thought about it a time or two, but I'd never want it to *actually* happen. You've worked hard, and I'd really hate for that to be destroyed."

Something soft flickers across his face before he masks it. "Thanks. I'll see you around, Brie."

And damn it, the way he says my name—low, deliberate—sends butterflies crashing into each other in my stomach like bumper cars. I don't *like* it. Except... I absolutely do.

"Bye, Logan," I murmur, softer than I mean to.

I stand there, watching his taillights disappear into the night, until the dark swallows him whole. Hating him is supposed to be easy. But it's getting harder and harder when he does things like this.

Brie

From behind the podium, I stare out at the crowd gathered in front of the not-quite-sad eleven and a half-foot Christmas tree. Okay, fine—maybe it *was* sad until Dad helped me jack it up another foot and a half. I even added extra Christmas presents underneath so the tree appears taller and bustling with extra holiday joy. It wasn't my first choice, but damn, I'm proud. The crowd is a sea of Santa hats, elf ears, and reindeer antlers. Mount Holly does not do Christmas halfway. Generations of townsfolk smile back at me like they've been waiting all year for this moment. I know I have. A thwack rolls over the crowd as I tap the microphone. Everyone quiets, giving me their undivided attention.

"Thank you for coming. The tree lighting is my favorite part of the Holly Jolly Festival. It kicks off the entire Christmas season. We have fun games, activities, vendors, and contests. New this year is the Holly Jolly Ice Rink. Every night, we'll have open skating for everyone to enjoy."

Cheers ripple through the crowd.

"And of course," I continue, "our local businesses came through with some amazing prizes."

"You can win one of my brand-new, super-duper power shovels. Only available at Holly Hammer Hardware!" my dad yells from the crowd.

The audience erupts with laughter and applause. I shake my head. "Thanks, Dad. Who *doesn't* need a super-duper power shovel?"

I gesture Vanna-White-style at the tree. "Big thanks to Henry and Reindeer Ridge for this beauty."

An applause rolls over the audience.

Near the back of the crowd, I spot Josie's head towering over everyone else. My gaze drifts down to the shoulders she's sitting on. Logan's staring back at me with a wide smile on his face. Even in the cold, my cheeks warm. Lauren clears her throat, getting my attention. She points to the tree. "Oh. Right. Let's kick off the Holly Jolly Festival! You ready?"

The entire crowd joins in the countdown. "Five! Four! Three! Two! One!"

I flip the oversized fake switch as Lauren hits the real one, and the tree explodes with red, blue, green, and white twinkling lights. The star blazes at the top, fireworks crack overhead, and for a second, I can't breathe. It's perfect. It's everything. Maybe, just maybe, I'll land this promotion. I scan the area where Logan was, but he's not there. Maybe it wasn't him after all.

Lauren murmurs, "Oh, it's beautiful."

"Yeah," I manage. But my chest is too tight to mean just the tree.

When you've convinced yourself of one thing for so many years, you become conflicted when you realize it was a lie. That's my situation with Logan. I've spent years cultivating my Logan Crawford Hate Club membership. But lately? My card has been revoked. When he's not around, I miss the bickering. When he *is* around, I can't decide if I want to argue or kiss him. Night after night, I replay the almost-kiss in the snowbank and every time I regret it didn't happen.

The next morning, I wake up tangled in thoughts of Logan. Again. I'd bet all my Christmas ornaments he was at the tree lighting. But why? He's got his own carnival kickoff. Which I'm sure will be big, extravagant, and over the top because Logan knows nothing different. Unless he was there to steal my ideas. Obviously, I can't ask anyone if he was there; that would insinuate I'm thinking of Logan in more than an I-don't-hate-you kind of way.

At the festival grounds, the crowd is... underwhelming. Sure there are a few families, young and old, wandering around, enjoying cookies, and hot chocolate. While others play games to win stuffed Santas and snowmen. But it's only one-fourth of Mount Holly, tops. My stomach knots.

"Brie! Brie!" Lauren jogs toward me, flushed. "Sorry I'm late. Traffic was insane near Snowflake Lane."

My brows furrow. "Traffic?"

She nods. "I saw a sign about a hockey tournament."

Damn. I know where everyone in town is. I pull out my phone and send a message to Willa.

BRIE

What are you doing?"

WILLA

Closing down the diner. Town is empty.

BRIE

Hockey tournament. Want to check it out?

WILLA

Oh, that's right. I totally forgot. That explains the lack of customers. I never expected you to go to a Logan Crawford event voluntarily.

BRIE

All our friends are playing. I want to be supportive.

WILLA

Not because you want to see a certain professional hockey player?

BRIE

No, but I like hockey, and I want to watch him lose.

WILLA

Nope. I checked my receipt. I didn't buy any of your bullshit.

BRIE

Better check again. Because that's what it is.

WILLA

HA! Alright, I'll meet you there.

I shove my phone in my pocket and turn to Lauren. "You can hold down the fort for a little while, right?"

Pure panic takes over her face. "Uh. Um."

"Great! You have my number if there's an emergency!" Before she can respond, I spin around and sprint down the walkway and out of the festival.

I meet up with Willa at the only available parking, which is a quarter of a mile from the carnival entrance on the side of Snowflake Lane. Thankfully, the sun is shining, and the temperatures are above zero. When we enter, it's bustling. Minnesota loves hockey, no matter if it's professional, junior hockey, high school, or in this case a fun weekend tournament. There's no way I'd be able to compete with this. Might as well enjoy it while I'm here.

"Who knew Mount Holly would love watching a bunch of thirty-somethings play hockey?" Willa says over her shoulder as we meander through the crowd.

Four sections of bleachers are full of spectators. People are even standing shoulder-to-shoulder along the boards. A thin netting surrounds the entire rink to protect the crowd from flying pucks. A few rows up, she finds us an empty spot on the metal bleachers.

She pats the bench. "This is fancy. He sprung for the extra luxurious foam padding." Both of us sit, our butts sinking into the vinyl-covered extra-soft foam.

Immediately, I scan the players on the ice, mostly searching for one in particular. It takes less than five seconds to find him gliding across the rink.

Willa leans over, playfully bumping my shoulder. "I dare you not to stare at Logan while we're here."

I scoff. "You say that as if it's a challenge."

Willa laughs. "We'll see."

Players get ready for the next game and skate around the ice taking practice shots into the net. Logan's on the far end. I'm mesmerized by his effortless gliding across the ice. His powerful thighs push him forward. I imagine his thrusting force is just as powerful. He lines up a shot, flicks his wrist, and the puck smacks the top corner of the net with surgical precision. My breath hitches.

"I should have placed a bet," Willa whispers.

"Huh?"

"You're staring."

"No, I wasn't." I drop my gaze and tug my knit cap farther down on my head.

"You're glued to the left side of the rink. Guess who's the only player there?"

There's no way I can lie my way out of this one. "Fine," I grumble. "I was staring. But he's a professional athlete. It's hard not to."

She smirks. "Because he's so hot and manly. All you want to do is rip all his pads off and play with his stick."

"No." I groan. "That's not—" Except yeah, it is. Exactly that. "He's a professional hockey player. It's hard not to stare when he's on the ice."

"Suuure," she teases.

I hate that there's a teeny tiny part of me that doesn't hate the way my chest flutters every time he's near. Or how his stupid dimple makes my knees weak. That he thinks of tiny things—like dryer sheets. How my heart skips a beat every time I see him being the best dad to his daughter. Or how my skin prickles with goosebumps every time he touches me. I hate I want it, all of it. All the time.

Willa nudges me and points to the far end of the rink. "Isn't that the Christmas blogger over there?"

I squint toward the far side of the rink. "Yes. Emma. What is she doing here? There's nothing Christmas about the hockey tournament."

"That guy is wearing a Santa hat over his helmet, so

it's kind of Christmas-y. You should go talk to her. Get that meeting so you can gush about the Holly Jolly Festival."

"I should! I'm going to go do that right now!" Leaping from my seat, I scoot past the row of people until I'm racing down the stairs while maintaining a visual of Emma's position. Once on solid ground, I weave through the crowd of people.

"Oh, Brie! Brie!"

I ignore my name and quicken my steps.

"Brie! I have a question."

Oh, my god. I didn't know Mrs. Albertson could move so fast for being an eighty-year-old woman. I grind to a stop and paste on a smile. "Sorry, I didn't hear you calling."

"That's okay, dear. I wanted to ask are there still three rounds for the Christmas cookie bake-off?"

"Yep, there sure are. We've always had three rounds." My gaze flicks over her head. I still have Emma in sight.

"Oh, good. Betty believed there were only two. Sheryl thought there was just one."

"Nope. There's still three. I haven't changed it." I bounce on the balls of my feet, not wanting to be rude, but also I need her to speed up this conversation.

"Great. I'll let them know. Thanks, dear."

"You're welcome." I rush past her and weave in and out of carnival goers.

"Brie!" I pinch my eyes shut when I hear my name again. I glance over my shoulder, and Mr. Jacobson is waving like he's hailing a taxi. "Oh, Brie! You have to thank your father for the brand-new snow shovel he sold me. It works like a dream. He had the perfect display showing me the good, better, and best of all the shovels. Of course, I had to get the best."

"Oh, that's great, Mr. Jacobson. I'm so glad it's working out for you."

"Yeah, when we got that snow the other night, the snow shovel came in handy."

"Fantastic." I flash him a fake smile. "I'll be sure to let my dad know." I peer around him to make sure I don't lose Emma.

"Thankfully the snow came a few nights ago instead of today. Otherwise, we wouldn't have such a beautiful day."

"Yes, I agree. If you'll excuse me." I slide past him and continue beelining it toward Emma.

"Hi Brie! I'm so glad to see you."

Kill me now. "Hi, Mrs. Parker."

"Is the Christmas parade still at noon?"

"It is, yes. It's always at noon."

"How long do you think it'll last? I've heard there are some extra floats this year."

"Thirty minutes."

"Okay, great. Thank you."

"You're welcome." I flash her a quick smile before weaving around her. I don't even make it two steps before a hand on my forearm stops me.

"Brie. It's so good to see you, dear. Tell your mom thank you for the cookies she dropped off. Harold has already eaten half of them. But your mom makes some of the best cookies."

"Great, I'll pass that along!" I spin, craning my neck. And… dammit. Emma's gone. If at first you don't succeed, you call your friend for a favor. I pull my phone from my pocket and dial Valerie.

After a few rings, she answers. "Thank you for calling the Fa La La Inn. This is Valerie. How may I help you?"

"Val, it's Brie. I need a favor"

"Anything. What do you need?"

"There's a Christmas blogger in town, and since you're the only lodging in Mount Holly, I need you to tell me if Emma St. Claire is staying there."

"Well, I can do anything but that. It goes against policy."

"Okay, how about cough once for yes, cough twice for no?"

"That's me pretty much telling you."

"It's you telling me without telling me. I just need to know. My boss wants me to schedule a meeting with her, and every time I see her in town, she's distracted by Logan. I need to pin her down where he won't be, and I don't expect him to be staying at the inn." She coughs into the speaker. "Is that a yes?" She coughs again. "No?"

She blows out a breath. "Start over." She coughs again. And then it's silent.

"Thank you, Val. You're the best. I'm going to swing by and casually run into her."

"Just try not to frighten the other guests."

"You got it." I hang up the call. Before exiting the carnival, I tell Willa I'm leaving. On my way out, I spare a glance at the rink. Logan skates by, and we lock eyes. My heart flutters in my chest. Stay and watch him play or go find Emma? Priorities. Don't get distracted. I peel my gaze away and leave before I change my mind.

At the Fa La La Inn, I sit at a small two-person table in the dining room, pretending I'm here for a casual breakfast and not a stakeout. Totally normal. Just a girl, sipping tea, and definitely not glancing at the door every four seconds. Out of all the years, why does everything have to occur this year? The one time when everything is on the line. My livelihood. I've worked so hard, and one slip-up could ruin it all.

Emma finally breezes in, and she sits down at a table

on the opposite side of the room. With my eyes trained on her over the rim of my teacup, I give her time to settle before ambushing her. Times up. I push my chair away. *Brie. Be cool.* I circle the room and fake a double-take. "Miss St. Claire? Is that you?"

She looks up. "Oh, hi. Brie, right?"

Oh my God, she remembers me. "Yes! Fancy seeing you here."

"Likewise. Especially at a bed and breakfast."

"I occasionally come here for the breakfast."

"Isn't it customary to have a bed too?"

"Yessss," I draw out. "Sometimes I like a staycation, to get out of the house, go somewhere new for a night." She nods. I hope she buys it. "If you're not busy, perhaps we could sit down, and I can tell you all about the Holly Jolly Festival."

Her brows lift, amused. "Well, sure. Sit down." She waves to the chair across from her. "Tell me about the Holly Jolly Festival."

"The Holly Jolly Festival is a tradition that spans decades here in Mount Holly. The entire town joins in the Christmas celebration. Over the years, it's evolved into something bigger, grander. And this year, especially, will be the biggest festival of them all."

"Do you find it difficult competing with another Christmas carnival?"

"Not at all." Because I'm going to kick Logan's ass. He wouldn't know a Christmas carnival or festival if it smacked him across the face. This is my territory. He may have won the battle with a hockey tournament, but I will win the Christmas war. "The townspeople of Mount Holly have grown to love the Holly Jolly Festival, and every year, their support grows more and more. I know they will do the same this year. The carnival is new. They don't know what the town wants or needs in a Christmas celebration."

She leans forward. "Is it true you and Logan have a history?"

What's with the Logan questions? This is supposed to be about the Holly Jolly Festival. "Yes. We've known each other for quite a while. Since we were kids, actually."

"And how has that affected your festival?"

Finally, back to the festival. "Well, if I had to say so, I don't think it's affected it one bit." *Unless you count that every time I see him, I want to strangle him… or kiss him. Hard.*

"Do you think he'll draw a crowd?"

"Of course. He's a local hockey legend. He is charming, charismatic, and oddly thoughtful. And he's a wonderful dad. So sweet to his daughter. It would be hard for people not to like him." Shit. Shit. That's too much. "However, the Holly Jolly Festival should have an amazing turnout. We're projecting a thousand more visitors than in previous years."

"That's wonderful. It's reassuring to hear that small-town festivals haven't lost their charm."

"Yes! My sentiments exactly. I plan on doing everything in my power to not only keep the tradition going but to make it bigger and better each year."

Val strolls by, shooting me a subtle *are you done yet?* look. I shake my head.

Emma peers over her shoulder and waves her over. "Excuse me? Can I order breakfast? The lemon ricotta blueberry pancakes sound divine."

"Yes. Certainly. I'll get those going for you right away." Val scribbles the order, throws me an apologetic glance, and retreats.

Emma directs her attention to me. "If you'll excuse me, I have to make a phone call."

"Thank you for sitting down with me to chat about the Holly Jolly Festival. I hope it's inspiring enough to make it onto your blog. The townsfolk would love it. They'd think they were famous."

"Yes. It's a wonderful story. It was nice to meet you again, Brie." She holds out her hand for me to shake.

"Same." She loosens her grip and exits the room.

Once she's out of sight, Val slides back in, soft-eyed. "Sorry, Brie. I didn't want her thinking we were slow on service in case she mentions the inn on her blog."

"It's fine." I sigh. "Thanks for letting me crash."

"I hope you get the article you want."

"Me too." I might get something, but I don't know how much of it will be with regard to the festival since my big mouth can't stop turning every conversation into one about Logan. And if I'm not careful, my heart's about to follow.

Logan

To say the hockey tournament was a success is an understatement. All weekend from midafternoon until well past dusk, the stands were packed with people cheering on every team in the tournament. The entire town of Mount Holly shut down and came out for a weekend of hockey. I couldn't have asked for a better kickoff to the carnival. To my surprise, Brie was even in the stands. It was hard to keep my eyes off her as I skated around the rink. Normally, I'm not the guy who gets distracted while on the ice, but there she was in the winter sun, brown hair loose over her shoulders, laughing at something Willa said, and my chest went warm in a way that felt… dangerous. We locked eyes for half a second. It hit me like a clean check. God, I'd missed that feeling.

After we won our first game, I scanned the crowd for her, but she was gone. When I caught up with Willa, she told me Brie left to talk to the Christmas blogger, and an unfamiliar hollow ache settled in my chest. I was hoping to see her and talk to her. Hell, I would have even argued with her if it got me near her. Maybe that's karma for slipping away after the Holly Jolly tree lighting—Brooke's favorite tradition at home—but seeing her on stage knocked the air out of me. I had to leave.

We played one more game before the tournament came to an end. It was a close one, but we squeaked out a win with a top-shelf rip from Carson at the buzzer. Back at my truck, I'm tossing my hockey equipment into the back when something black shoved under the seat draws my attention. Reaching under, I pull out a black top hat. Brie's snowman. It's naked without it. And Mount Holly doesn't need naked snowmen.

I hop in my truck and drive past her house, but all the lights are off. As I drive past the Crooked Reindeer, her SUV isn't in the parking lot. I decide to check one more place. I pull onto the festival grounds, and everything is dark. Off in the distance, a soft glow illuminates a window in one of the buildings. As I drive closer, Brie's SUV comes into view. Parking next to her vehicle, I grab the top hat from my passenger seat and climb out. Christmas music plays softly from inside the building marked Santa's Workshop. Snowflakes flutter down from the sky, calmer than my erratic pulse. Lifting my hand, I rap my knuckles against the wood. I don't know why I'm here or why I have to give the top hat to Brie now, but I just want to see her. Even if it's for a second before she slams the door in my face. I want to inhale her sweet lavender scent so I can go home and dream about it.

The door opens a few seconds later. Brie's whiskey-colored eyes light up. "Logan. What are you doing here?"

Relief washes over me. No bitter words spewed my way. But she asked me a question, and I need to answer. "Well, when I went to exchange the stolen goods that you failed to come to, I forgot this." I hold up the black top hat.

"Oh. Um. Thanks." She plucks the hat from my grasp.

"So why didn't you show up that night?"

A gust of wind sends snowflakes swirling around us. Her shoulders scrunch as she fights a shiver. "Come in. It's a little too cold to heat the outdoors." She opens the door wider and motions for me to come inside. Once I get through the doorway, the door closes with a soft click.

Inside, a small portable heater sits in the corner of the one-room wooden building. Along one wall sits a fake fireplace with stockings on the mantel. A big red high-back chair sits in another corner next to a fully decorated Christmas tree. Wrapping paper and ribbons cover the floor and table. She sets the top hat on the table next to a wrapped present and bites her lip. "Would you believe I was washing my hair?"

I shake my head. "Cut the bullshit. For once, I actually thought we were moving past all this. Whatever our history is, it was years ago. It's time to get over it."

She throws her hands up in the air. "Easy for you to say, Mr. Gets Everything He Wants With the Snap of His Fingers."

"Not everything," I mumble.

"What was that?"

"Not everything," I say, steadier. "So… why didn't you come?"

She turns, then faces me again like she'd changed her

mind mid-spin. "Because I don't know what to do anymore."

"About your festival and my carnival?"

"No." Her gaze searches mine, raw and unguarded. "About hating you. I've held onto it so long it felt like truth. But lately?" She swallows. "Lately all I want to do is—"

"What?" I stepped closer, heat from the little heater brushing my back. "Say it."

"Kiss you."

All the air is sucked from my lungs. I can't say anything. I can't breathe. The only telltale sign I'm alive is the thumping in my chest.

"Please say something," she whispers.

I step closer so we're chest to chest. Reaching out, I clasp my hands around her cheeks and crash my lips to hers. My chest swells with something that feels like the sun's first rays bursting over the horizon. No shocks of electricity or dramatic crescendos, but something softer, more intimate—like finding your favorite song again after years of forgetting it. Her hands slide up my chest. I'm convinced she's going to push me away, call me an asshole. Instead, she fists the fabric, holding on like a lifeline. At least it's true for one of us. I pull back a breath, resting my forehead against hers. "I wish I had kissed you the night after the bar."

"Me too." This time she tugs me to her and presses her lips to mine. It's soft, then hungry. It's the kind of kiss that makes you forget your own name. Fuck, I need her. More than ever right now. She tears apart the buttons of my fleece jacket and slides her hands over my shoulders until it hits the floor with a thud. With desperate fingers, my hands roam across her back, playing with the hem of her sweater. Walking backward, we knock into a table. Glancing over her shoulder I spot wrapping paper, ribbon, tape, and scissors on the surface. With a swoop of my arm, I shove everything off, and it scatters all over the floor like confetti. I hoist her onto the empty table.

"Hey, that's my—"

I silence her with a kiss, my hands sliding to her waist as I nestle between her thighs. "Worth it," I mutter against her lips.

Her legs hook around my hips, pulling me flush against her. I groan at the contact, burying my face against her neck as she grinds against me.

"You think you're going on Santa's nice or naughty list?" I mutter against her heated skin.

"Definitely naughty." My gaze lifts to hers and she pushes her lips to mine in a ravenous kiss. She's as desperate as I am, and it's never made me feel more alive.

We're nothing but frantic hands and limbs, tearing at each other's clothes. Our lips fuse together, only breaking apart so I can lift her shirt over her head. Her fingers curl around the hem of my hoodie and pull it up, taking my shirt with it. Since her arms aren't long enough, I help her the rest of the way. I cup her breast over her red lace bra, and she moans into my mouth.

I want this. God, I want *her*. I've been craving Brie for weeks, and yet—I need to be sure. Pulling back just enough, I whisper against her lips, "If this is too much, tell me and I'll stop."

Her answer is immediate. Fingers sliding into my hair, tugging me closer. "Don't you dare stop."

That's all the permission I need. Heat pounds through me as my mouth trails down her neck, across her collarbone, tasting her skin. She grinds against me like she can't get close enough.

"Logan," she breathes, her voice half warning, half plea.

My control snaps like a brittle candy cane. I curl my fingers around the cup of her bra and tug down, exposing her hard nipple to the cool air. She inches closer to me, rocking her denim-covered pussy over my straining cock. Now it's my turn to moan. I've dreamed of touching her like this, and hands down, the reality is much better. I brush my thumb over her stiff peak, and she arches into my touch. My dick twitches at how responsive she is. Breaking away, I drop my head to her chest, placing kisses over her soft, smooth skin. I swirl my tongue over her stiff nipple, and she sucks in a sharp breath. She leans back on her hands as I continue to nip and suck on one tit while my hand plays with the other.

She moans. "It feels so good. You're supposed to be my enemy."

I grin against her skin. "Then I'm the worst kind of enemy. Because I want to worship you with my mouth. One place in particular." When I look up, her gaze is locked on mine, wide and expectant. Slowly, I drag my hands down her stomach, every inch leaving a trail of goosebumps in their wake. When I reach the button of her jeans, I pause, silently asking. Her mouth parts, her breath catches, and then she nods.

That's all I need.

I pop the button and tug the denim down her hips. She lifts herself off the table, helping me shove them the rest of the way until they hit the floor. My cock jumps when I see her panties—red, the same ones from Sip and Sleigh. Like she planned this, though I know she didn't.

"Fucking gorgeous," I rasp, my gaze roaming over her. She bites her lip, fighting a smile, but I see the flush creeping up her throat.

I press my thumb to the fabric covering her, circling slowly. It darkens with each pass. "Already so wet for me."

Reaching down, I undo the button of my jeans to give my straining dick more room.

"Yes," she moans, head tipping back.

Bending over, I hook my finger around the fabric and tug it to the side, exposing her glistening pussy. With my hand on her other thigh, I open her up wider. I lower myself to her spread legs and press my lips to her inner thigh, tasting her skin as I move closer. Licking, sucking, teasing until her breath comes in shallow gasps. Her scent wraps around me, thick and heady. "You want me to lick your pussy?"

"Yes." Her response comes out breathy.

I trail my nose along her thigh, stopping just shy of her center, then repeat the torture on the other side. Drawing it out. Savoring her. *Melting the Ice Queen,* I think with a wicked grin.

"Logan, please." She bucks her hips, begging me to lick her.

"I love that you're just as frantic as I am." I spread her open, exposing her clit. Using the flat of my tongue, I run it up her center.

"Oh yes!" she gasps, her entire body shivering.

From between her legs, my gaze wanders up her torso, watching her tits rise and fall with every ragged breath, until I meet her eyes. They're wild, pleading.

"Shhh. You have to be quiet. Someone walking by could hear you."

I continue to lap at her pussy, making sure not an inch of her goes untouched. Her fingers clench in my hair, guiding me exactly where she wants me. My dick is suffocating in the confines of my jeans.

"Oh god! Logan!" she moans. "Fuck me with your tongue."

I pull away and stand.

"Hey!" she protests, propping herself on her elbows, flushed and panting. "I was enjoying that."

"Yeah, and I told you to be quiet." I lift a brow.

Her teeth sink into her bottom lip before slowly sliding it free. "What are you going to do about it?"

I glance around the room, searching for something—anything—that'll keep her quiet. My gaze lands on a bag of plush toys in the corner. Perfect. I pluck a reindeer from the top and carry it back to where Brie waits, her chest heaving, eyes dark with want.

"Open up and bite down on this."

Her brows pinch together. "But that's for the kids who visit Santa."

I shake the reindeer, and its legs flop back and forth. "Do you want me to lick your pussy, or would you rather argue with me?" She stares at me for a beat before her gaze drifts to the reindeer. As each second ticks away, I'm convinced she's going to tell me to go to hell and kick me out. "Do you trust me?" Her gaze flicks to me, and my heart thunders in my chest. Maybe I've gone too far. Slowly, her lips part.

Relief and heat flood me at once. My mouth curves into a grin. "Good girl."

I slide the toy between her teeth, the plush legs resting against her flushed cheeks, and then I drop to my knees. My palms brace her thighs, pushing them wider, and I lower my head, continuing my exploration of her pussy with my tongue. Using the tip, I circle the edge of her opening before shoving inside her.

Her muffled moan sounds behind the cotton stuffing. Her hand goes between her legs, and she rubs her clit while I fuck her with my tongue. "Mmm."

Her hips buck, and I do it again. Glancing up, her back is arched, and her other hand pinches her nipple. Fuck, I love she's giving herself pleasure while I'm doing the same. My cock strains painfully in my jeans. With my free hand, I shove them down enough to free myself, pre-cum already leaking. Using it as lube, I slowly stroke myself.

"Hold these. I want your clit." I guide her hand to her panties, and she holds them aside while I take over. With my lips sealed around her clit, I suck. Hard. Her muffled moans vibrate through the room as she writhes under my tongue. With a shudder, her orgasm tears through her as she cries out against the plush reindeer. Her chest heaves as she props up on her elbows, staring down at me with glazed eyes. I don't stop, licking her through every aftershock, savoring the way she trembles under my mouth.

She rips the reindeer from between her teeth. Her voice is hoarse but sure. "I want to see you."

I rise slowly, wiping my mouth with the back of my hand. She scoots closer to the edge of the table, her legs parting as I stand to my full height. My cock is hard and aching in my fist as I stroke myself. Her gaze drops instantly, and her tongue darts out to wet her bottom lip.

"I want to touch you," she whispers, nudging my hand away, replacing it with hers.

My dick throbs the second her delicate fingers close around me, and I groan. "Fuck, Brie." I clutch the table for balance. "Spit in your hand."

She obeys before going back to stroking me. Her thumb sweeps across the crown. The friction makes me hiss through my teeth. "God, you feel so good jacking me off." Leaning in, I kiss her hungrily, her moans spilling into my mouth as we touch each other.

A tingling, sharp and fast, builds at the base of my spine. My legs tremble. "Oh fuck. Lay down," I rasp. She drops her hand and reclines against the table. With my elbow, I nudge her legs open farther, putting her pussy on full display as I fist myself. "Touch yourself. Let me see you."

Her fingers find her clit, rubbing in quick, desperate circles. The sight destroys me. "Oh fuck, yeah," I groan. "Just like that." Seconds later, all my restraint snaps, and my orgasm rips through me. Spurt after spurt of cum lands on her stomach.

When the last tremor fades, I rest a shaky hand on her thigh. "Sorry for the mess," I murmur, still catching my breath.

"It was kind of hot watching you lose control like that." Her teeth sink into her bottom lip.

Reaching up, I free her lip with my thumb, my cock already stirring again. "You've got to stop giving me that look. Unless you want round two."

She flicks her tongue against the pad of my thumb, sending another shiver through me. I'm tempted to pull her off the table and bend her over the edge.

"I have a packet of tissues in my coat pocket."

She pulls me out of thoughts of burying myself balls-deep inside her. Glancing around the room, I spot her coat draped over a chair. I return with a handful of tissues and clean her up before depositing them off to the side. Leaning down, I press open-mouthed kisses up her hip and along her rib cage.

"So," I murmur against her skin, "what do you say we call a truce to all these pranks?"

"Why? Because you're ahead."

I huff a laugh. "You're actually keeping score?"

"I am."

"Fine," I say, nipping under her breast just to hear her suck in a breath. "How about this—one orgasm on my tongue, and we're even."

She whines dramatically. "That only makes us even. I prefer winning."

I grin. "Two orgasms, then. Final offer."

She shakes her head, though her body arches when I suck her nipple into my mouth. "Tempting. But you can't bribe me with orgasms."

"Are you sure?" I lift my head, arching a brow. "I'll give you a sample, and then you can decide if you want to take the deal." I suck her nipple into my mouth, and she arches into me, a soft moan falling from her lips. Her fingers thread through my hair. I'm convinced she's going to shove my head back between her thighs and demand another orgasm, which I'd be more than willing to give, but she tugs instead.

"As much as I want to continue violating Santa's Workshop with you," she says, cheeks flushed, "I have to call a raincheck. I really need to finish wrapping all these presents so I can get home at a decent hour."

"Only you would pass on an orgasm to wrap presents. Not even real ones."

She doubles over laughing, her belly shaking. "What can I say? Wrapping is a turn-on. The paper crinkling, silky ribbon sliding through your fingers, tape ripping—mm, hot."

"No wonder this is your favorite time of year."

"Oh my god, I was joking!" She shoves at my shoulders until I'm standing.

I scoop up her underwear and jeans, passing them over, then yank my shirt on while she wriggles into her clothes. When I tug her sweater into place, she quirks a brow. "I've never had anyone help me put my clothes back on."

"I took them off," I say with a grin. "Figured it's only fair. Though admittedly less fun."

Brie's phone chimes from the other side of the room.

"That's probably Willa asking if I'm done yet." She strolls to the opposite side and pulls her phone from her purse.

In the meantime, I swipe the reindeer off the table and shove it into my coat pocket. When I glance up her posture stiffens. My humor fades, and I lean against the table, ankles crossed. "What's wrong?"

Her head lifts slowly, and the light in her eyes is gone, replaced by something sharp and hollow. "What's the real reason you came here tonight?"

I straighten. "To return the top hat."

"It wasn't for us to… to do this."

I scrub a hand over my jaw. "No. It kind of snowballed into that."

Her voice cuts like ice. "You didn't come here to sleep with me just to get me to back down?"

"What are you insinuating?"

She thrusts her phone toward me. On the screen in big, bold letters: *A Tale of Dueling Christmas Celebrations.*

I scan it, brow furrowing. "I don't get it. Both our events are in the article. Isn't that good?"

Her gaze burns into me. "She quoted you. Said, *'It would be a lot easier if I could break her icy exterior.'*"

Her voice shakes as she spits the words back at me. "So tell me, Logan—was this you breaking my icy exterior?"

Brie

His eyes widen. "No! Why would you even think that?"

"Because of this." I shove my phone into his hand. He squints at the screen, brows knitting.

"Why the hell would she publish that?"

"I don't know. Maybe because *you told her*?" My pulse thrums in my ears. "Why else would she write it? For once, it would be nice to get something I've poured my heart and soul into without facing a mountain of difficulties. But no —you show up, and suddenly everything is harder for me and ten times easier for you."

Logan leans against the table, arms folded, maddeningly calm. "Are you… jealous?"

I rear my head back. "Jealous?" The word echoes in

my head. It's a legitimate word that perfectly explains my life. "You know what? Yes. Yes, I was, or am, jealous because I worked so damn hard all the damn time and all you had to do was show up, and everything was handed to you. In elementary school, you got to be the Christmas star in the school play without even trying out. You got all the easy words during the spelling bee, like kale. While I got asparagus." I spin away from Logan and pace from one side of the room to the other while he leans against the table, arms crossed over his chest. God, why am I shaking? It's not like I haven't fantasized about telling him off since fifth grade. All of it building up like a dam about to burst. Here it goes. "In high school, you were valedictorian even though I saw you goofing off with your friends all the time while I was in the library studying my ass off. Any girl who blinked at you wanted to be your girlfriend. Everyone bought you Valentine's Day suckers from the high school fundraiser. You had a whole plethora of suckers. You know how I know? Because I had to pass them out. Lastly, you host one carnival, and suddenly a world-renowned Christmas blogger comes to town wanting to interview *you*."

As I pass by Logan, he grabs my wrist and pulls me to his chest.

If he smirks right now, I might actually throw my phone at his perfect, smug face.

"You realize none of that matters now."

"It does to me," my voice cracks, "because this festival is my one shot, and it's being ruined by you. Again. I hate how much you get under my skin."

His fingertips skim my arm—barely there, but enough to send a rush of goosebumps chasing after them. "Or maybe," he murmurs, voice low and threaded with something that steals the air from my lungs, "I get under your skin because I'm the only one who actually knows you. The real you. Not the easy stuff anyone can guess—your favorite food, your coffee order. What I know is that you're smart. Stubborn. Fierce. A fighter. You don't back down, even when the odds are stacked against you."

His gaze pins me, warm and unrelenting.

"Those are the things I know about you," he finishes softly. "Everything else? I can learn. But those… those are the things that matter."

I freeze. His eyes—soft, unguarded—pull at something in me I don't want to admit exists. Shit. What if he's right? Maybe all the bickering and one-upping is just… knowing each other too well.

"You know what, Brie?" His thumb strokes my cheek. "Can I kiss you?"

I blink. "What? Why?"

"Yes or no. That's all I need."

"That makes zero sense. I just confessed a lifetime of hating you, and now—"

"I'm giving you five seconds. If you don't say no, I'm kissing you."

"Logan, you can't—"

"Five. Four. Three."

"You're not serious."

"Two."

My eyes narrow to slits. "You wouldn't dare—"

"One."

Before I can finish, his hands cradle my face and his mouth crashes to mine. The kiss is molten—slow, deep, devastating in the best way. So this is what it's like when your enemy detonates your brain with his mouth. It melts years of irritation into something hotter, something that makes my knees weak and my head spin. The man who's mastered pushing my buttons is now nailing every single one that turns me on.

He pulls back, but he doesn't let go of my face. Instead, he brushes his thumb over my cheek, tender and careful. "We've fought about a lot of stupid things. But none of that's real. This? This is."

He lifts my phone, scrolling. "She twisted my words for clicks. What I *actually* said?" He holds the screen up. "That you're smart. Beautiful. Generous. That's why I'm here tonight—because I can't stop thinking about you. And if it's you against the world, I want to be right there at your side."

His eyes wander over me like I'm the answer to a question he's been asking his whole life. I don't even know the question, but I desperately want to be the answer.

His finger slides over my temple as he tucks a strand of hair behind my ear. "For the past few weeks, you've been the best distraction. I've been able to get out of my own head for once."

"Life has certainly been more…" I purse my lips together, searching for the right words, "entertaining since you've come back to town."

He cups my cheek, and I lean into his warmth. "We have a connection. I feel it. I know you feel it. I don't want to fight it anymore."

Twisting my head, I press a kiss to his palm. He's right. Whatever hate I've harbored toward him has shifted to something that's the complete opposite. "I believe you." We've been through a lot, not only regarding the festivals, but our whole lives. I lift my chin, my lashes fluttering open with my gaze lingering on his.

"If you keep looking at me like that, we'll be staying in Santa's Workshop until the sun comes up." He presses his lips to my forehead in a chaste kiss. "I'm glad you believe me. If you didn't," he rests a finger under my chin, forcing me to meet his eyes, "I'd have to give you another orgasm to show you how much you should believe me."

"Fine." I hop onto the table, spreading my legs with a wicked grin. "I don't believe you."

His laugh rumbles against me as he steps between my thighs, cupping my face. "God, I want nothing more than to feast on you all night. But I have to pick up Josie. I'm already late."

My eyes scan his, searching for any signs of insincerity. Earlier, he asked me if I trust him, and I do. Since whatever is happening between us is so fresh and new, I haven't even had the chance to fully wrap my head around it. Again, I spent so many years believing one thing about this man, and I was completely wrong. "Are you going to tell them about this?"

"Do you want me to?"

"Actually, what if we just keep this between us for right now?"

"Oh, so you just want to go back to hating me again?"

"It's kind of fun. And we haven't gotten to the hate sex yet."

"You best believe I will hate sex the fuck out of you. Just tell me the time and place."

A giggle bursts out of me. I'm half tempted to say right now, but I need to deal with one emotion first before I bring on a slew of others. "For now, you should get going so you're not any later. Then you'd really have some explaining to do."

"Fuck. You're perfect." He grips my chin and presses his lips to mine.

He pulls away, but I don't want him to. Instead, my lips chase his like an overeager puppy. When my lashes flutter open, he's staring at me with a look that shouldn't belong to my supposed rival—adoration. "I'm really not."

"To me, you are," he says like he's stating a fact.

My brain short-circuits. So naturally, I go for humor. "Get out of here before I tie you up with Christmas ribbon and keep you as my sex hostage."

His grin tilts, cocky. "If that's a threat, it's a pretty bad one."

I laugh, pushing at his shoulders. "Go."

"Okay, okay." He chuckles as I spin him toward the door and shove. "I'm leaving."

The second he disappears into his truck, I sag against the door, grinning like an idiot. Logan and me putting aside our differences for a common goal. Never say never. Granted, I didn't expect that goal to be orgasms, but honestly? Best. Goal. Ever.

I push off the door. I need to finish wrapping presents so I can get home and go to bed. Tomorrow is the snowman-making contest, and it will be the biggest one yet; over two hundred people have signed up.

The next morning, I wake up dry-humping my pillow with vivid flashbacks of Logan's tongue. The man put his mouth to *very* good use last night. Better than all the hours he's spent arguing with me. But if he wants to use that tongue after every argument, I will pick a fight with him *every single day*.

After I dress, I swing by Sip and Sleigh. A coffee is exactly what I need before heading to the festival grounds. Lauren has been doing a fantastic job managing the graphics and marketing, which is helping to build excitement for the festival. I don't think I could have done all of this without her help. Even her taking the reins on organizing the sleigh ride has been a blessing.

The bell jingles as I step inside, still smiling like someone who got thoroughly… well, distracted.

Sloane zeroes in on me, her eyes sparkling. "You've got a little extra pep in your step. And I doubt it's because you love snowman contests *that* much."

"Maybe it is," I say, the words sounding braver than I feel.

She rolls her eyes. "Ooor maybe it has something to do with me overhearing the Gigis this morning and their fresh batch of hot gossip."

Shit. Hot gossip could be anything, and nothing's hotter than what Logan and I did last night. Don't blush. Don't blush. Oh look, I'm blushing so hard I might combust and take the croissants with me. Perhaps it's something else. At least I can pretend. "Let me guess. Mr. Holter's lawn gnomes went missing again, when in fact, they're only buried by the snow."

"Nope." She pops the *p* for extra emphasis.

"Mrs. Haugan inquired about the non-delivery of her mail. Again."

She shakes her head.

I sigh. "I give up."

"It's about how a certain hometown hockey hero's truck was spotted next to yours outside Santa's Workshop for an unreasonable amount of time to be considered a casual conversation."

Heat creeps up my neck. I yank at my scarf, like that'll help. "Oh."

"Exactly." She quirks a brow. "So, why was Logan's truck outside Santa's Workshop for an *unreasonable* amount of time?"

"He dropped off my snowman's top hat. And we wrapped presents." Not technically a lie.

"Uh-huh. Just wrapping presents?"

I can't tell her he gave me a Christmas present he unwrapped with his tongue that sent me into orgasm bliss several times. "That's it," I spit out. I don't know what Logan and I are doing. Besides the one-time exchange of orgasms. I'd hate for it to be only one time. But everything between us is so new. We haven't even discussed what we're doing. As far as I know, it will be a one-and-done situation, and later he'll forget it even happened, and we'll go back to sabotaging each other's events.

She tilts her head to the side. "Is that why you have a hickey on your neck?"

Did he give me a hickey? My hand flies to my neck. My fingers meeting the crocheted fabric of my scarf instead of skin. Dammit. It would be impossible for her to see if I had a hickey.

Her smile goes full supernova. "Yup. Got my answer."

"Don't say anything," I hiss.

"As long as you give me *all* the details later." She straightens, all professional again. "You know, people take the Gigis words as gossip, but I'm thinking they're more like truth bombs. They detonate at the perfect time, exploding all over Mount Holly." She slides a paper cup toward me. "Here's your coffee. Enjoy your *splendid* day…" she leans in, voice dropping to a whisper, "thinking about Logan."

Another wave of heat scorches my cheeks. I snatch the cup, muttering a thanks, and head for the door. Splendid day, indeed. Twelve full hours of trying not to daydream about Logan Crawford and failing.

Logan

Brie wanders from one group to the next, her breath visible in the cold air as she inspects each snowman like she's running a covert investigation. Honestly, I have no idea how someone cheats at a snowman competition—but if anyone could find a way, it'd be the Dillards. I'm convinced they've got secret spray bottles in their pockets to polish the snow until it gleams. She stops by a cowboy snowman and smiles, bright as sunlight hitting fresh snow.

"Dad! Dad! You're not helping." Josie's mitten smacks against our snowman's torso.

Her voice jolts me out of my staring. "Yeah. Right. Sorry. What do you need me to do?"

"He needs more snow on the back of his head. It's not round."

"Got it." I crouch and patch the back with handfuls of snow.

"Hi Brie!" Josie chirps.

My head shoots up.

"Hi, Josie. Wow, your snowman looks amazing." Brie's gaze lingers on Josie's creation… and then slides to me.

"No thanks to my dad," Josie adds with a dramatic sigh. "Maybe you can help me instead. He's kind of useless."

Brie laughs, and my dick jumps. Her laughter shouldn't be so sexy, but damn if it doesn't do me in.

"I'd love to," she says, "but I'm judging the contest. If I help, it's cheating."

"So when do we get crowned snowman champions? I already cleared a spot on the mantel for the trophy." I playfully rub my gloves together.

Brie teases, "Confident, are we? You've got stiff competition. But over the next few days there will be a judges vote and a community vote. After those are tallied, we'll make an announcement."

"How about you come over tonight and we can build a snowman together?" Josie turns her attention to me, big hazel eyes boring into mine. "Dad, can Brie come over later?"

"Uh." Brie's gaze whips to mine. I rub the back of my neck. I glance from Brie to Josie and back to Brie, praying Josie gets distracted and forgets she asked, but she's like an unwavering stone. "That's up to Brie." Ha. Deflection. Now it's in her court.

"Um." Brie pinches her lips together.

"I had so much fun building one with you the day we

baked cookies. And my dad can even make his famous chicken and wild rice hotdish," Josie pleads.

Brie chuckles. "Oh boy. That's hard to turn down."

Her finger taps her bottom lip, and my focus zeroes in. God, I want to kiss that spot.

"Alright," she says softly. "Snowman building and hotdish it is."

Josie jumps up and down. "Yay!"

Shit. She said yes. My palms sweat in my gloves. Date? Not a date? Either way, I'm wildly out of practice. "Um. What time are you free?"

"I can be at your place at four. That will give us a little time to build a snowman before it gets dark. Is that okay?" Brie drops her gaze to Josie.

"Yes!" Josie exclaims.

"Since my snowman-making skills are lacking, I'll cook dinner," I say.

Brie's eyes catch mine, something sparking there. "Then I'll see you at four."

"Bye, Brie!" Josie waves her snow-covered mitten.

"Bye, Josie." Her dark-brown eyes lift to mine. "Bye, Logan." She flashes me a sultry smile.

Fuck. I want nothing more than to tackle her in the snow and do what we did in Santa's Workshop, but this time with Frosty watching. Santa's definitely putting me on the naughty list.

Four o'clock on the dot, Brie's walking up my driveway. My heart thunders in my chest like it's seeing her for the first time, and it's only been three hours. I glance at the street, but it's empty. No SUV. My brows draw together. Did she walk? If it was summertime, sure, our houses are only a mile apart, but it's winter. I yank open the door. "You're punctual. I like it."

She holds up wine and cookies. "Luckily, I had these at home. Didn't have to make a pit stop."

"You didn't need to bring anything." I take the offerings and stand to the side to let her in. "Where's your car?"

Her shoulder brushes mine as she slips past, close enough that my blood heats. "Parked around the corner.

"You could have parked it in the driveway."

"Then the speculations would fly about why my car is in your driveway."

"So you're my dirty little secret?"

"Only if you do dirty things to me." She gives me a salacious grin.

Fuck. Don't think about last night. Do not think about last night. I adjust myself and shut the door before she notices. A part of me enjoys bickering and arguing with Brie because she's quick-witted, but the sexy flirting with Brie is way better.

She follows me into the kitchen, and I set the wine and cookies on the counter. "Josie put together a snowman-making kit."

Josie climbs onto a stool. "I didn't have a top hat, but I have one of my dad's hockey hats." She points to a knit beanie. "I also got a scarf, some charcoal for eyes, and even a carrot for the nose."

"Wow, this is perfect." Brie's eyes sparkle as she looks over the collection.

"Josie, why don't you get your stuff on, and we'll go outside," I say.

Once outside, Josie scoops snow into her mittens and squishes it into a ball while Brie does the same. I stand off to the side, supervising, where it's safe.

"Let's start with yours, Josie." Brie collects the snowball from Josie's grasp, sets it in the pristine snow, and rolls it.

With each turn, more and more snow collects, growing the ball. "Now the trick is as you're rolling, you also shape it. It'll help save time later."

Brie smooths the sides of the ball before she continues rolling it. As Brie bends over, her ass is straight in my line of sight, round and perfect. She glances over her shoulder and catches me staring, I bite back a laugh. Busted.

"Why don't you start another snowball for the head?" Brie asks.

"Alright." I grab a handful of snow and carefully compact it into a ball. "There you go." I hold out my open palm with the snowball nestled on top.

"Dad, your ball is weird!" Josie scolds as I present my lumpy, egg-shaped effort.

"Can't we shave it down later?" I study the lump of snow in my palm.

"Dad! You're doing it wrong. It's best to start with a ball," Josie huffs.

Brie giggles. "Here, let me." She takes my hand, molds it over the snow, then covers it with hers. "Like this."

My heart stammers in my chest. She's focused on the snowball, but I'm focused on the warmth of her hand over mine. On the flush in her cheeks. On the smile tugging her lips.

When her gaze flicks up and collides with mine, I nearly lean down and kiss her right there.

Instead, I clear my throat. "Looks like you two have this covered. I'll, uh, get dinner started."

From the kitchen window, I watch Brie and Josie smile, laugh, and playfully throw snow at each other. Josie deserves this kind of joy that I can't give her alone. I hate she'll miss out on pivotal mother-daughter moments. First school dance. First boyfriend. First heartbreak. Wedding dress shopping. I'm a poor substitute, even though I'd be by her side if she wanted. Brooke would be better.

The sizzle of chicken and onions fills the kitchen, the scent of garlic and butter drifting through the air. When I glance out the window, Brie and Josie are in the yard, already laughing over their third snowman. I shake my head, grinning. They look like they've been doing this together forever.

A little while later, the patio door bangs open, and the pair tumble inside, dusted in snow.

"Alright, alright," I laugh. "Brush it off before you track half the yard into the kitchen."

They stomp their boots in unison, giggling as they swat snow from each other's coats.

"Dinner smells delicious." Brie shrugs out of her jacket.

"Dad always makes it with extra cheese," Josie pipes up proudly.

"You can't go wrong with extra cheese." Brie winks at me.

I fake a groan. "Hey, don't go giving away all my secrets." That earns me another round of laughter—Brie's light and warm, Josie's bubbling over.

"Josie, why don't you wash up? Dinner's almost ready," I say.

"Okay!" She bolts for the bathroom.

When she's gone, Brie leans back against the counter, arms folded, eyes tracking me as I chop a tomato for the salad. "You know, I kind of wish I'd stayed in here to watch you cook. There's nothing sexier than a man who knows his way around the kitchen."

I set the knife down, heart thudding harder than it should. "Next time, I'll make sure you've got a front-row seat. I've got more than one famous dish."

"Oh, so you're already assuming there'll be a next time?" she teases, voice lilting.

"I'm hoping," I counter, stepping closer.

Her teeth catch her bottom lip, and I forget how to breathe.

"You've got that look again," I murmur.

She tilts her head. "What look?"

"The one that makes me believe I need you more than air." My gaze flicks to her lips. I'm leaning in, seconds away, when the oven timer beeps, interrupting our moment.

Brie's whisper is amused. Breathless. "Dinner's done."

I blow out a laugh, dragging a hand over my face. I've never had my willpower tested so many times in one day. "Yeah, it is. Go grab a seat before I lose all self-control."

"You're serving me too?" She raises her brows. "Careful, Crawford, I could get used to this."

"Just one of my many talents."

"Oh, I'm definitely learning what they all are."

Josie races back into the kitchen, grabs a chair, and places it right next to Brie. "We made three snowmen today."

"I saw that. You two were busy." I set a bowl filled with salad and a plate with hotdish in front of Brie, followed by a plate for Josie.

"It's a family. One's me, one's you, and the other's Brie." She digs in like she hasn't just dropped a bomb.

Brie and I exchange a startled look, then she gives a tiny shrug and a soft smile, rolling with it. At least she's not high-tailing it out of here.

"This looks amazing. I can't wait to try it." Brie shoves a forkful of the chicken and wild rice hotdish into her mouth. Her eyes drift closed and she hums like I've just served her a meal from a Michelin Star restaurant instead of hotdish. "Oh yeah. This is so good."

I bite back a grin, shoulders relaxing. Never in my life did I imagine Brie in my kitchen, eating my cooking, and enjoying it.

Halfway through dinner, Josie launches into jokes. "What does a nosy pepper do?" She bounces in her seat while she waits for us to guess.

Brie and I share a look before shrugging. "I don't know," we say in unison.

"It gets jalapeño business!" Josie throws her head back in laughter.

Brie giggles.

"That's a good one," I say. "I have one for you. What did the snowman order at the Mexican restaurant?"

"What?" Josie asks.

"A brrr-ito."

Josie cackles, practically falling out of her chair, while Brie just shakes her head with a smile that makes my chest feel too tight.

"It's a good one." I wiggle my eyebrows.

Under the table, I stretch my leg—and my foot bumps into something solid. Brie's eyes flick up, startled, then soften when she realizes it's me. A teasing smile curves her lips. I graze her toes with mine, just a brush, but heat flares through me like I've touched a live wire. She nudges me back playfully, and a pink blush warms her cheeks.

I clear my throat before Josie notices the electricity crackling between us. "Speaking of snowmen, how'd the rest of the contest go?"

Brie sets her fork down, turning toward Josie with a proud grin. "So many great entries—including yours. You've got serious snowman-building skills." She bumps Josie's shoulder.

The two of them launch into a conversation about cowboy snowmen, glitter glue accessories, and one entry that looked suspiciously like Elvis. I lean back, half listening, half lost in the way Brie's laughter lights up the room. My foot keeps brushing hers, and she doesn't pull away. She plays along, toes tangling with mine under the table. This is exactly what Josie should have had growing up. Family dinners. Easy laughter. A woman's voice mixing with ours at the table. The ache in my chest twists, sharp enough to make me shove my plate away.

"You're done already?" Brie's brows pinch.

"Yeah, I had a big lunch."

She eyes me but doesn't push. Instead, she finishes her last bite and stands. "Here, let me grab the dishes."

"I've got it. You're my guest."

"And you cooked. At least let me help."

"I'll help too!" Josie hops up like it's Christmas morning.

I stare at her suspiciously. "You never volunteer for dishes." Leaning toward Brie, I whisper, "What have you done to my daughter? You should probably come over more often."

Brie giggles.

Josie pipes up, "Yes! Dad makes the best pancakes."

Brie's eyes sparkle as she turns to me. "Oh, so now we're moving on to breakfast."

As I pass Brie, I bend down, my nose running along the shell of her ear, and whisper, "I'm not opposed to making you breakfast."

Her breath catches, and satisfaction zips through me.

We form an assembly line at the sink—me rinsing, Josie handing things off, Brie sliding them into the dishwasher. It feels… dangerously domestic. Like something I could get used to.

"Brie, you should stay for a movie," Josie says. "Dad can make popcorn. It'll be like a slumber party."

A flicker of hesitancy crosses Brie's face when she glances at me. Does she want to stay? I'd love to have Brie share my bed, but maybe it's too much. Too fast. I rest a hand on Josie's shoulder, and she peers up at me. "I'm sure Brie would like to sleep in her own bed tonight."

Brie smiles softly. "But I'd love to stay for a movie."

Josie cheers and bounds into the living room.

Once she's gone, Brie's gaze lingers on me. "If I'm overstaying my welcome, just say so."

"No, I'm enjoying your company. But I hope to have that sleepover someday."

Brie's fingertips trace down my arm, and my heart leaps into my throat. "And I hope to get pancakes."

I'm seconds away from saying to hell with it. She can stay over, and I'll cook her all the pancakes she wants in the morning, but I haven't been with a woman since Brooke, let alone had one stay the night. Josie seems to like Brie, but I don't know how she would take my being with someone else. Sure, she's only a kid, but she's my daughter. What I do affects her as well. I can't just leap. Not yet.

After making the popcorn and dumping it into a giant bowl, we stroll into the living room where Josie already has the movie up on the screen and has turned the couch into Blanket Kingdom.

"The Taylor Swift Eras Tour." Brie nudges me with her elbow, smirking. "Never pegged you for a Swiftie."

"I do it for Josie," I deadpan.

"Dad can sit here, and then Brie can sit here." Josie pats the cushion next to my spot.

"Where are you going to sit?" I ask.

"On the other side next to Brie."

Brie points toward the recliner in the corner. "Maybe I should sit there."

"No, sit here for optimal TV viewing. It's the best spot in the house. At least that's what Dad says."

Brie bites her lip, trying not to laugh. "Well, I can't argue with the best spot in the house."

The three of us squeeze in. Brie shifts, her thigh brushing mine, and a jolt of heat shoots through me. God help me. Her scent, her warmth, her smile tugging at the corner of her lips—it takes every ounce of my being to keep my eyes glued to the TV instead of her mouth. A month ago, we were mortal enemies. Now? The only war I'm fighting is keeping my hands to myself.

During the first five songs, Josie shimmies on the couch, Brie's belting lyrics into an invisible mic, and I'm tapping my foot like I'm not secretly the biggest Swiftie in the room. If anyone asks, I'll deny it.

Halfway through, Josie hops up. "I'm going to grab something from my room."

"Want me to pause it?" I ask.

She waves me off. "I know what happens." Then she scampers upstairs, leaving me alone with Brie.

"She's a great kid," Brie says softly. "You did an amazing job raising her."

"Thanks. But honestly? She came out amazing all on her own." My voice drops, unguarded.

Two more songs pass with no sign of Josie. "I'm going to check on her." I jog upstairs and peek in her room. It's mostly dark, with the only light coming from a small nightlight in the corner. Blankets drape over the bed, forming the perfect outline of a tiny body. My daughter is plotting something but now is not the time for a discussion. Silently, I close the door and return downstairs.

"I guess she went to bed."

"Maybe the snowman marathon wore her out," Brie says, tucking one leg under herself on the couch.

"Maybe." I drop onto the cushion beside her. "Though if I let her, she'd be awake until four in the morning playing on her tablet. How is everything else going with the festival?"

Brie laughs, then sighs. "Good. Stressful. But good."

"I thought you thrived at this planning stuff. What has you so stressed?"

She fiddles with a loose strand of hair. "For starters, Mrs. Kingsley has given me impossible task after impossible task, which makes it slightly more difficult on top of organizing the festival."

"Like what?"

"After she heard about Emma St. Claire being in town, she insisted I get an interview with her."

"You did that. So it wasn't impossible." I rest my arm on the back of the couch.

"But it also wasn't the most newsworthy blog post. I wanted the focus to be on the festival, not my personal life. Mrs. Kingsley also wanted me to find a new Santa, which, let me tell you, was not an easy feat two weeks before Christmas. And on top of it all, I'm still trying to prove I deserve the event coordinator position. I've always been second place. Always the bridesmaid, never the bride. And now you waltz back into town with your carnival, and suddenly I'm scrambling to keep my dream alive."

"I didn't mean to take the spotlight off you by any means. This was something I needed to do for myself and Josie."

"It's okay. Luckily, I had a few extra activities tucked up my sleeve to help draw a crowd. But this is my one shot. Possibly my last shot at getting this position. The Holly Jolly Festival needs to be the biggest and best event this town has ever seen. Or I might as well throw in the towel and give up."

I reach over, brushing my fingers along her shoulder until they tangle in her hair. "I've been a competitor my entire life, especially with hockey, and I think the one thing that made me even better was competition. Made me sharper. Someone set the bar, and I figured out how to shatter it. Don't think of it as me ruining your chance, but I'm pushing you to exceed your expectations." Her chin tips up, eyes locking on mine. Warm, defiant, vulnerable. "I think you might be a little surprised at what you can do." She nods but doesn't say anything. I hope she believes me. I didn't come back to Mount Holly to ruin any chance she had with the festival and a promotion. Poor timing.

She leans against the back of the couch and tips her head toward the ceiling. "You know, I always loved this house. Well, from the outside, anyway. I never got a chance to see the inside until I brought you home from the Crooked Reindeer."

I mimic her pose. "Is that so? What made you love it so much?"

"The wrap-around porch," she says dreamily. "I pictured myself with a book on the swing in the summer or stringing garland and lights around the railing at Christmas."

I turn to face her and lower my voice. "I have the swing in the garage. All it takes is a couple of hooks."

Her eyes flick to mine, laughter bubbling in her throat. "Are you talking dirty to me right now?"

I lean closer, brushing her knee with mine. "I might even have a spare set of lights out there too."

She snorts, her cheeks flushing. "You really do know the path to a girl's heart." But then she sighs, reluctant. "It's late. I should head home. Tomorrow's the cookie bake-off, and I'll be busy making sure Mrs. Walters doesn't bake with her son's cannabutter again."

I chuckle. "I would've paid money to see that judging."

"Nonstop giggles," she confirms, shaking her head.

"Let me walk you to your car."

"You don't have to. It's just around the corner."

"It's dark."

"And it's Mount Holly."

"Will you just let me walk you to your vehicle?"

She rolls her eyes but smiles. "Fine. If you insist."

"Let me just go check on Josie real quick." I rise to my feet and jog up the stairs. When I reach her door, I twist the knob and peek my head in. Josie's blanket is puffed up like a tent. "I know you're not sleeping." She peeks her head from under the blanket, a sheepish grin on her face. If I had to guess, she's playing on her tablet. "I'm going to walk Brie to her car. When I get back, we'll talk."

"Okay."

I shake my head, but I can't fight the smile on my lips. She's too smart for her own good. And I'm going to be in trouble. Back downstairs, Brie's waiting at the door, coat zipped and cheeks rosy. I tug on my boots, shove a knit cap over my head, and lead her outside. Our breaths curl in white clouds as we walk shoulder to shoulder down the quiet street.

"I had a really good time tonight," she says. "You'll have to thank Josie for inviting me."

"I'm glad you came." Our fingers brush once, twice, and sparks skitter through me.

At her SUV, she hits the remote start. The engine rumbles to life. I open the driver's door, but instead of stepping back, I brace one hand against the frame and cage her in with the other.

Her breath catches.

"I want nothing more than to kiss you goodnight," I murmur.

Her lashes flutter. "I don't think that's a good idea. Someone could see."

"If the neighbors are watching from behind their curtains, we should at least give them something worth gossiping about." I rest my forehead against hers, her lips so close I can feel the whisper of her breath.

She leans in first, closing the distance. Her mouth meets mine, soft at first, then deeper, warmer. She melts into me, and every muscle in my body screams to pull her closer, to forget the streetlights, the neighbors, the risk. But I force myself to keep it PG-13.

Reluctantly, I pull away. "Night, Brie."

"Goodnight, Logan," she whispers before climbing into her SUV.

I close the door, watch her taillights fade into the night, and laugh when I spot the rustling of a curtain across the street. Mount Holly never misses a thing.

Back inside, I head upstairs to Josie's room. She's propped against her headboard, blanket pulled up to her chin, eyes wide with fake innocence.

"So," I say, sitting on the edge of her bed, "what was that all about?"

She shrugs. "I wanted you two to spend time together."

"Is that why you invited her over to make snowmen and dinner?"

"No. I actually needed help. Your snowman skills are… bad." She holds up her hands in a circle. "This is what a snowman should look like. Yours looks like this." She squishes her fingers into an oval.

"Snowmen come in all shapes and sizes."

"Only yours."

I laugh. "Fair enough."

She tilts her head. "Do you like Brie?"

The question hits harder than a shoulder to the ribs. I consider lying, but she's too smart for that. "Yeah. I do."

Her grin is pure mischief. "I think you *really* like her. You get this dorky face whenever she's around."

"I do not!" Do I? I never noticed. Then again, I'm too busy staring at Brie whenever she's near to know what my facial muscles are doing.

"Yes, you do. It looks like this." She cocks her head to the side. Her eyes go as wide as her grin, and she bats her eyelashes. "Grandma says she hasn't seen you laugh and smile as much as you have when you're around Brie."

"So Grandma said that, huh?"

"Yup, but it's true. I see it too."

I groan. "Sometimes I think you're too smart for your own good."

She smirks. "One of us has to be."

I press a kiss to her head. "Go to sleep, Peanut. Love you."

"Love you too, Dad."

When I close her door and lean against the railing at the top of the stairs, my chest squeezes. I haven't felt like this since Brooke. And the truth? It terrifies me.

Brie

Yesterday was a curveball I never saw coming. Josie inviting me over. Logan cooking dinner. The movie. And that kiss. That kiss. We're in some strange limbo of *is this real or just temporary insanity?* Because how do you admit you've developed feelings for your lifelong nemesis? Logan today isn't the Logan from eighteen years ago, that much I know. I don't know how long this will last, but for now? I'm buckling in and enjoying the ride. Worst case, we go back to hating each other later.

When I step into the Jolly Biscuit, the warm smell of coffee and pastries wraps around me like a hug, but my brain is busy replaying Logan's lips on mine. A smile sneaks across my face before I can stop it.

"You're the talk of the town this morning," Willa sing-songs, wiggling her brows the second I walk in. "And your grin says it all."

I bite my cheek, fighting it. "What are you talking about?"

"Have you checked the Shenanigans group? It's more entertaining than any soap opera or tabloid magazine."

"No." Curiosity wins. I pull out my phone, scroll, and —yep. There it is. The top post started last night.

Margret: Whose car is this? I haven't seen this car parked on my block before.

Larry: Isn't that Brie McKenna's car?

Margret: I thought her car was blue. This one is black.

Sue: It's dark out. Maybe it looks black. Go outside and snap a closer picture.

Leslie: Does it have a Holly Jolly Festival sticker on the back?

Margret: *Posts a picture* It does. But why is she parked in front of Finn Whitlock's house? I thought she was seeing Logan.

Larry: Someone better tell Logan.

Leslie: I thought Finn was with Vana.

Margret: I thought it was Valerie.

Sue: What if they're in one of those thruples? I learned about it on a TV show. It's an interesting dynamic. But I don't think I could do it.

Margret: Oh. Someone's coming. Wait. It's two people. The car just started up. They're standing in front of the open door. I need better glasses. I can't see.

Sue: What if it's four of them? Would that be a quadthruple?

Leslie: Get the binoculars.

Margret: They're kissing. I think. Or he's putting a necklace on her.

Larry: Why would he be putting a necklace on her?

Margret: I don't know. I can't see.

Leslie: Who's the guy?

Margret: She drove off. I'm pretty sure it's Logan. If I squint any harder, my eyes will be shut.

Sue: It still doesn't answer whether they're in a thruple or quadthruple.

Clearly, we're not very good at staying incognito. I slide my phone back in my pocket. "Fine. There may be something happening between Logan and me."

"That's not screaming at each other?" She arches a brow.

"There may be screaming, but it's definitely not at each other. And I assure you it's not a thruple."

"Brie!" Willa screeches.

"Shhh!" Reaching over the counter, I slap my hand over her mouth. "I'll fill you in later, but for now we're keeping it quiet."

"And obviously you're doing a terrible job at it." She laughs. "Girls' night. And I want all the dirty details." She holds out a paper bag. "Here's your sandwich. Now go do amazing things, especially if you're doing them with," she glances around the diner and mouths, "Logan."

"On that note, I need to get to the Holly Jolly Festival grounds to get ready for the cookie bake-off. I need to watch Mr. Saulter like a hawk so he doesn't add extra ballots into his box." I turn around and saunter toward the door.

As I head out, Willa calls after me, "Happiness looks good on you!"

Great. Now I'm grinning so hard my ears are probably blushing.

By nightfall, the cookie contest is over, and I'm up to my elbows in tablecloths and stray sprinkles. People get more competitive every year—royal icing, edible glitter, even stained-glass sugar cookies. I tug at a red cloth when a loud *bang* outside freezes me in place.

There's another thud, even louder.

I shove into my coat and push open the door. Through the crack, I peer to my left and then to my right. A coal-sized lump gets lodged in my throat. Brad. The woolly menace himself is headbutting the side of the hot chocolate stand like he's auditioning for a demolition derby.

"Brad! Stop it!" I yell, hoping he understands.

He peers up at me. I tilt my head. Maybe he does? He turns his head toward the snowmen from the contest and back to me. He *baaa*s.

"Oh no. Don't even think about it," I warn as he turns toward the ski-goggle snowman. He *baaas* at me— mockingly, I'm sure of it, before flouncing toward the snowman. "Don't do it." I dash after him, the cold air stinging my face as my boots kick up plumes of snow. "Brad!" He stops next to the snowman and licks its torso. "Stop violating the snowman!" When I'm a few feet away, Brad bolts, tearing the hockey snowman's arm clean off and licking under the arm pit. I lunge at him, but he dodges my advances. When did sheep become so sprightly? I take off in a sprint toward Brad, and he *baaa*s and darts toward the feather boa snow queen. "Brad! Get back here right now!"

Headlights slice across the field of snowmen before coming to a stop on me. Relief floods me. It's Logan.

"Is this a new holiday tradition?" he calls. "Running with the snowmen?"

"Brad's loose!" I gasp. "He's licking all the entries! Judging hasn't even started!"

Suddenly, I'm shrouded in darkness. Speckles of light dance behind my eyelids with every blink. A door slams, and a few seconds later, Logan's silhouette forms out of the darkness, jogging across the snow. "Where is he?"

"Using his ninja skills to evade me. But he can't ruin the snowmen."

"Then let's catch him."

We fan out, weaving in and out of the snowmen like a Christmas-themed obstacle course. Brad, of course, is loving it—darting between us, baaing like it's his personal victory anthem.

I come to a stop, doubled over with my hands on my knees. I pant, "We need a new plan."

Logan stops next to me. "What's that?"

"I," inhale, "don't know."

"I think we need to trap him somehow."

"Yeah. Because outrunning him is not working." I rise to my full height and peer over a snowman. Brad stares at us from behind a snowman wearing a cowboy hat, wielding a lasso. If only cowboy snowman could wrangle Brad like a bull. I glare at Brad. My gaze shifts to another snowman, then to the hot chocolate stand. "I got it. I'm going to steal a snowman head and lure him into the hot chocolate stand, and you'll slam the door."

"You're sacrificing a snowman?"

I press my lips together. "It's for the greater good. Their death won't be in vain." I pluck the head off the nearest snowman. A gold crown tumbles to the snow, and I cringe a little. "Sorry, snowman. I'll be sure to tell everyone about your bravery." I wave it at Brad, getting his attention. He *baaa*s and takes a step closer. "That's right, Brad. I know you want this delicious, water-filled snowman head." I take a step backward, urging him to follow me, which he does. Inch by inch, I get closer to the hot chocolate stand. Brad's walk turns into a trot. Seconds later, it's a full-fledged gallop. My eyes widen in terror as Brad charges after me.

"Run!" Logan yells.

I shriek, sprinting with the snowman head tucked like a football. Brad thunders behind me, closing in. Logan's a few steps behind Brad. At the last second, I adjust my grip and hurl the head into the hot chocolate stand. Brad barrels after it, hooves clattering against wood.

"Now!" I scream.

Logan slams the door shut with a crack that echoes across the festival. Brad's muffled, indignant *baaas* rattle the walls.

"We did it! We did it! Ha!" I throw my arms in the air, half-laughing, half-screaming. Adrenaline makes me reckless, because the next thing I know, I leap into Logan's arms like I scored the winning touchdown. My legs wrap around his waist. "Brad can't outsmart us!"

His arm clamps tight around my back, the other sliding low to cup my butt. His fingers dig in, firm, possessive, and I gasp. *Oh yes.*

"I called Henry. He's on his way," he says, voice rougher than it should be for just wrangling a sheep.

I hook an arm around his neck, strands of hair falling between us as I look down. His hazel eyes have gone molten brown, all heat and hunger. My chest heaves—not sure if it's from sprinting after Brad or the way Logan is staring at me like he's already undressing me. His fingers flex against my ass, sending sparks racing across my skin.

"Fuck it," he mutters, and suddenly I'm pinned against the hot chocolate stand, sliding down his solid frame until my mouth is inches from his. His warm, mint-tinged breath skims my lips. "I want to kiss you," he whispers.

My brain sputters out a weak protest. "We shouldn't—"

"Which makes me want to even more."

"Fuck it," I echo, and crush my mouth to his.

The kiss starts soft, but within seconds it's ravenous, desperate, addictive. My hips grind against his growing erection, my body greedy for friction. His tongue teases mine before claiming it, and I melt, wrapping tighter around him. The cold night air is no match for the fire roaring between us. He thrusts his hard cock against me, hitting the right spot. I pull away, a moan escaping me.

His warm lips a stark contrast to my cool skin as he kisses down my jaw, grazing my ear. "I want you, Brie. I want you so fucking bad." His hips thrust against mine, making me moan. "Too many clothes," he growls. "I want to feel your tight pussy around me, strangling my cock."

My nipples instantly pebble and not because of the cold. Logan can talk dirty to me anytime. "Oh. God. Yes. I want that too."

The wood creaks as he presses me against it, giving himself better leverage. He grinds against me, rough and carnal. With one hand still under me, he rests his palm against the wall beside my head. A wave of pleasure washes over me as he sucks on my neck. The friction against my clit increases, a rising crescendo of sweet torture. I'm seconds away from detonating in my pants. "Oh, yes!"

A sudden, sharp squeak makes every muscle in my body tense. As if someone turned the lights on, a spotlight blazes over us. My eyelids snap open, and I'm immediately blinded by the intense glare of headlights. "Oh, shit," I murmur.

Logan freezes, lips still against my neck, hand tightening on my ass.

From across the lot, Henry's voice bellows, "Looks like you two made up!"

Logan slaps the wall beside my head. "She seems sturdy. Nice construction. Don't you think, Brie?"

I swallow a laugh. "Yep. Very… strong."

Henry laughs. "You two are full of shit. I'm glad to know everyone can stop whispering behind your backs about when the first hookup will be."

Logan lowers me to the ground, and I fumble with my jacket. "There's one thing wrong with that," I say. "People in this town don't whisper."

Henry smirks. "Fair point. But now they'll just move on to planning your wedding and naming your kids."

"Uh, considering it was just a kiss, I don't think I'm pregnant yet." I shoot Logan a sideways look. "Unless you've got a superpower you haven't mentioned." Shit. Do I want kids? Does Logan want more kids? Do I want kids with Logan? I mean, we've only just started this. Why am I thinking about kids? "I was joking, by the way."

Logan chuckles. "Yeah, I got it."

"Alright, well I'll collect Brad and let you two," Henry waves a hand between us, "continue what you were doing. Hope he hasn't done too much damage."

"There are a few snowmen who will have some trauma to work out, but overall, I think it's okay. Also, don't be alarmed if Brad's poop sparkles. He found the glitter snowman and went to town." I shrug.

"Maybe I can place a horn on his head and call him a unicorn," Henry chuckles.

After we help Henry load Brad into the trailer, he drives away. Only the silvery moonlight shines down on us.

Logan steps closer, thumb grazing my cheek, sliding

down to tilt my chin. My pulse trips over itself. "Hope you haven't had too much excitement tonight," he murmurs, eyes dark, "because I'd like to continue this."

My lips curl into a smile. "What do you have in mind?" *Please let it be filthy.* My body's buzzing for more. The night in Santa's Workshop was fun. Amazing. Mind-blowing, but I want to feel him inside me.

"Come back to my place," he says, voice husky. "Josie's at my parents'. I want to lay you out on my bed, spread you open, and feast until you can't remember your own name—before I finally give you a proper orgasm."

My entire body lights up like the Christmas tree at the festival. "Lead the way."

Logan

When we reach my house, I click the garage opener clipped to my visor, and the heavy door groans as it rolls up. I pull my truck in front of the closed third stall, then motion for Brie to park in the empty space.

"You can pull in here," I say, pointing to the open bay. "That way nobody drives by and sees your car sitting in my driveway."

She nods and pulls into the garage, the low purr of her engine echoes against the walls before she shuts it off. The second she steps out, I jog through the opening, hit the button next to the door, and the garage rumbles closed behind us. Once it's shut, I can't wait another damn second.

I grab her by the back of the neck and crush my mouth to hers. She melts into me instantly, her hands slipping inside my coat, fingers brushing heat into my back until goosebumps scatter across my skin. Her soft moan vibrates against my lips, and I swallow it down like it belongs to me.

I pull away just long enough to rest my forehead against hers, breathing hard. "We should go inside before I fuck you against your SUV." My nose drags along hers, and she shivers.

"Tempting," she murmurs before slipping out from under my arm with a wicked little smile. She saunters toward the door, pausing halfway up the short set of stairs to glance back over her shoulder. She bites her lip, her eyes glinting with pure lust.

Jesus. My cock jerks against my zipper at that one look. In two strides, I'm scooping her up, and throwing her over my shoulder like I've just claimed my prize.

She squeals, laughter bubbling out of her. "Logan! What are you doing? Put me down!"

I smack her ass lightly, loving the way she wriggles. "You're mine now, Snowflake. I'll carry you wherever the hell I want."

She kicks her feet, giggling harder. "You're ridiculous. I can walk, you know."

"Yeah, but this way I get to do this." My palm lands on her ass again with a satisfying crack, followed by a slow, deliberate rub over her denim-clad curves.

Her mock outrage dissolves into breathless laughter. "Caveman."

"A caveman who's about to fuck you senseless." At the door, I kick off my boots and tug hers off, each one hitting the floor with a heavy thud. I march us through the kitchen and up the stairs like a man on a mission.

"Patience is not your strong suit." She giggles.

"Not when it comes to needing you."

When I reach my bedroom, I drop her onto my bed. She's flushed and panting from laughing. Her hair fans out across my pillows, messy and perfect.

"I can't believe you just carried me up here," she says, sitting up on her elbows.

"It was the best way to get you where I want you." I tear off my coat and drop it to the floor. Reaching down, I slide hers off before gripping the hem of her sweater, but she stops me with her hand on my wrist.

"Wait." Her gaze locks with mine. "You called me Snowflake. That's what you called me the night I brought you home from the bar. So you do remember."

I scrub a hand over my jaw. "It may not be as hazy as I made it seem."

Her brows rise. "So you pretended to forget?"

"No, I mean technically yes, but," I blow out a deep breath, "I wasn't in the right headspace. I had to work through a few feelings first."

"And those feelings are…"

"Worked out." I cup her chin, my thumb brushing her bottom lip. "Now, I want us to work out a few things… together."

Her sultry smile could burn down the whole damn house. "I'll have you know, I'm very good at working things out." She grabs my shirt, tugging me closer until I'm standing between her spread thighs. Her fingers drift down to the waistband of my jeans. Through her dark lashes, she peers up at me as her teeth sink into her bottom lip. The look nearly sends me over the edge. It's so tempting, alluring, and it ignites a fire within me. She pops the button of my jeans and slides the zipper down with a gentle hiss.

"Brie…" My voice is gravel as she pushes the denim

down my hips. My cock strains against my boxer briefs. Thick and hard. Wanting her. Only her. My snowflake. Her hand skims over my bulge, a teasing stroke that makes me jerk in her palm. Reaching behind me, I rip my shirt over my head. Her fingers trace the elastic waistband, grazing my skin, causing goosebumps to sprout over my body. Before she dips inside, I stop her with a hand on her wrist. "You're wearing entirely too many clothes."

She smirks. "Then take them off me."

Challenge accepted.

I hook my arms under hers, pull her to her feet, and crash my lips to hers. Our tongues slide against each other. Soft. Rhythmic. Like a slow dance I never want to end. She whimpers into my mouth, the sound driving me even closer to the edge. I undo the button on her jeans and slide them over her hips. Without breaking our kiss, she shimmies out of them as I drag her sweater up. I reluctantly pull away and continue sliding it up. She raises her hands to help, but once it's over her head, I stop, trapping her in the tangled fabric. I bend down and press open-mouth kisses to the swells of her tits.

"Not fair."

"For who?" With one hand, I hold her hostage in her sweater, and my other hand tugs down her bra cup, freeing her peaked nipple. Bending down, I take it into my mouth, sucking hard until she cries out, arching into me.

"Logan…" Her moan is pleading, needy.

I repeat the action on the other side while nipping and sucking on her soft skin. I skim my hand down her rib cage to the front of her panties. She parts her legs slightly, giving me more room. I rub her clit over the soft cotton.

"Oh yes. Logan." She bucks her hips, rubbing herself against me.

I slip my hand inside the elastic and over her bare

pussy. "I think you like being tied up and blindfolded. You can't see what I'm going to do next."

"Logan, I need you. Please."

"What do you need, Snowflake?"

"Touch me."

I slide my finger over her clit and down through her wetness. When I reach her opening, I circle my finger around the hole. She bucks her hips trying to spear herself on my finger. "Now I think it's you who needs a little patience."

"No. I want you to finger fuck me."

"Yeah? Like this?" I slide a finger inside her warm heat.

She moans. "Oh, yes."

My cock throbs at her words. I thrust in and out of her tight pussy. When I pull out, I add a second finger, stretching her even more. She rocks her hips against my hand, letting my palm rub against her clit. I'll never tire of how wild she gets even from my fingers.

Her breath hitches. "Yes. Just like that."

"You think you can have an orgasm on my hand?"

Her head drops back, exposing her neck as she exhales a soft whimper. "Keep going. Don't stop." As I continue thrusting in and out, her breathing turns into short pants. "Logan."

My name drips from her lips like honey and it makes my cock throb so hard I swear I could come just from her voice. "Say it again. Just like that."

"Logan…" Her voice is drawn out this time, shaky and drenched in need.

I rip her sweater the rest of the way off, needing to see her face when I make her fall apart. Her lashes flutter, eyes blown wide with lust, as my thumb circles her clit. Her moan rips through the air, her pussy clenching around my fingers as her orgasm overtakes her. She shudders, head thrown back, the sound of my name breaking from her again as she rides it out.

I don't stop until she collapses against me, boneless and gasping.

"That was… so good."

I grin against her cheek. "Snowflake, I'm just getting started."

Reaching behind her, I unclasp her bra. The straps fall off her shoulders and it hits the floor. I hook my thumbs in the waistband of her panties and pull them down while she does the same to me. With my arm around her lower back, I pull her to the center of the bed, kissing a path along her jaw before sucking hard on her neck. "You're the first person I've been with in three years."

Then she stiffens. "Wait." She pushes at my shoulders, holding me back. "You haven't had sex in three years? How is that even possible?"

I shrug. "Um, I just didn't."

"You're hot. Like, how could no woman want to have sex with you?"

"Well, it's not for lack of them trying. I just was never in the right headspace. I wasn't going to lead anyone on." I brush my lips along her cheek. "But this. I want this. Fuck, I want this. I want you."

She giggles. "You're only saying that because it's been three years since you've had sex."

"I'm saying it because I waited three years to have the perfect moment with you."

"And you have lines for days."

"Not a line." My voice roughens. "The truth. It's been a long time since I've felt like this, and it's because of you. But it's not just sex. That's just the cherry on top." I roll us so she's straddling me, her bare pussy gliding over my cock, and my head falls back with a groan. "Top drawer. Condoms."

Her grin is pure sin as she leans over and fishes through the drawer. When she pulls out the stuffed reindeer instead, her brows shoot up. "You kept this?"

I nod. "It has sentimental value now. Every time I open the nightstand, I think back to the night I fucked you with my tongue."

Her smile turns wicked as she gently places it on the bed, then reaches back into the nightstand. After some rustling, she sits up, a condom pinched between her fingers.

"Put it on me," I rasp.

She tears it open, slides down my body, and wraps her hand around my cock. I hiss through my teeth as she strokes me. Slow. Teasing. "I'm getting you ready."

"Snowflake," I grit, "I am beyond ready."

Her tongue peeks out, wetting her bottom lip, as she rolls the condom down my length. It's cute as fuck. Once it's in place, I reach down and pinch the tip. "Come up here." I nod. "I want to feel you slide down on my cock."

She rises up on her knees, and I position myself at her entrance, rubbing the tip of my dick through her slick pussy. Once in position, she slowly sinks down my length. Inch by inch.

"Fuck," I groan, eyes slamming shut.

Her breath stutters, lips parting. "Oh my god."

"Just a couple more inches, Snowflake. Take all of me."

When she bottoms out, her nails dig into my chest. "I feel so full."

I thrust up, and she moans, her nails digging into my stomach. Reaching over, she grabs the reindeer and holds it up. Her eyes glitter with lust. "Do you trust me?"

Normally, I'm the one in control. But with Brie, I'd

hand it over in a heartbeat. She used the same words I used with her. *Do you trust me?* There's no one I trust more. I open my mouth, and she pushes the reindeer in, muffling me.

"Good boy," she purrs, rolling her hips. "Now your neighbors won't hear you scream as I ride your cock."

Slowly, she rocks her hips over me, my cock sliding in and out of her. Her grip loosens on my stomach as she continues to ride me. With each stroke, her pace grows more ravenous. My fingertips dimple her soft skin as I guide her movements. Glancing down, I watch as my dick disappears inside her warm pussy. A thrill shoots through me, my senses alight as the pleasure intensifies. She rolls her hips in a slow, sensual circle. A deep groan rumbles through my chest, the reindeer muffling the sound as her pussy clenches around me.

Her hair falls around us as she leans down. "I'm close."

With each thrust, her breaths become increasingly ragged. I wrap my arms around her back, holding her to me. From below, I slam up into her.

"Oh! Oh yes! Fuck me. Don't stop."

A tingle shoots through my entire body. My orgasm on the brink of exploding.

Her back arches. "I'm coming!"

Her pussy clamps down, strangling my dick. The tightness rips my orgasm from me. A myriad of fireworks exploding behind my eyes as I bite the reindeer so hard I almost cut it in half. I continue thrusting into her as her pussy milks me for every drop. Once I'm spent, I slow my pace before coming to a stop. I spit the reindeer from my mouth, and it falls to the bed. Her body collapses on top of mine.

I press my face to her neck, my nose tracing the curve of her delicate skin. The words tumble out before I can stop them. "Stay the night." I freeze. Did I actually just say that? But the truth is, I want her here—want to fall asleep with her tangled up in me, want to wake up with her smile as the first thing I see. "Josie's not expected back until tomorrow evening, so we'd also have all morning alone."

She pushes off my chest and her gaze drops, lips pressed together as though she's weighing something. Then she looks up with soft eyes. "Okay."

Her lips find mine in a kiss so tender it undoes me. I wrap my arms around her, roll us onto our sides, and she curls against my chest like she belongs there.

We talk until the early hours. Not only did I learn her favorite color is red but also that she's terrified of turtles. Apparently, a turtle almost took off one of her toes as a kid, and now she'll never dangle her feet in the water off a dock. I tell her about my fear of heights. We laugh, we tease, and share another round of orgasms before finally drifting to sleep.

I stir awake to a warm body draped on top of me. Her leg slides higher up my thigh, inching closer and closer until it brushes against my semi-hard erection. A groan rumbles from deep in my chest.

"Sorry," she whispers, though her sly little smile tells me otherwise.

"Are you?"

"Not really." She does it again, slower this time, on purpose.

"Snowflake," I grit, "you're playing with fire."

"And what are you going to do about it?" Her hand

slips under the blanket, fingers curling around me. My cock twitches, all the blood in my body surges south.

"Nothing. Absolutely nothing," I groan, already undone by her touch.

She disappears under the covers until she's nestled between my legs. With the flat of her tongue, she licks up the underside of my shaft. My head thuds back against the pillow, eyes squeezing shut as I surrender to the wet heat of her tongue. A faint noise—a door somewhere—barely registers. She hums around me, the vibration shooting straight to my balls. Holy fuck. Another sound. This time inside. My eyes snap open. Panic cuts through the haze of pleasure. I tap her shoulder and lift the edge of the blanket. She glances up, my cock still between her lips.

"Someone's in the house," I whisper.

She releases me with an audible pop. "What?"

"Logan?" My mother's voice. Clear as a bell. In my house. "Logan, are you home?"

The whites of Brie's eyes grow, taking over her irises. I shoot my gaze from one side of the room to the other. There's nowhere for her to hide. "Stay there. Be still." I shift the blanket and lift my knees and attempt to tent the blanket to hide her body.

A soft knock sounds on the partially closed door before it swings open. "There you are. I've been calling your name. Why is your truck in the driveway? You never leave your—" My mom's voice cuts off, her gaze dropping to the suspicious mound of blankets. Her smirk says it all. "Oooh. You're not alone."

Before I can stammer out a reply, Josie barrels into the doorway. "Daddy! Daddy—"

My mom's reflexes kick in before she can get a step farther. She grips Josie's shoulders and rotates her in the opposite direction. "Sweetheart, why don't you go get your tablet, and Dad will see you in a few."

"Okay!" Josie scampers off.

My mom leans on the doorframe, arms crossed. "That's some pretty pink toenail polish Josie picked out for you." She eyes the blanket. Brie jerks her foot back under the covers. Then my mom grins. "And that red sweater is cute, but it looks a little too small for you."

I manage a tight smile. Fuck me. This is not a conversation I want to have right this moment, but I know she'll be hounding me for answers later.

"Well," Mom says, far too pleased with herself, "I'll let you two get back to it. I'll be dropping Josie off at six. Just so you know." She winks and shuts the door.

Through the closed door, I hear Josie in the hallway. "Dad! I want to tell you about the reindeer!"

"Your dad is busy right now, but you can tell him all about it later tonight," my mom says. The clatter of feet descending the stairs followed by the click of the front door sounds through the house.

I lift the blanket; Brie's staring up at me. "Sorry. Now there's one more person who knows about this."

"Don't be sorry." She crawls up my body, her chin resting on my chest, amusement sparking in her eyes. "You let Josie paint your toenails?"

"She likes the practice," I mumble.

"That's actually really sweet." She tilts her head, suddenly shy. "Should I… go?"

"Why would you?"

"I don't know. Maybe your mom walking in on us killed the mood?"

I roll her beneath me, pinning her with a grin. "You heard her. I've got until six o'clock. And I don't plan on wasting a single minute."

As much as I wanted to keep Brie in my bed all day, she had to get to the festival for the mini-reindeer race. People harness their dogs to mini sleighs with stuffed Santas, and the dogs race for the Reindeer Cup. She showed me pictures from previous years, and it looks fun. Some even have their dogs wear reindeer hats for authenticity. After Brie left, I got ready and went to the carnival to make sure everything was running smoothly. Before six, I arrive back home just as Josie barges through the front door.

"Hey Dad!"

"Hey Peanut! Did you have fun with Grandma?"

"I did! It was a blast! We got to pet the reindeer, and we went Christmas caroling, and then saw the reindeer race, which isn't actual reindeer, but dogs!"

Glancing at my mom, a Cheshire grin fills her face. I shift my gaze back to Josie. "Why don't you put your stuff away and then you can tell me all about it?"

"Okay!" she grabs her backpack and climbs the stairs.

"So," my mom says casually, "who is she?"

"Just a girl."

"Mm-hmm. Well, if you won't tell me, I can always ask around town. You know how fast news spreads in Mount Holly."

"Thanks for the blackmail, Mom."

"That's what mothers do." Her smile softens. "So, are you going to tell me?"

I scrub my hands down my face. "I'm pretty sure you already know."

She nods. "I wanted confirmation. I'm so happy for you. Beneath all that bickering and hostility, I sensed a burning passion between you two.

"Mom, don't say 'burning passion'."

"Fiery lust."

"Not any better."

"Steamy connection."

"Nope, you can just stop right there. We're just seeing where it goes. No need to be saving any dates or anything."

"Either way, I'm happy for you." She wraps her arms around me in a tight hug only a mother can give. "You deserve a little joy in your life."

"Thanks, Mom." I hug her back. "Also, don't tell anyone. Everything is new, and we haven't even discussed what it is between us."

Josie races down the stairs. "Bye, Grandma!"

After they say their goodbyes, I open the door for my mom, and she strolls to her car. For the rest of the evening, I sit on the couch with Josie while she tells me everything she and my mom did. As soon as she goes to bed, I spend the rest of the night thinking about Brie. About her laugh, her kisses, the way she feels curled against me. And about the fact that, for the first time in years, I actually want more.

Logan

They say time apart makes the heart grow fonder. I'm hoping twenty-four hours qualifies as time apart, because I haven't stopped thinking about Brie since she left my house. Sure, the sex was incredible. Life-changing. And yes, I want nothing more than to do it again. But also, I love talking to her. She's like a fireplace in the middle of a snowstorm, melting the chill right out of me. When I'm with her, the rest of the world falls away until it's just us— our own bubble where everything feels safe, easy, right.

When I spotted a red scarf with silver snowflakes while shopping for Josie, I bought it for Brie without hesitation. Red for her favorite color and snowflakes for me.

Would I be pushing the line toward stalker territory if I

just drove past her house to see if she was home? Probably. Am I going to do it anyway? Yup. I turn the corner onto Mistletoe Street, looking for a place to make a U-turn, but the bright lights shining from the festival pique my interest. Instead of turning around, I continue driving down the road. After a few blocks, Brie's SUV comes into view. I grin, pulling in beside it. Guess I don't need to be a stalker tonight.

A light dusting of snow floats from the sky, twinkling in the rink lights. On the far side, a figure clings to the boards like a newborn deer on stilts. I laugh under my breath. Hopping out of my truck, I grab my skates and hockey stick from the back seat before strolling down the path leading to the opening. Brie stands up on wobbly legs. Staying out of sight, I slide my shoes off and replace them with my skates. Once they're on, I walk to the opening of the rink and glide over the smooth ice. I drop my shoes off at the bench next to her belongings. Pulling the puck from my pocket, I toss it onto the ice. The scrape of my blades on the ice makes her head whip up. She gasps, knuckles whitening against the wall. Whizzing past her, I twist around so I'm skating backward.

"What are you doing here? Come to watch me embarrass myself?" She rises to her full height and loosens her grip.

"Saw the lights on and thought I would toss the puck around. I didn't know you skate."

"I don't," she says, laughing at herself. "These skates have been buried in my closet since high school. I figured now is a perfect time to break them out."

Skating beside her, I smirk. "They'll work better if you glide instead of walk."

"Easy for the hockey pro to say."

"Fair. So what did you tell everyone about the snowman?"

"I feigned surprise, and now the entire town thinks there's a vandal on the loose. They're locking their doors, and I overheard something about starting a neighborhood watch group."

A chuckle escapes me. "I'm shocked there isn't something already set up."

"Don't worry, they'll be knocking on your door asking you to join soon enough."

I glance down the ice. "This is a nice rink you've got. Way more glitz than mine. And the tree at the end?" I point to the towering spruce haloed in twinkle lights. "That's a showstopper."

"I needed a little spectacle. And since I couldn't achieve that with height, I added extra twinkle lights." She shoots me a sideways smile. "It's hard to compete with Logan Crawford."

"It doesn't have to be a competition."

She snorts. "Between us? It's always a competition."

"Maybe back in high school."

Her gaze dips to her skates. "Anyway, I'm soaking this in while I can. The rink punted my budget straight into what-the-hell-was-I-thinking territory. We might have to cancel the Valentine's Bouquet Drop, the Leprechaun Hunt, and—brace yourself—the Christmas in July Jamboree."

I clutch my chest. "Not the Jamboree."

Her laugh fogs the air in a pale cloud. "I know. The town will be so disappointed. One thing I didn't anticipate when installing an ice rink is the upkeep it requires to maintain it. The ice wasn't even in my budget, let alone the funds to keep it operational. I guess I'm enjoying it while it lasts. Because it won't be around much longer."

I hate she might lose the rink. Rival or not, I don't want to see her defeated over something like this. "How much do you need to keep the ice rink afloat for the rest of the year?"

"Like… all of it." She huffs out a humorless laugh. "Seeing as I'm already over budget for this entire festival, my chance of securing the event coordinator promotion is slowly slipping through my fingers."

Shit. The budget issue is news to me. With all her hard work, I can clearly see how passionate she is about her job. "You've put on one hell of a festival. Josie's been loving all the contests you've had."

"Thanks. Every year, I try to think of new, fun ideas for the community to enjoy." Her skates chop at the ice as we move along the boards.

"I could help you with your skating, if you want."

"This wall is doing a pretty good job."

I laugh as she inches herself, hand over hand, along the edge of the rink. I push forward until I'm in front of her, skating backward.

"Show-off." She smirks. "I have to give credit where credit is due. Your rink idea was really great, and starting the Mount Holly Cup Tournament drew a lot of attention."

"Former hockey player rediscovers hockey," I deadpan. "Real creative."

"I suppose." She makes it three careful shuffles before her blade betrays her. I dart forward, catching her before she faceplants. She lands against my chest, soft and warm, her breath misting between us. "Thanks," she mutters, "That could have been bad."

"Wouldn't be the first time I've saved you." I wink, then nod at her feet. "Come on. Try again. Glide, Snowflake."

"Come on. Try again. Glide, Snowflake."

"Walking works just fine for me."

I skate backward, extending a hand. "Just try. Come to me." She hesitates, then pushes off the wall. Her eyes stay glued to her feet. "There you go. You got it."

After a few feet, she peers up at me. "Oh my god. I'm skating!" Her smile hits me square in the chest. Then her blade zings sideways. She flails, I reach for her, but she overcompensates. We hit the ice in a heap; Brie sprawled on top of me.

"Oomph," I wheeze, all the air exiting my lungs.

"I'm so sorry! Are you okay?"

I meet her eyes and forget what pain is. "Yeah. I think so." My hands find her waist, drifting to the sweet curve of her hips. I never expected to find myself falling for someone after Brooke passed away, but more and more every day, Brie is showing me life continues whether we want it to or not, and that happiness is real again. I tilt my chin up, so my lips are centimeters away from hers. One by one, the rink lights shut off, shrouding us in darkness.

A beat of silence passes before she laughs. "I forgot the timers."

My fingers flex against the soft fabric covering her ass. "What do you say we get out of here?"

She bites her lip. "Want to come over to my place?"

"And my truck?" Might as well keep up the secretly-hating-each-other ruse. Even though I think the town is catching on. But I'm enjoying the bubble we're in. It feels safe.

"Park it in my garage."

After leaving the rink, I follow Brie to her house. On the drive, I make a phone call to my bookkeeper to arrange an anonymous donation to the Mount Holly Festival. Now she won't have to worry about budget problems. When I arrive at Brie's house, I step into the foyer from the garage.

A pungent scent hits me in the face. "It smells very piney in here."

Brie tosses me a grin over her shoulder. "Welcome to my tour of trees."

She shrugs out of her coat, and I catch it halfway down her arm, tugging it free and hanging it beside mine.

"This is the first stop." She sweeps her arm over her modest living room. A TV hangs on the wall with a couch and loveseat angled in front. With her hand in mine, she leads me to an eight-foot tree in front of a bay window. "This is my traditional tree that I have every year."

"Wow. This is quite the tree. A little more elaborate than mine." My gaze roams over her intricately decorated Christmas tree. Not an ornament is out of place.

"It is my favorite holiday, so I go a little over the top." Next, she leads me into the kitchen. "This is my baking tree. I decorated it with ornaments related to baking."

My gaze wanders over the gingerbread man, apron, and rolling pin ornaments. "You just had these lying around?"

"It was a great excuse to purchase new ornaments. Plus, I couldn't have a naked tree."

"Nobody wants a naked tree," I agree solemnly.

Her laugh bubbles up, soft and sweet. "Come on. The tour continues."

We exit the kitchen and stroll down a short hallway and through a doorway. A perfectly made bed sits against a wall in front of us. I lean down, lips brushing her ear. "If you wanted me in here, all you had to do was ask. No Christmas tree bribes required."

Her smile is wicked. "Behave. Tour first, bribery later. But for now, this is my North Pole themed tree." She waves her hand over the tree perched in the corner of the room.

"It's decorated with ornaments featuring stockings, Santa, and reindeer."

I inspect the various ornaments scattered over the tree. My gaze snags on one of Santa sitting in a big red chair with a list in his hand. "So Santa really does watch you while you sleep."

"Obviously." She wiggles her brows.

"Tell me—have you been naughty or nice?"

"Wouldn't you like to know?"

I slide behind her, pressing a kiss to her neck. "I'd bet on naughty. Probably while thinking of me."

Her laugh shivers against me, but she points back at Santa. "Careful. He's watching."

"Good thing Santa's into voyeurism."

She swats my chest, still laughing. "Later. There's one more tree left on the tour." She escorts me out of her bedroom and down the hall to another room. "This one's not as extravagant. It's more of a hodgepodge of all my other leftover ornaments."

Another tree sits in the corner, but my attention veers left. "Forget the tree. What is this?" I slip out of Brie's grasp and stalk toward a row of tables covered in porcelain buildings, tiny streetlamps, and enough fake snow to bury a small country. "Is this how you're planning world domination—one miniature city at a time?"

She laughs. "No. It's just a small hobby of mine."

"This isn't a hobby. This is a holiday takeover." I lean down, squinting at the little figurines.

"Just wait."

She moves to the opposite side of the display and flips a switch. The whole village hums to life—buildings glowing, streetlamps flickering, skaters gliding in endless loops across a frozen pond. My jaw drops.

"Hold up." I point at a square building with *Hardware*

Store painted across the front. A few figurines down—*Coffee Shop.* Then, at the end of Main Street, the town square and a rink suspiciously like the one we just left. My eyes widen. "Wait. This isn't just *a* village. This is Mount Holly. You've built a replica of the town."

Her gaze flicks to the table as she fiddles with a tiny Santa figurine. "Don't be ridiculous."

"It's all right here." One by one, I point to the buildings. "You have the hardware store, the coffee shop, the diner. There's a tea shop."

"We don't have one of those in Mount Holly."

"Yeah, that's because they probably don't make miniature bars. That's exactly where the Crooked Reindeer is."

"Alright, that's enough. No more analyzing my Christmas village. Isn't there a hockey game on? We should go watch it."

I laugh. "Trying to use hockey as a diversion?"

"It's not as fun as watching you play, but yeah." She links her fingers with mine and drags me back to the living room.

"Wait—you watched me?"

"I begrudgingly stared at the TV while you skated around showing off."

"Good to know."

The warmth in my chest spreads. Maybe she didn't hate me as much as she wanted me to believe. I drop onto the couch and open an arm. She hesitates a beat before curling against me, soft and warm.

"We've come a long way," I murmur, pressing my lips to her temple. "No more hating each other."

She aims the remote at the TV. "I kind of miss hating you. This," she waves between us, "feels unnatural."

"Get used to it. It's our new normal."

Her mouth curves, and she kisses me. I kiss her back—until a blur of motion on the screen catches my eye. Jason Malone, the right winger for Chicago, propels himself down the ice. He's always had killer speed and an even more wicked slapshot. Malone is one-on-one with Florida's goalie. He dekes him and sends the puck into the net. "Yes!"

Brie groans. "I should have known better." She laughs, shaking her head.

I steal a quick kiss. "Hey, you still get my undivided attention… during commercials."

"No, no, I did this to myself. But I'm happy right here." She curls deeper into me.

"I'll make it up to you later. I promise." While keeping my gaze locked on the screen, I press another kiss to the top of her head.

By the second period, my eyelids grow heavy. Brie's curled up next to me. Her soft, rhythmic breathing almost lulling me to sleep. I press a kiss to the top of her head before turning my attention back to the TV. During the next commercial break, I lower my lids for a couple of seconds. I don't need to watch a boy band sing about laundry detergent.

I lift my eyelids and blink a few times to clear my vision. The TV comes into focus. The game is long gone—replaced by a blender infomercial. Carefully, I lift my arm from around Brie's shoulders and stretch my limbs.

Brie stirs awake, stretching her arms above her head. "What time is it?"

I check my phone. "Two in the morning. I should probably get going. Chances are high fewer people will see me leaving now than at seven."

She stretches, sleepy-eyed and gorgeous. "Good idea.

Mrs. Emerson across the street loves to spill the tea. I'd rather not give her an overflowing kettle."

She rises off the couch, and I do the same. We stroll to the foyer, and I put my coat and shoes on. I wrap an arm around her waist, my fingers brushing warm skin where her sweater rides up. "When can I watch hockey with you again? And maybe not fall asleep."

"My schedule is pretty busy until after Christmas with the festival. Maybe New Year's?" She smirks.

"You say that as if you don't think I'll wait. New Year's it is." Her hands rest on my chest. Bending down, I brush my lips over hers. "Good night, Snowflake."

"Good night, Logan."

She opens the garage door for me, and I get in my truck and drive home. Living in Mount Holly is getting better and better every day.

Brie

I yank open the front door, already late, mostly because after Logan left last night, sleep never came. All I wanted was to curl against him, let the rise and fall of his chest lull me under. Instead, I spent two hours staring at my ceiling, shivering in sheets that suddenly felt much too big.

Before I can step outside, I freeze. Sitting on the "Merry AF" doormat is a perfectly wrapped box—red paper, silver bow, no card. My brows pinch together. I scoop it up, give it a shake. Nothing. Hold it to my ear. Silence. Not even a threatening jingle. I carry it inside and slowly tug at the ribbon, bracing myself for confetti, glitter, or worse, a spring-loaded Santa clown. But it's none of those. Instead, nestled inside red tissue, is a postcard.

This is truly the superior Christmas treat.

I peel back the tissue paper to reveal a flawlessly decorated Yule log under a plastic dome. My grin hurts my cheeks. Logan. This has Logan written all over it. I tuck the box into my fridge before heading to the festival grounds.

The days leading up to Christmas Eve are always the busiest. All the kids are desperate to get their last-minute wish lists to Santa, parents frantically buying cookies for parties, and me, running around like my life depends on it. Which, career-wise, it sort of does. And I only have two days to prepare. Today is our annual bake sale. Vendors line the pathways with cookies, cakes, pies, bars, and breads. Later this evening, the Crooked Reindeer will host the annual Christmas ham bingo.

When I arrive at the festival, the grounds are already bustling with people wandering from stand to stand.

"Brie! Brie!"

I spin to see Lauren barreling toward me, breath puffing like a steam engine. "What's wrong? Don't tell me Mr. Coleman is hiding free samples in his pockets again. He's running out of warnings."

"No." She doubles over, catching her breath. "It's about the budget."

My stomach nosedives. "Oh no. Please tell me we don't have another expense. I don't think I'll be able to recover from this year." Scenarios of bills from contractors race through my head. I shouldn't have strayed from last year's plans. Then none of this would have happened, and maybe my promotion wouldn't be in jeopardy.

She shakes her head, grin spreading. "No. An anonymous donation came in this morning. The festival isn't in the red anymore."

I blink. "Wait… what?"

"Everything's paid for. *Everything.* Plus, there's enough left to keep the rink open through February. Isn't it amazing? It's a Christmas miracle!"

Anonymous donation. Ice rink. Miracle. My breath hitches. "I have to go. You've got things covered here?"

Lauren frowns. "Yeah, but—where are you going?"

"Taking care of something." I sprint through the festival, dodging townsfolk and their "Merry Christmas!" greetings. First the Yule log. Now this. Only one person could have done it.

I jump in my SUV and race across town, breaking a few traffic laws along the way. I need to see him and get confirmation in person. Once I reach his house, I kill the engine and jump out. I jog up the walkway and pound on the door. "Logan!" *Bang. Bang. Bang.* "Logan!" *Bang.*

On the fourth knock, the door swings open, and Logan's standing in front of me, brows furrowed. "Brie. What are you doing here?"

"Did you get me a Yule log?"

His lips curve into a smile. "I did."

"And the donation?"

"I wanted you to have the festival you deserve—"

That's all I need. I launch myself at him, hands cupping his face, and crash my lips to his. He catches me instantly, arms banding tight around my waist. With our lips still fused together, I push him through the doorway. Once we're inside, I kick the door shut and spin us around until his back hits the door.

I pull away a fraction of an inch. "Are you here alone?"

"Yes."

"Good." I press my lips to his in a lingering kiss. "You didn't have to do that." *Kiss.* "It's amazing." *Kiss.* "So kind." *Kiss.* "And thoughtful." *Kiss.* "And the most generous thing someone has done for me."

"It was only a Yule log." He smirks.

My fingers graze the short hairs at the back of his head as I press my body closer to his. His warmth radiates into me. "No, the donation. Logan…" My throat tightens. "No one's ever done something like that for me."

He brushes a strand of hair from my face, eyes steady on mine. "You deserve the best festival Mount Holly's ever seen."

My eyes lock on his, and every day it's the same truth—falling for him is both the easiest and most dangerous thing I've ever done. My lips curve into a smile before I crash them against his. His hands slide inside my jacket, slipping it from my shoulders until it puddles on the floor. I toe off my boots, kicking them aside like they've personally offended me.

"I want to show you how much I appreciate you," I murmur, tugging him toward the living room.

He plants his feet, that infuriating grin tugging at his mouth. "Or we could head upstairs. Just in case my mom makes another surprise visit."

He's not wrong. The last one was bad enough. It's not an encore I need. "Bedroom it is."

We barely make it up the stairs before I'm tugging at his clothes. His shirt hits the floor. My pulse kicks when my gaze snags on the hard line of him pressing against his gray sweatpants. I hook my thumb under the waistband and shove them down like it's Christmas morning and he's the only present I care about.

His cock springs free, thick and heavy. My fingers curl around his shaft, stroking once, twice, loving the way his head drops back as a groan rumbles from his chest.

"Fuck, Snowflake. I love your hands on me."

A bead of pre-cum glistens at the tip, and I swipe my thumb across it, nerves sparking with anticipation. This isn't new—we've had sex before—but the air is different today. Hotter. Sharper. More vulnerable.

His fingers fumble at my jeans, and I help, shimmying out of them along with my underwear. My sweater goes next, then my bra, until I'm bare under the heat of his gaze. His lips part, eyes dragging over every inch of me like I'm the only thing he'll ever want. Warmth blooms in my chest.

I shove him back onto the bed, climbing over his thighs. "I want you, Logan. So much." I grind against him, my slickness sliding over his cock.

He groans low and dangerous. "As much as I want you to show your appreciation, I want your sweet pussy first." His grin sharpens. "Sit on my face."

My nipples tighten at the command. I crawl up, bracing my hands on the headboard. His palms cup my ass, guiding me exactly where he wants me.

"Grab on, Snowflake," he growls. "Ride."

Before my fingers can even curl around the wood, his tongue runs up my pussy. "Oh, fuck." The words rip out of me. He licks hard, roughing his tongue up my slit. His lips seal around my clit and he sucks until stars burst behind my eye lids. My grip on the headboard tightens, turning my knuckles white as I grind against his mouth. A raging inferno burns in me as he eats me out like a man having his last meal. His finger slides between my cheeks and circles my puckered hole. A gasp escapes me, the surprise sensation sending a shiver down my spine. It's new and foreign, but I don't hate it. The pad of his thumb circles the hole teasingly. Adding more pressure. The unexpected touch rockets through me, shattering the last of my control.

"Logan—don't stop—" My mouth falls open in a gasp. My spine goes rigid as pleasure tears through me in relentless waves. His fingers dig into my ass as he holds me down, licking me through every aftershock until I'm trembling. Once he's done, he presses his lips to my inner thigh. My chest heaves as I slide down his body.

He kisses me, the slightly sweet but also salty taste of myself lingering on his lips sends another pulse of heat between my legs. Coming from him, it's kind of a turn-on.

"You've ruined me," I pant. "That orgasm is seared into my brain forever."

"Good." His chuckle is wicked. "Means I get to ruin you again and again."

"Now it's my turn to ruin you." I pepper kisses along his jaw, down the column of his neck, and over his chest. My fingers trail over his pecs, and I lick a path down his stomach. His fingers thread through my hair. When I reach his cock, I wrap my fingers around the base, stroking as my tongue circles the crown.

"Fuuuck," he groans.

I slide my lips over the tip. The bead of pre-cum is salty on my tongue. He bucks his hips, thrusting into my mouth. The tip hits the back of my throat, and I slide back up, lightly dragging my teeth over his soft skin. I peer up at him through my lashes, and he's resting on an elbow, eyes heated with lust as he concentrates on my lips wrapped around him. Keeping my gaze locked on his, I slide down his cock.

"Fuck. You look perfect with your lips on me." His hand fists in my hair, guiding me as I take him deeper, moving in tandem with my hand. "Fuck. Just like that."

I moan around his shaft, his words spurring me to go faster, sucking harder.

He rocks his hips, tunneling his cock in and out of my mouth. "Fuck. Absolutely perfect. Mmm. Fuck. Brooke—"

I freeze.

He does too, realization hitting like a slap.

My heart plummets, heat draining from my body. His wife's name. He just called me his wife's name. I release my grip on him and sit up. There's no way I can pretend he didn't say it.

"Shit." His voice cracks. "I'm sorry. It just—slipped."

"Uh. Yeah. Totally understandable. We're having a moment. You called me your wife's name. Perfectly normal." I ease myself off the bed.

He throws his arms over his eyes. "I'm sorry."

"I think I should go."

He jackknifes off the bed. "Please don't go."

"I think it's for the best if I do." My voice cracks, but I force it steady. With one arm clutched across my chest I bend to snatch my bra off the floor, and I slip the straps over my shoulders with fumbling fingers. Next, I find my jeans and sweater. What was I thinking? He's not over her. How could he be? She was his wife. The mother of his child. Every time he looks at Josie, he sees her. I'm not competing with a ghost—I'm not competing, period.

Logan yanks the blanket away and crawls to the end of the bed. His fingers wrap around my wrist, and he spins me around. "I didn't mean it. I'm sorry. Please. Understand." The words are a frantic plea, tumbling over each other. "Brie—"

The sound of my name, ragged on his lips, almost undoes me. Almost. My chest aches as I inhale, shaky and hollow. I had reservations about Logan for many reasons, and this is what happens when you don't trust your gut. "I've taken second place in a lot of things in my life, but I won't be second place in someone's heart."

His eyes flash, desperate, pleading. "It wasn't like that. I didn't mean it. Please——"

"I get it." I blink back the tears. "She was your wife. Your *everything*. You don't just get over that. And I'm not asking you to. But I can't be second choice. This was fun." I wave a hand between us. "Maybe I'll see you around." Before he can answer, I wrench free and bolt, practically flying down the stairs. I did the right thing, right? He called me another woman's name.

By the time I jam my feet into my boots, there's a loud thump upstairs, followed by frantic footsteps. I fumble with the deadbolt, swing open the door—just as Logan barrels down the stairs, bare-chested, boxer briefs, all muscle and regret.

"Brie! Wait!"

I slam the door before he can reach me. My SUV beeps open, and I dive inside, shoving it into reverse without a warm-up. Out the windshield, Logan stands on his porch, shoulders sagging, heartbreak etched across every line of him.

Two blocks down the road, I veer my SUV toward the curb, and with shaky hands throw it into park. The adrenaline crashes, leaving nothing but ache and angry tears streaking down my cheeks. What the hell was I thinking? Why did I not see this earlier? Why did I even get involved? Why? I was fooling myself to think there could be something between Logan and me. I deserve more. I deserve *first place*. Not a consolation prize. Not a placeholder. I won't settle. Not with this. In my gut, I knew I should have stayed away. Logan Crawford is nothing but trouble. Sexy, caring, kind, compassionate, a great kisser, even-better-in-bed kind of trouble. It's even worse when he holds my heart in his hands and won't let go.

Back at my house, I'm sprawled out on my living room

floor, staring up at a twinkling pink ornament spinning on my Christmas tree. He said his wife's name. Honestly, I don't even know if it would sting less if he'd said some random ex's name… or even a celebrity crush. At least then it wouldn't mean so much. But his wife? The woman he built a life with, the mother of his child. That's a whole different kind of pain. Was he thinking of her the entire time we were together? Every kiss. Every touch. Every laugh. I've never had someone call me the wrong name before, especially while in bed together. It's a little disorienting. One thing is clear. He's not over her. How could he be? He was with her for fourteen years. Then one day—gone. Not coming back. I can understand. But that doesn't make it easier. And I don't want to be someone's second choice. Been there, done that, collected all the silver medals along the way. I want to be someone's first. Not a warm body to pass the time. I want gold. I want first place in someone's heart. I want to be chosen. And I won't settle for anything less. As much as I've come to enjoy Logan's company—his smile, his laugh, the way he makes me feel —I can't keep pretending it's enough. Because it isn't.

My phone chimes with an incoming message, jerking me out of my spiral. My heart lurches. Logan? I pull it from my pocket and glance at the screen and frown. Instead, it's a message from Willa.

WILLA

Where are you? It's Christmas ham bingo night.

BRIE

Sorry. I'm not feeling the best. I'm going to stay home.

Her reply pings back instantly, but I don't look.

Wallowing is the only thing I want to do tonight. I nudge the ornament with one finger, watching my fractured reflection warp and spin along with the room. It feels fitting—my life, spinning in circles. A month ago, I was on track to land my dream promotion. My favorite Christmas blogger was in town. I was on the verge of falling in love. And now? I'm lying on the living room floor, poking at an ornament while everything unravels. My promotion is slipping through my fingers. I practically stalked a woman for an interview that turned into an exposé on my personal life. I couldn't get the Santa my boss really wanted and instead had to settle for a second-rate Santa. And the man I let myself fall for is still not over his deceased wife. This is what I get for losing sight of my priorities. I should have focused on the festival, not Logan. Merry freaking Christmas to me.

Logan

By the time I get my shit together and bolt down the stairs, her SUV is already halfway down the driveway. I come to a halt on the porch, the wood planks like ice against my feet, and watch helplessly as she disappears around the corner. A bitter wind slaps against my bare skin. Shit. I'm only wearing boxer briefs. Across the street, Mrs. Smith freezes mid-mail grab. Her hand clutches her chest, eyes going wide as a smile forms on her lips. Mr. Smith hustles out, glances at her and then me, eyes narrowing before tugging her back inside. Nothing they haven't seen if they saw the underwear ad I did several years ago, minus the erection.

Spinning around, I enter the house, slam the door, and

collapse onto the couch. My head drops into my hands, fingers digging into my hair. "Smooth, Crawford. Real smooth." I don't know why I said Brooke's name. I certainly wasn't thinking about her at that moment. It just slipped out of my mouth. I can't blame Brie for leaving. I would have done the same, if not worse, if she had called me some other guy's name. I've heard the locker room horror stories—guys who said the wrong name in bed. I laughed. Called them dumbasses. And now? Guess who's the dumbass.

Lifting my chin, a photo album filled with pictures from Christmas four years ago sits in front of me. The last one with Brooke. Josie asked for a picture of her mom to turn into an ornament. My chest tightens. Maybe I'm not over her. Maybe I'll never be. Fuck. I don't know anymore. There will always be a part of my heart that belongs to Brooke. And Brie's right. She deserves more than I can give her. But at the same time, I don't want to give her up. She makes me want to try. She makes me believe I can have more than grief and guilt. She's my Snowflake. My second chance. If she hasn't given up on me yet, I'll be damned if I give up on her.

I take the stairs two at a time, dragging on clothes with one hand while jabbing at my phone with the other. Every call to Brie goes straight to voicemail. Each text message unread. Once I'm dressed, I circle her house, but it's dark. Next, the festival grounds. Nothing. The Crooked Reindeer's parking lot is overflowing. My pulse spikes. If she's anywhere, maybe she's here. I crawl the rows, searching for her SUV. Nothing. I need to find her. Talk to her. Two blocks away I squeeze into a parking spot and jog down the icy sidewalk, my breath clouding in the frigid air. By the time I yank open the door, heat and noise slam into me all at once—laughter, voices raised over the bingo caller, glasses clinking. I scan the crowded room, eyes darting from table to table, searching for a glimpse of her hair, her coat, her smile. Nothing. I shoulder past a couple of regulars and step up to the bar.

Simon spots me immediately, his brows lifting in surprise. "Hey man. I didn't know you liked Christmas ham bingo."

I lean in, my throat tight. "I don't. I'm looking for Brie. Have you seen her?"

Simon shakes his head. "I haven't. Which is weird, considering her friends are here." He nods toward a high-top where Willa and Sloane sit.

"Alright, thanks. Also, I know you didn't ask her out." I glare at him.

He laughs. "But it served its purpose."

I shake my head. The move was effective. I'll give him that. I push away and weave through the crowd until I reach them. "Where's Brie?" The words rip out sharper than intended.

Both women whip around like I've just suggested Santa was overrated.

"She's at home," Sloane says cautiously.

"I drove by. Lights were off." My eyes flick between them, desperate for a tell.

From behind me, someone shouts, "Sit down, I can't see the board!"

I ignore it. "So where is she really?"

Willa shrugs. "She bailed on bingo, claimed she was sick. Which is bullshit. She has shown up half-dead with influenza just to play. Clearly, she wants to be left alone. And if you wanted to be left alone, would you keep your lights on?" She arches a brow.

"I need to talk to her. It's important."

"Take a seat or get out!" another voice bellows.

"You better listen to them. It's bingo night, and they take it very seriously," Sloane says.

"B-five," the bingo caller announces.

"Quiet up front!" another person roars.

My jaw clenches so tight it aches. "I don't care about bingo! Is she going to be at the festival tomorrow?"

"More than likely." Willa shrugs, eyes narrowing. "What did you do, anyway?"

"Nothing," I blurt. Which, let's be honest, is basically everything.

"Quit yapping! We can't hear the numbers!" someone else hollers.

My jaw clenches and I twist around. "B-five!"

"Your reaction doesn't say 'nothing,'" Willa says.

"O-sixty-nine," the caller announces.

I pinch the bridge of my nose. Chances are Brie's going to tell them what I did anyway. "I messed up, okay? I need her to hear me out, and she won't answer my calls."

"Still can't hear!" someone else shouts.

Willa leans in. "Give her time. She'll come around. But you better get out of here. Someone may shank you with their pocketknife bingo dabber."

"That's a thing?"

"Do you want to stay and find out?" Sloane adds.

I huff. "Fine. If you see Brie, tell her I need to talk to her."

"Sure thing," Willa says.

I turn around and stomp toward the exit. "I'm leaving. You can go back to bingo." The entire bar applauds.

Back in my truck, I scrub a hand over my face, contemplating driving to Brie's house, pounding on the door, and demand she talk to me. What do I even say? "I'm sorry. Please forgive me." Already tried that, and she's still icing me out. Fuck it. Willa and Sloane say she's at home, so that's where I'm going.

Standing at her doorstep, I lift my hand and knock on her front door. "Brie! I know you're home. Please open up." I knock again. "Brie!" My forehead drops against the door, the wood cold against my skin. "If you won't open, then maybe you'll just listen. I'm sorry. I don't even know why I said it. It was an accident." The ache in my chest goes hollow. I spin and slide down the door until I'm sitting on her "Merry AF" doormat. With my elbows resting on my knees, I rake through my hair. Snowflakes fall from the sky and accumulate around me. "Moving back to Mount Holly has been one giant change," I murmur into the night. "Hell, the past three years have been nothing but change. But this past month with you? Brie, you were the change I didn't know I needed. You made me believe I could… breathe again." My breath fogs white into the cold, vanishing as quickly as it forms. "Brooke will always be a part of me. I can't erase that. I'll always love her. But she's my past. Maybe I'm still healing, but being with you has been the first time I've felt alive in years. I don't know if I'm the man you deserve, but damn it, I want to try." I sit up and lean my back against the door. For the first time, I actually feel how numb I've been.

Above me, a click echoes. The door creaks open—and suddenly I'm flat on my back in Brie's entryway, staring up at the ceiling while the doorplate digs into my spine.

"Oh!" Brie jumps back, then crouches beside me. Her eyes are puffy and red, and guilt slams through me. She's been crying. Because of me.

"Are you okay?" she whispers.

"Yeah," I say quickly, scrambling upright. "I'm sorry."

"I know." Her lips press together, trembling.

"I like you. A lot. And I don't want to throw this away."

Her eyes flicker with something soft before hardening again. "I like you too. But now isn't the best time for us. I appreciate everything you said, but I think it's best we put the brakes on this." She waves a hand between us. "It's been a lot and fast. I understand Brooke will always be a part of your life, and that's okay. But also, I need to look out for myself. The last few days of the festival are the most important, and that's where all my attention needs to be."

I nod because what else can I do? She's right. She deserves more than I can give her.

"I'm sure we'll see each other around. It's Mount Holly, after all." She huffs a laugh that's half-hearted at best, then pushes to her feet. "Thanks for coming over."

"Thanks for listening."

She rises to her tiptoes and presses a kiss to my cheek—sweet, final. I lean toward her lips, but she pulls back. "Bye, Logan." The door closes, leaving me outside in the dark.

Not the ending I wanted. Hell, I don't even know what ending I wanted. But at least it's better than her ignoring me altogether.

By the time I slump into my truck, the ache in my chest has settled into something sharp. I drive on autopilot to my parents' house, the whole ride one endless loop of *what ifs* and *if onlys*.

I rap my knuckles against the door before pushing it open. "Hello?"

My mom peeks her head around the corner. "Hey, Logan. Come in."

I toe off my boots and hang up my coat and meet her the kitchen. "Smells good."

"Swedish meatballs," she says, already pulling out an extra plate. "Are you hungry?"

She slides it across the kitchen island, and I add it to the empty spot at the table.

She leans closer, lowering her voice like she has some top-secret intel. "How are things going with… Brie?"

I collapse onto the stool, rubbing a hand over my face. "Over."

The potato masher clatters into the pot, and she turns on me with a glare that could crush a grown man. "What did you do?"

"Why do you assume it was me?" I ask, but the look she gives me is answer enough. "Fine. It was me."

Her expression softens. "Logan, what happened?"

I scrub my hands down my face. "Maybe it's best I don't start dating yet."

She rests a hand on my arm. "Sweetheart, I say this with love—it's been three years. It's okay to move on."

"I *am* moving on. I sold the Chicago house, moved back here for Josie, for a better life. I'm moving on."

But even as I say it, my chest feels heavy. Because maybe moving on and moving forward aren't the same thing at all.

Mom arches a brow. "Only to organize a Christmas carnival that wasn't even your idea. I want to make sure you're doing it for the right reasons. You've never been Mister Christmas Spirit. So why now?"

"People change."

"They can." She tilts her head. "Let me ask you this. What do you want?"

Her question lands like a weight in my gut. What do I want? It should be easy. Everyone should know what they want. But the truth? My life feels like it's hovering at an intersection with no street signs.

I fidget with the corner of a kitchen towel, then force myself to meet her eyes. "I don't want to be a shell anymore." My voice is rough, but a piece of me feels lighter just saying it. "I want to live. Really live. I thought finishing Brooke's carnival dream would finally put her memory to rest. But it's not my dream. It never was. And you're right. The carnival isn't me."

"In cases like this," she says gently, "it's okay to be selfish. Brooke's legacy already lives on—in Josie, in every memory you two made. You don't have to complete her dream to prove you loved her. And if she's watching, she's definitely calling you an idiot for even trying."

My lips twitch. Yeah. That sounded exactly like Brooke.

Mom smiles, softening. "When your dad passed away, I found his bucket list. Only one thing wasn't crossed off."

"What was it?"

A smile tugs at her lips. "To go skydiving. I spent a lot of time contemplating whether I should finish his list for him."

"Did you?"

"Jump out of a perfectly operational airplane? No! His list stayed unfinished, and I know your dad would want it that way. He was stubborn, but he never wanted anyone else to live his life for him."

I can't help it—I smile. She's right.

Her gaze flicks to mine, warm but firm. "There was a time I thought I'd never find anyone again either. But then I met John. He made me laugh again. He reminded me that life wasn't over just because a chapter ended. And now I want the same for you."

I lower my head, her words sinking in deeper than I want to admit.

"I know you buried yourself in hockey so you could avoid the silence," she continues. "I did the same when your father passed. All those school fundraisers I helped organize, volunteering at the Mount Holly Community Club, I didn't do those things for fun. It kept my mind off losing your father. But, Logan"—she squeezes my hand—"this past month, since Brie, I've seen something in you I haven't seen in years. A real smile. Not the fake one you plaster on for show. The one that reaches your eyes. The one that tells me you're happy."

She releases my hand and gestures toward the back door. "Now, go grab John and Josie from the yard and wash up. Dinner's almost ready."

I stand, but her words echo in my chest. For as much as Brie drives me insane, she also makes me feel—everything. With her, the past doesn't drown me. When she smiles, I remember what it's like to actually want a future.

And for the first time in years, I know exactly what I want. Her.

Brie

The next morning, I'm at the festival grounds before the sun has breached the horizon, triple-checking every detail in Santa's Workshop. Presents stacked just right, garland fluffed to within an inch of its life, candy canes angled at exactly forty-five degrees. It's perfect. Or it should be.

But as I line up the last gift box, flashes of Logan hit me like a reel I can't turn off. Him between my thighs, his mouth on me. The night we were finally honest with each other. It feels like forever ago, when in reality, it's been—what?—less than a week.

Last night after Christmas ham bingo ended, Willa and Sloane came over to tell me Logan was seconds away from being shanked for interrupting the bar. They insisted I tell them why he was looking for me, which makes sense why he showed up at my door, using it like a confessional. After peeling myself off the floor, I pressed against the other side of the wood, listening. A part of me melted. The bigger part—the one that knows I'm not his first choice—iced over. I can't be the rebound. I can't be the woman he's with while secretly still living in someone else's memory.

Which means it's better to pull the plug now before my heart loses any more pieces. I need to focus on the festival. No distractions. Especially not six-foot-two, hockey-god-shaped ones.

I smooth the final bow into place and march across the grounds to the changing area to check on Santa. When I step inside, it's empty. Pulling my phone from my pocket, I glance at the clock, and my pulse spikes. He's thirty minutes late. I pace from one side of the changing room to the other while I dial his number. Straight to voicemail. Again. My face burns hot with irritation. This is what happens when you trade in reliable Santa for "fresh and new." Santa better not have ghosted me on Christmas Eve. Because if he did, I will personally smother him with his own big, red sack.

Finally, my phone rings. Scott. My Santa. I stab the answer button. "Where are you? You're late."

"I was in the emergency room with a broken ankle."

I blink. "What do you mean you broke your ankle? Santa doesn't break bones." This can't be happening. Not today of all days. Not Christmas Eve. Nausea turns in the pit of my stomach.

"I'm sorry, Brie. They have me in a boot, and I'm not supposed to put weight on it."

"You're Santa. You sit in a chair. Can't you hobble over here and sit all day? That's what Santa does."

"I'm sorry, Brie. I hate to do this, but I just can't."

My vision goes red. I have no Santa. A cold sweat prickles my skin as I squeeze my eyes shut. It's not like he did this on purpose. Right? "Okay. Get better soon." Santa is gone. On Christmas Eve. The one non-negotiable day of the year. This is it. Career over. I shove my phone into my pocket and do everything in my power not to scream. Of course, this would happen. Why wouldn't it? For the first year, everything, or almost everything, goes as planned. This is karma. Revenge for all the bad things I did in my life like stealing a candy bar when I was five. Yelling at other drivers who don't know how to zipper merge. Not rounding up my grocery bill so the few extra cents get donated to charity. Oh god. I drop into a chair and fold myself in half, head between my knees, as stars dance at the edge of my vision. "Goodbye, promotion," I whisper to the floor. "Hello, lifetime career in selling snow shovels."

Bootsteps creak across the wooden floor, and Willa's MUK LUKS appear in my eyeline. "What's wrong?"

"Christmas is ruined, and it's all my fault." Sitting up, I wrap my arms around my waist and rock back and forth. Anything to keep myself from bursting into uncontrollable tears.

"Why is it your fault?" She kneels beside me, resting a hand on my knee.

"I'm Santa-less. For the first time in festival history, there will be no Santa on Christmas Eve. The children of Mount Holly are about to stage a mutiny, and I'll be the first casualty."

Her brows knit. "Oh no. What happened?"

"Santa broke his ankle. And instead of hobbling here to sit his jolly ass in a chair like a champ, he bailed. Now I have no Santa, no backup, and apparently no foresight to book a backup." I press my hands to my temples as the pounding intensifies.

"I'm sorry. What about Henry? Simon? Mason?"

"Henry's wrangling sleigh rides. Simon's at the bar, drowning in toy donations. Mason's on fire duty." I groan. "And me? I'm about to be the only event coordinator in history who tanked her shot at the job by having no Santa Claus." I flop backward dramatically, hand to my forehead.

"It's not that bad. We still have, what, an hour? We'll find you a Santa. This will be the best Christmas Eve this town has ever seen." Willa's voice is an octave higher, but her enthusiasm is faker than snow in Aruba.

"Thanks," I mutter. "But it's too late."

"Nope." She jumps to her feet. "It is *never* too late. The Brie McKenna I know does not get defeated."

"The Brie McKenna you know just did." My head droops forward, my shoulders sagging. "Story of my life. Second place, every time."

Her eyes light up with dangerous glee. "What if *you* played Santa?"

I stare. "That's absurd. I could never pass as Santa." Could I? This might be my only option. Luckily, the suit is here. Jumping to my feet, I sprint to the rack and yank the red coat free. "Okay. Maybe I could shove some pillows under here. Lower my voice. You know, ho ho ho!" My attempt rumbles low in my throat.

"Totally believable!" she squeals.

I jab a finger toward a stack of throw pillows. "Hand me those." She passes them over, and I shove them under my sweater, puffing out my belly until I look less jolly old elf and more lopsided snowman. "Hmm. Kind of looks like Santa needs medical attention." I squish the pillows around, trying to smooth the lumps. "Maybe the jacket will cover it?"

Willa hands me the beard, and I hook it over my ears. She fluffs the synthetic strands, then steps back, pursing her lips. "Maybe Santa's on a diet. Mrs. Claus told him no more cookies." She shrugs.

"Ugh." I flop onto a chair, burying my face in my hands. The fake beard tickles my palms. "Why did I ever think this would work?"

Willa's phone chimes with the message. "Santa's at the workshop!"

My head snaps up. "Wait—what? Scott? He made it?"

"All Sloane says is Santa's there."

I shoot out of the chair, yanking off the beard, coat, and pillows in record time. "Doesn't matter. Let's go." We dash across the festival, cutting through the crowd. Parents and kids line the paths, craning their necks, waiting for the sleigh's grand arrival. "Change of plans, everyone!" I shout, waving my arms. "Santa's already at the workshop and eager to see you! Follow me!" The line snakes all the way to the hot cocoa stand by the time we get there. I stand at the front of the crowd, waving my hands until the chattering fades. "Alright, I'm just going to go check and see if Santa's ready to take all your wish lists!"

I push open the door and peek inside. There he is, perched in the big red chair like he's been waiting all along. "Oh my god, I'm so happy you made it. I was five seconds from cardiac arrest." My gaze drops automatically to his leg. "Where's your boot? Did you not need one after all?"

He gives me a hearty ho ho ho!

"Okay, not very chatty," I mumble. "Guess you're really leaning into the character." I admire the enthusiasm.

I push open the door, and children from two to ten rush inside. All afternoon, Santa chats with the kids as they tell him all their last-minute Christmas wishes and get a picture taken. I pass out candy canes as they leave. By the end of the afternoon, the workshop is buzzing with holiday magic. To call it a Christmas miracle would be an understatement. This is more than a miracle. It's a miraclemas.

But as I watch Santa pose for another photo, my chest tightens with a thought I can't shake. What's the point of getting exactly what I want… if it isn't *him*?

Logan

"Dad! Dad! Dad!" Josie barrels into the makeshift dressing room.

I wrestle the red coat onto my shoulders and glance down. "Whoa, what's all the dads for?"

Her boots squeak to a stop. Eyes wide. "Dad! There's no Santa!"

Confusion takes over as I stare down at my outfit. "Santa?" I point to myself.

"No! Not you!" Josie whines. "The festival. Brie doesn't have a Santa. I overheard Amanda talking about it."

"Shit," I mutter.

"What do we do?" Josie throws her hands up like the world's ending. "She *needs* a Santa."

And she's right. No Santa equals no promotion for Brie. And Brie deserves that damn promotion. I can't let that happen, not if I can help it. "Jump in the truck. Santa's relocating. She needs a Santa more than we do." Josie beams up at me. Outside, I flag down the first volunteer I see. "Tell everyone Santa's overbooked. He's now at the Holly Jolly Festival."

The girl blinks at me like I've grown a third eye but nods. "O-okay."

Minutes later, Josie and I are fishtailing down the snowy road in my truck.

"Dad?"

"Yeah?"

"I really like Brie."

The corners of my lips curve into a smile. I more than like her. "Me too." Josie smiles at me before turning her attention to the window as Mount Holly flashes by.

When I slam the truck to a stop near Santa's Workshop and jump out, Sloane rounds the corner. She freezes. "I thought Santa drove a sleigh, not an F-250."

I glance over my shoulder at my truck. "Times have changed. Where's Brie?"

"Probably hyperventilating into a paper bag." Her eyes sweep over me. "What's with the suit?"

"I'm Santa. The hat and beard don't give it away?"

She snorts. "Oh, I got that. I meant—what are you doing here dressed as Santa?"

"I heard Brie needs one."

She lets out a laugh so loud a passing elf startles. "She's going to lose her mind when she finds out it's you."

"About that. Do me a favor? Don't tell her. Not yet, anyway."

Her grin turns sly. "Okay. But I'm going to tell her she doesn't need to look for a new job yet."

"Deal. Do you know where I can finish getting ready?"

"Follow me."

Sloane leads us to another building adjacent to Santa's Workshop. After I wriggle into the rest of the suit, and adjust the beard, I'm ready to be the best damn Santa this festival has ever seen. As we stroll into Santa's Workshop, Josie is skipping alongside me, handing out candy canes like she's running for mayor. I ho ho ho at the kids, trying not to think about how just last week Brie was spread out on a table beneath me, my face between her legs while she moaned my name. Not exactly Santa-appropriate. Focus. I need to channel my inner Santa. In the far corner, I plant myself in the big red chair. Josie leaves to venture around the festival with her friends, plus her being here would give away the surprise. A few seconds later, Brie bursts in. My heart pounds wildly in my chest. I divert my gaze and focus on the wrapped presents scattered around the room. Luckily, she mistakes me for a guy named Scott and is too distracted by the line of eager kids to notice who's really in the chair.

All afternoon, kids sit on my lap, get their picture taken, and tell me all the toys, gadgets, and electronics on their wish list. Brie hovers nearby, running the show like the pro she is. When the last kid leaves, she collapses onto the edge of the table and exhales a deep breath.

I clear my throat and deepen my voice. "It's your turn."

Brie spins around to see who else is here, but it's empty. "Me?" She points to herself.

"Ho ho ho! Why don't you tell Santa what you want for Christmas?"

She lets out a laugh, crossing her arms. "What I want and what I got are two very different things."

"Santa didn't ask you what you got but what you want."

"Does Santa always refer to himself in the third person?" She lifts an eyebrow.

I nod. "Santa does."

She shakes her head, smiling despite herself. "What do I want…" She taps her chin but stays rooted.

I pat my knee.

She freezes and glances at my leg. "Oh. I'm not sitting on your lap."

"Your wish only comes true if you sit on Santa's lap."

Her expression flickers, then falters. "Doesn't matter. My wish can't come true anyway."

"Why not?"

She moves across the room, fiddling with fake presents. "Because I'm falling in love with a man who still loves someone else. I shouldn't even love him. I spent my entire life hating him. It was much easier to do that than deal with him not being in my life now. But I can't be with someone who doesn't see me as first place. I can't do that to myself." She stops on the other side of the small room. "Sorry to unload all that on you."

My chest twists. Enough pretending. "What if he does see you as first place?" My real voice slips out.

Her head whips toward me.

The air crackles as she strides over to me. Her fingers grasp the white strands of my fake beard and yank, exposing my face.

"Logan?" She releases the beard, and the elastic snaps back, smacking me in the lip. I flinch. Her hands fly to her mouth. "Oh! I'm sorry!"

I pull the beard off my face and it slips from my grasp, snapping me in the chin. "Shit. That's going to leave a mark." I rub my jaw.

She giggles, covering her mouth. "Come here." Together, we wrestle the elastic free.

Once off, I set the beard to the side and grab Brie's hand, curling my fingers around hers. "What are you doing here?" she whispers.

I tug her closer until she's between my legs, perched lightly against my knee. My arms circle her waist, holding her steady. I brush my thumb over her thigh as trepidation shines in her glossy eyes. I push past the lump in my throat. "You are my first place. After coming back to Mount Holly, spending time with you—it gave me new life. My snowflake. For once, my days didn't feel like the same loop on repeat. You make the world less heavy. And all this"—I pull the Santa hat off and toss it onto the armrest—"none of it matters compared to you."

Her brow furrows. "What about the carnival?"

"It's not important," I admit. "You are. The carnival was never my dream—it was closure. Brooke is my past. She'll always be my past. But you…" My voice dips as I trail my hand up and down her thigh. "I want you to be my future. Josie deserves someone in her life to do all the baking, nail painting, and eventually all the boyfriend talks. I'll need someone else to be the voice of reason; otherwise, I'll tell her she can never date until she's thirty. I'm sure that won't go over well." I blow out a breath, my gaze falling to my hand. "But I don't want her to forget her mom either."

Her fingertip nudges under my chin, lifting my gaze back to hers. "Logan… a part of me is terrified when you talk about a future with me. But whatever happens, I need you to know—I don't ever want to replace Brooke. I couldn't. That's a bond you'll always share with her, and same for Josie. I just want to stand beside you. Not take over."

Fuck. She makes it so easy to fall in love with her. "Josie and I are a package deal. You're okay with that?"

Her smile is soft and steady. "I more than adore Josie. Honestly, I think I'm getting the better end of the deal."

Warmth cracks open in my chest, the kind I've been starving for. "Also, I'm willing to take this as fast or slow as you'd like, but I want to be by your side while we do it. I love you too, Brie."

Her lips curve into a mischievous smile. "See, I said I was *falling* in love. I never said I was *in* love with you."

I shake my head and tighten my grip around her. This is the exact reason why I adore her. "Is this what you're going to argue about with me?"

"Yes."

"Perfect." I wrap my hand around the back of her neck and haul her to me, pressing my lips to hers. She breaks away, breathless. "You never answered about the carnival."

"Not important." I kiss her again.

"But—"

"I'm hanging up my carnival hat. The Holly Jolly Festival will be the only holiday event in Mount Holly." I kiss her again.

She laughs against my lips. "You're not the person I thought I wanted. You're better. So much better." Her whisper is so soft, I almost miss it. "Also, I may have already fallen. I love you too."

"I know." My grin is shameless. "Come spend Christmas with us."

Her forehead rests against mine. "I don't know… don't you and Josie do a family thing? I don't want to intrude."

"Our family thing is sitting around in pajamas, watching movies, and arguing about which Christmas cookie is superior." I brush a quick kiss against her mouth.

"The only rule is—you have to wear Christmas-themed pajamas."

She giggles. "All I have is this ridiculous flannel set with Santas and reindeer all over it."

"I guarantee it won't be more ridiculous than what I'll be wearing."

Her voice softens. "And Josie? She'll be okay with me crashing?"

"She'll be thrilled. But I'll ask her to make it official." Her fingertips graze my cheek, and I lean into the warmth. "I'll call you after I talk to her." I kiss her again, slow and lingering, until I force myself to pull back. My forehead rests on hers. "We should stop, or I'm going to lay you out on the table and repeat the first night I made you come on my tongue."

Her breath hitches, but she rises from my lap, tugging me to my feet. "Then consider that my Christmas present."

I smirk. "Christmas present. Day-after-Christmas present. New Year's Eve present."

Later in the evening, after talking to Josie, she was more than excited to invite Brie over for Christmas. So much so, she wanted to be the one to invite her. I pick up the phone and dial Brie's number. After two rings, she answers.

"Hello again."

"Hi Brie, I got you on speakerphone, and Josie wants to ask you something."

From beside me, Josie leans over and yells into the phone. "Do you want to come over and spend Christmas with us? Please, please, *please*."

Brie giggles. "I would absolutely love to."

Josie bounces on the stool. "Yes! And you have to wear Christmas pajamas—it's the rule."

"You know," Brie teases, "I think I might just have the perfect pair."

"Yay!" Josie whoops. "I'm putting mine on right now!" She takes off up the stairs before I can stop her.

I take Brie off speaker and lift the phone. "She wanted to do the inviting herself."

"It was sweet. She's an amazing girl."

I lower my voice. "Also, just so you know, once you're in my bed, the pajamas come off."

"Oh, so you're assuming I'll be spending the night?"

"Might as well pack for the entire weekend."

When I mentioned the idea to Josie, she jumped around the house. She listed everything we could have for breakfast, games we could play, and movies we had to watch. I love that she's just as excited about Brie as I am. Maybe more.

Her laugh bubbles through the speaker, warm and teasing. "Bye, Logan."

Not long after, a knock rattles the door. Josie launches off the couch and flings it open. "Brie!"

"Hi, Josie. I hope it's okay I wore my pajamas over." Brie tugs her coat open to reveal red-and-green flannel pajamas plastered with Santas and reindeer.

Josie gasps. "Yes! We match!" She flips up the hood of her Christmas onesie, complete with stuffed antlers.

"That's absolutely adorable," Brie coos.

I push off the couch. "Josie, maybe let Brie in before she turns into an icicle."

"Oh. Right!" Josie scrambles back, and Brie steps inside, removing her coat.

"My dad has the same pajamas," Josie declares.

Brie arches a brow, eyes skating over me from head to toe. Her lips twitch like she's fighting a laugh. "Oh, that's a sight."

"Wait—it gets better." I yank on the hood. The antlers flop from side to side, and when I press the tip of the hood, the red fuzzy nose lights up.

"You look good as a reindeer." She smirks.

"Not just any reindeer, but Rudolph. Don't worry, next year, we will get you your own pair. You can be Vixen."

"I can hardly wait."

Grabbing her overnight bag, I set it near the staircase. "We were just about to start the first movie. Honestly, I wasn't sure you'd actually come. Figured you'd be knee-deep in planning your Christmas world domination for next year." My hand finds the small of her back as I guide her into the living room. Even that tiny touch lights me up like the nose on my hood.

"The Christmas takeover can wait a day or two." She sits, curling into the couch cushions. "Besides, I won't know about the promotion until next week."

"If you don't get it, I'll stage a protest."

Josie pops up from the makeshift bed on the floor. "I'll make posters!"

"Thanks. I'm happy to know I have your support." Her phone chimes with a message. She glances at her phone, brows pinched together. "There's a new blog post from Emma St. Claire."

"What does it say?" I lean closer, our legs brushing.

"*Mount Holly, Minnesota, is bursting with Christmas cheer all thanks to the Holly Jolly Festival,*" Brie reads. "Then she gushes about all the events—the cookie contests, the over-the-top decorations, the way the whole town turns into a snow globe come to life. Oh, and—" She grins. "There's even a quote from Mount Holly hockey legend, Logan

Crawford: *'The Holly Jolly Festival is the best damn festival in the country.'"*

A smile tugs at my lips. "Good. She added that part."

Josie bolts upright. "Dad! She didn't even mention the carnival."

"That's okay, Peanut. I actually wrote a strongly worded email to her to focus on the festival."

Josie's mouth drops. "But I wrote her too! I even entered the carnival in a contest so she'd come here!"

I sit straighter. "What?"

"When we moved here, I saw a Christmas magazine at Grandma's. I filled out the form and sent her an email." Josie's bottom lip wobbles.

"Ohhh," Brie murmurs, nodding. "So that's why she showed up."

I tug Josie gently between my knees. "Peanut, that was very sweet. But you can't email random strangers on the internet, okay?"

Her chin drops. "But it was for the carnival."

"I know. I love the thoughtful gesture, but you're too young to be emailing strangers."

"I'm sorry." Her gaze drops to the floor. "Am I in trouble?"

"No. Just… don't do it again." She nods, and I kiss the top of her head. "Now, why don't you pick the first movie?"

"Okay." I pass her the remote, and she goes back to her spot on the floor. She scrolls through the various Christmas movies until she lands on Dr. Seuss' The Grinch. "We forgot the snacks!" Josie hops up.

"Can you grab them?" I ask.

"I'll help," Brie says, following her into the kitchen.

I sink into the couch, a smile pulling at my lips. Never thought my life would look like this. I came to Mount

Holly for Josie. To heal. To start over. What I found? Brie. Fierce, determined, stubborn as hell—and the best thing that's happened to us. We've both grown and changed over the years. Sure, both of us will always be competitors, but now we'll also be cheering for each other. She's turned my world right-side-up again. Their laughter drifts from the kitchen before they reappear, Josie carrying a tray of cookies, Brie balancing two bowls of popcorn.

"We couldn't pick between sweet or salty, so... both," Brie announces.

Josie passes an English toffee cookie to each of us before setting the tray on the end table. Brie sets the popcorn down, then settles beside me.

I slip my arm around her shoulders, tugging her close. Leaning down, I whisper, "I think my kid likes you more than me."

Brie grins, snuggling in.

And the truth? I wouldn't have it any other way. Because having both of them here—my two favorite girls —is all the happiness I need.

Brie

My lashes flutter open. Heat radiates around me—but it's not mine. A heavy arm is draped across my waist, pinning me down like a weighted blanket. Except this one smells a whole lot better. Fresh and clean. Logan.

I roll carefully onto my other side to face him, and his arm tightens, pulling me closer like I might try to escape.

He nuzzles against my neck, voice still husky with sleep. "I like waking up and finding you here more than I want to admit. I vote we stay like this all day."

A warmth blossoms in my chest. Waking up next to Logan is my new favorite thing and certainly something I could get used to. "But it's Christmas Day. Isn't Josie going to be bouncing on her toes to unwrap her presents?"

"Oh, she's definitely under the tree by now, shaking every box like a detective in training." His hand slides beneath the blanket, tracing up my thigh under the oversized Boston College shirt I borrowed last night. I wasn't ready to push my luck by sleeping in his bed naked like he requested. Instead, I borrowed—stole—one of his old shirts.

A knock interrupts us. "Daddy, can we open presents now?"

I meet Logan's gaze, biting back a smile. He shrugs. "Or… standing outside the door." He calls to her, "Five minutes, Peanut. We'll be right there."

"Okay!" The patter of little feet thunders down the stairs.

"We're on a timer and what I want to do to you will take more than five minutes, so we better not keep her waiting." He nuzzles my neck.

I giggle. "I can settle for a raincheck." I run my fingers across the stubble on his cheek. Being here with Logan is surreal. If someone had told me two months ago I'd be lying in bed next to him, I would have asked if he was hogtied with Christmas lights because that's the only way we would be this close. But we've come a long way. Eighteen years is a long time, but there isn't anyone else I'd rather spend Christmas with.

He brushes his lips against mine. Too quick. Too tempting. Then he swings out of bed in nothing but red boxer briefs, muscles flexing as he pulls on the Rudolph onesie from last night. Somehow, the man manages to make polyester antlers look indecently hot.

"You're staring," he teases.

"Bold of you to assume I could stop." I wink.

He tosses me my Santa-and-reindeer pajama set. "Tradition."

As we stroll downstairs, Josie's waiting by the Christmas tree with a present barricade surrounding her like a fortress fit for a princess. For the next twenty minutes, we watch in delight as she tears into all her presents, her excitement growing with each one.

Her joy is infectious. She's been through so much, and yet she's here—laughing, squealing, happy. My chest aches with the realization that I get to be part of this.

Then Logan points under the tree. "Looks like there's one more. Josie, can you grab it?"

She dives under the branches, emerging with a snowflake-patterned box. "To Brie. From Santa."

My heart skips. "Logan, you didn't have to—"

"Not me." He grins. "Santa."

I shake my head but take the box, pulse racing as I peel back the paper. Inside is a red and silver scarf, soft as silk. I wrap it around my neck, letting it drape over my chest. "It's beautiful. Thank you."

He leans in, voice low. "Don't thank me. Thank Santa. My present comes later." The dimple flashes with his smirk.

Heat curls in my stomach. "You didn't need to get me anything."

"Oh, trust me. You'll enjoy this one too."

I laugh, shaking my head. "You're really making me feel like I failed at Christmas."

His eyes soften, voice gentle. "You being here is more than enough."

We tidy the living room, then head into the kitchen to make breakfast.

I offer to make snowman pancakes. Since, there's a plethora of fresh fruit in the fridge, I cut the strawberries to use as a scarf and blueberries for the buttons and eyes. Josie helps by making whipped cream top hats.

It's messy and chaotic and perfect. Between the laughter and the sugar high, it feels like I've belonged in this kitchen for years.

Logan glances at Josie. "Hey, Grandpa's coming to pick you up in thirty minutes so you can open presents with them too. Go get dressed."

"Are you coming?" she asks.

"We'll be over shortly."

"Okay!" She bounds up the stairs, leaving us in the warm, syrup-scented kitchen.

After John picks up Josie, the house is suddenly quiet. Just us.

He turns to me, eyes dark and playful. "It's time for your Christmas present." His arms hook around my thighs and I'm hoisted over his shoulder like I weigh nothing. A squeal escapes me, part laugh, part breathless nerves, as butterflies explode in my belly. Instead of going upstairs to the bedroom, he sets me down on the dining room table, right on the swirly red-and-gold snowflake runner. Slowly, he unravels the scarf from around my neck until both ends are in his grasp.

"Logan," I gasp, heat crawling up my neck. "This is where people eat."

"Exactly." His grin is sinful. "And I plan on eating."

When his thumb hooks into the waistband of my pajama pants, I don't hesitate—I wiggle and lift my butt to help him peel them down. My shirt follows. He grips the zipper of his pajama onesie and slides it down, freeing his arms until it pools at his hips. He takes a step back; his gaze drags over me like I'm something precious and all his. "Fucking gorgeous," he murmurs.

I curl my fingers around the fabric of the onesie and tug him to me, crashing my lips to his. Tilting my head, I deepen the kiss as he runs his tongue along the seam, and I open for him. Our tongues slide against each other like a slow dance. The kiss is everything—erotic, sensual, the kind of kiss that steals your air but sets you on fire in return. With desperate fingers he unclasps my bra, and when it slides away, my nipples tighten instantly under his gaze.

I expect him to climb over me. Instead, he drops to his knees. His big hands slide down my shins, catching behind my knee to guide me open. My breath hitches. His blond head lowers, and then his tongue—hot, rough, unrelenting—slides up my center.

"Oh, yes." The moan tears free before I can swallow it down. Leaning back, I brace my hands on the table, tipping my head back as my entire body tingles. His tongue flicks over my clit, and I buck into him. He spears me with two fingers, pumping in and out. Every suck, every stroke sends me higher until my toes curl and my body bows off the table. "Don't stop. Please don't stop."

He doubles his efforts, thrusting harder, licking faster. I pinch my eyes closed as a burst of stars explode behind my lids. I arch my back, thrusting my pussy into his mouth. "Oh, fuck, yes. Just like that. Oh, Logan." My release slams through me, it's white-hot, a rush so fierce I claw at the tablecloth like it's the only thing tethering me to earth.

He rises, wiping his mouth with the back of his hand, smug and unrepentant. "You're my favorite meal."

Merry Christmas to me.

I pull him closer, sliding the onesie off his hips until it drops to the floor. He kicks it away. I inch closer to the edge, guiding his thick, hard cock against my soaked pussy. The look in his eyes nearly undoes me.

His breath hitches, and he drops his forehead to mine. "I want nothing more than to slide into you… bare."

"I'm on birth control," I whisper, my lips grazing his jaw.

"I haven't been with anyone but you for three years, and I regularly get tested." His hands trail up my thighs, causing goosebumps to prickle my skin.

"I've always used protection."

He tugs on the ends of the scarf tangled in his fingers and yanks. My body collides with his. "Then we're about to put this scarf to good use." His kiss is fire—hungry, consuming, promising everything. With an arm around my back, he pulls me off the table and spins me around, so my back is facing him. I glance over my shoulder as he unwinds the scarf from my neck. The material is soft against my skin as he wraps it around my wrists instead. His finger slides between the scarf and my skin to make sure it's not too tight. "You're like a little Christmas present, waiting to be fucked."

My breath hitches, and my nipples tighten with anticipation. His hand dips between my legs, and his finger traces a path through my slick heat. "So wet for me. Are you going to be a good girl and be quiet as my cock stretches you?" His breath is hot against the shell of my ear.

"Yes," I moan as his finger circles my entrance. Slowly, he drags his finger up and past the tight muscle of my ass. A small whimper escapes me from the touch. This is the second time he's done that, and each time it's gotten more erotic. A shiver runs through me as his hand traces the curve of my body, finally stopping at my shoulder blades.

"Bend over for me, Snowflake." His voice is deep and gruff like his own restraint is seconds from snapping.

I do as he says. My nipples graze the textured runner, sending jolts of pleasure straight to my core. The scarf around my wrist tightens as he pulls my arms back. My back arches and then—he's inside me. Long, thick, filling me in one deep thrust that steals my air. "Yes!"

"Fuck. You feel incredible like this. Your pussy is so eager to take every inch of me." The table creaks with every powerful push, his grunts mixing with my moans. The sound is obscene, perfect, addictive. "Fucking gorgeous. Look at you taking all of my cock."

He comes to a stop still inside of me. "It's time for me to unwrap my Christmas present." He tugs the fabric around my wrists until my hands are free and fall to the edge of the table. He pumps into me a few more times, more leisurely like he wants to savor every second. "I want to see you when you come." With one hand across my chest, he pulls me so I'm upright. He slides out of me and spins me around. "On the table," he demands. With his help, I sit on the edge of the table. Glitter clings to my chest from the runner.

He nestles himself between my legs, the tip of his cock sliding against my pussy. He grips my chin and presses his lips to mine as he pushes his bare cock into me. My body jolts as my breath catches in my throat. I rock my hips, pushing deeper into him.

"Look at us," he groans, rubbing his thumb over my clit, driving me higher. "Perfect."

When he pulls out, he's glistening with my wetness, and the sight alone makes my teeth sink into my bottom lip. God, it's filthy and beautiful all at once—watching him disappear inside me again and again, owning every inch of me. He buries his head in the crook of my neck, his breath hot against my skin as his hips keep driving into mine. I lock my legs tighter around his waist, my heels digging into the firm curve of his ass, urging him to go deeper, harder.

A guttural groan vibrates through his chest. "I'm not gonna last like this. You feel too fucking good."

His hand slips between us, thumb finding my clit, rubbing tight, fast circles that make me cry out. My body writhes against his, desperate, greedy, clinging to him like if I let go, I'll float away. My nails score his shoulders, half-moon marks biting into his skin as pleasure builds, sharp and relentless.

"Yes, yes, more," I chant, my voice breaking as the pressure coils hotter and tighter.

He hauls me closer, one arm banded across my back, giving him the leverage to thrust deeper, rougher. The table creaks beneath us along with the sound of skin slapping skin in time with our ragged breaths.

"Come for me, Brie," he pants, each word a command, a plea. "Come all over my cock."

The words detonate something inside me. Stars explode behind my eyes, my pussy clenching down around him in pulsing waves as I unravel. My cry tangles with his guttural roar as he slams into me twice more, his cock spilling hot and thick inside me. His movements slow to a stop, both of us riding through the aftershocks until we collapse against each other, sweaty, shaking, and completely undone. My chest heaves against his as I try to remember how to breathe.

He's still buried deep inside me when he lifts his head, pressing a tender kiss to my swollen lips. His voice is rough but filled with something more than lust—something that makes my heart stumble. "Merry Christmas, Brie. You're the best damn present I could've asked for."

I smirk against his mouth, though my pulse is still racing. "You're not too bad yourself."

His laugh rumbles against my chest, warm and intoxicating, before he cups my face in both hands and kisses me again—slower this time, like he's sealing a promise neither of us is ready to let go of.

Technically, the office is closed until after New Year's. So when my phone rang Monday morning and Mrs. Kingsley asked me to come in, I knew one of three things was happening: I got the promotion, I'm fired, or I'm doomed to spend the rest of eternity in the same position I've been in for the past eight years. Honestly? At this point, I'd take the first two over the third. By the time I reach the third floor, the entire building is dark except for the glow spilling out from Mrs. Kingsley's office. This is the perfect setup for a firing. Call me in while everyone else is still on Christmas vacation to spare me the embarrassment of cleaning out my desk with pitying eyes on me.

"Hello?" My voice echoes down the empty hallway.

"Brie. Can I see you in my office?" Mrs. Kingsley says from down the hall.

My shoes squeak with every step as I approach her door. Great, now I sound like a clown heading to my own execution. My heart slams against my ribs, my palms slick as I smooth them down my coat. This is it. I'm about to be escorted out with a sad cardboard box filled with a fake plant and crushed dreams.

I step inside, and without looking up from her computer, she says, "Take a seat." Before sitting, I shrug my coat off my shoulders, but she stops me. "Keep it on. This won't take long."

Well, there's the nail in the coffin. I lower myself into the chair, my entire body bracing for impact. I had a good run. It's been fun while it lasted.

Then she turns, her face as blank as a freshly baked sugar cookie. Seconds tick by. Then her mouth twitches, and she smiles. "Congratulations, Brie. You're Mount Holly's new event coordinator."

I blink. Once. Twice. Maybe three times. Did she just—?

"Really?" My voice cracks. "I got it?"

"There's no one else I'd want to pass the position to."

The air whooshes out of me like a popped balloon. I grin so wide it's a miracle my face doesn't split in two. My arms twitch with the urge to vault over the desk and hug her, but instead I settle for bouncing in my chair like an over-caffeinated elf.

"You showed me what you're capable of under pressure," she continues, her tone softening. "You're going to do wonderful things for this town."

I clasp my hands together, trying to act professional, even though my insides are screaming like I just won the lottery. "Thank you. Truly. Mount Holly means everything to me. There was no way I could let an out-of-towner take over."

She chuckles. *Chuckles.* I didn't even know she had the muscle memory for that. "Between us? There was never an out-of-town agency."

I jerk my head back. "Wait… what?"

"I wanted to see how you'd handle the pressure. This job was always yours." She turns around and picks up six bulging three-ring binders and holds them out to me. "And now it officially is."

When she slides them toward me, I rise to my feet and collect the binders. My knees nearly buckle under the weight. But who cares? I'd carry a hundred binders if it meant this moment.

By the time I leave the office, I'm floating so high I swear the snowflakes part around me like confetti. I make it to my car, fling the binders in the backseat, and immediately do an undignified happy dance in the driver's seat, arms flailing, squealing like a twelve-year-old at a boy-band concert.

I call Willa. Then Sloane. But Logan? He deserves the in-person version. Once on his doorstep, I knock on the door. I wipe my expression off my face, wanting it to be a surprise.

The door opens. Logan's eyes take me in, his brows knitting. "Shit. What happened?" He drags me into his chest, wrapping me up like he's ready to storm the gates of town hall. "Who do I need to threaten? Point me in the direction."

I tip my head back, unable to hold back my smile any longer. "I got it."

His brows shoot up. "Wait. Really?"

I nod giddily

His entire face lights up. In one swoop, he lifts me off the ground and spins me in a circle, my laughter echoing through the cold air. When he sets me down, he kisses me breathless, his forehead resting against mine.

"I knew you could do it," he whispers, eyes burning into mine. "I'm so damn proud of you. You deserve this. I love you."

Tears prick my eyes. My heart somersaults. "I love you too."

Logan

Brie sits at the dining room table with Josie, the two of them bent over construction paper, glue sticks, and an ever-growing list of new Christmas activities for the Holly Jolly Festival. They look like co-conspirators planning world domination—if world domination involved glitter and gingerbread houses. Many have asked if I'm doing the carnival again this year, and every time, I tell them absolutely not. That was a one-and-done, thank you very much. I'll leave the festival chaos to Brie, the woman who actually thrives on it. The only thing I kept is the ice rink, which is my excuse to sneak in way too many hockey tournaments under the guise of "community engagement." Over the past year, it's even expanded into more of a sports complex. This year's big addition? A curling bonspiel.

Eight months ago, I asked Brie to move in with us. She was basically here every night anyway, but she hesitated, so I didn't push. Instead, I cleared out drawers, made closet space, and sure enough—every month she adds her things to the empty space. Pretty soon, she'll be moved in anyway.

Six months ago, I did something I never thought I'd do again. I bought a ring with the perfect plan already in place for when to give it to her. I never thought I'd want marriage again after Brooke. But Brie… Brie made me believe in forever again. She's the best thing that's happened to me in the past four years. I owe moving on to her. Do we still bicker? Absolutely. Half the time I think Brie does it on purpose just so we can make up afterward. The making up is my favorite part.

Of course, I ran every life-altering decision past Josie first. She was more than thrilled to have Brie move in. She said she now has someone to bake and do crafts with. I was excited, I no longer had to have my nails painted. The big question came when I asked Josie what she thought about me and Brie getting married and Brie being her stepmom. I've never seen her smile as big as she did that day, which really solidifies the idea that Josie likes Brie more than me. I'm okay with that. Josie even insisted on helping me pick out the ring, because, and I quote, *"I'm a girl. I know what girls like."* I couldn't argue with the logic, plus I liked having her as part of the process. We left the jeweler with a three-and-a-half-carat, three-stone, princess-cut diamond ring representing our past and our present flanking the largest diamond in the middle, our future. Thankfully, Josie was able to keep the secret even though she almost spilled twice. Once when we took a trip to the city, we passed the jewelry store, and Josie made a comment about going there. Luckily, I saved us by telling Brie we went there for a Mother's Day gift for my mom. The second time, she mentioned a big surprise for the Holly Jolly Festival. Again, I had another save, saying the big surprise was another hockey tournament, but going even bigger and longer.

Brie and Josie are practically inseparable. I feel like I have to pencil in time just to see them. But I love that Josie has a mother figure in her life and that Brie was so willing to take on that role. It's a difficult one. But she loves Josie as if she's her own.

Now, sitting at the table, I palm the ring box, nerves buzzing under my skin. I flip it open just enough for the overhead light to catch the diamonds. "Do you think she'll like it?"

Josie groans, flopping back in her chair. "Dad. Yes. I've told you, like, a hundred times."

"More like ten," I mutter.

"Exactly. Ten too many." She crosses her arms, but there's a grin tugging at her mouth.

I snap the box shut and tuck it into my pocket. "Alright, Peanut. Tonight's the night. You ready for your big moment?"

She nods, bouncing in her chair. "Just like we practiced. I'll be on the side of the stage."

I ruffle her hair, pulling her in to kiss the top of her head. "I love you."

"I love you too, Dad. But seriously—don't mess this up."

Later, Josie and I stand off to the side of the stage as Brie steps behind the podium. She's glowing, cheeks pink from the cold, eyes sparkling brighter than the string lights overhead. My chest tightens just watching her.

"Thank you, everyone, for coming!" Brie's voice rings out, full of that contagious holiday cheer that makes the whole town eat out of her mittened hand. "This is my favorite event of the Holly Jolly Festival—the lighting of the Christmas tree to kick off this year's festivities!"

The crowd erupts into applause. Brie grins and lifts her hand toward the towering evergreen, which is much taller this year since I stopped hording them.

I step onto the stage, boots crunching on the wooden planks, and sneak up behind her. She jumps, spinning around, eyes wide.

"If I could," I say, reaching for the mic, "I'd like to say something."

Her brows knit together. "Um, yeah, sure." She passes me the microphone, suspicion written all over her features.

I turn toward the crowd, their expectant faces glowing in the twinkle lights. "Now, growing up, the Holly Jolly Festival meant family. It meant being together, year after year. It was always special." The cheers rise again, warm enough to rival the bonfire. "But tonight, I want to make it even more special."

When I face Brie, she mouths, *What are you doing?*

The small velvet box is smooth under my fingertips as I pull it from my pocket. The crowd gasps when I flip it open and drop to one knee. "Brie," I say, my throat tight, "will you join our family and spend every Holly Jolly Festival with us? Marry me."

Her hands fly to her mouth, eyes shimmering.

I wave Josie over, and she dashes across the stage, breathless and grinning. "Please," she says, tugging on Brie's sleeve. "We want you to spend every Christmas with us."

My pulse pounds so loud I swear the mic picks it up. Seconds stretch into eternities. She hasn't said yes. Panic claws up my throat. Did I misjudge this? Did I—

Willa

My best friend's getting married! I squeal so loud I nearly pop an eardrum and do a little jig in the snow. She's going to say yes. She *has* to say yes. If she doesn't, I'll march up there and say yes for her. My phone buzzes in my pocket. I pull it out and glance at the screen, skimming the message. "Son of a bitch!"

Gasps ripple through the crowd. My head jerks up. Every single face is staring at me. Including Logan. Including Brie. Including the giant diamond sparkling under the stage lights.

Crap. I said that out loud.

I wave my phone in the air like a white flag. "Sorry! Not about them! Just… a terrible text message. Carry on!"

Brie finally laughs through her tears, her voice carrying across the mic. "Yes. Of course I'll marry you!"

She launches herself into Logan's arms. Josie barrels into them, and Logan wraps both of them into a hug. The entire town cheers, whistles, and claps. It's like a Hallmark movie climax—only real.

And me? I shove my phone back into my pocket, the weight of that awful text pressing against my thigh. How could he do this to me? He knew it meant a lot to me to have him by my side for Christmas, and what does he do? Bail!

I'm fucked. Now for the entire holiday, I'll have the

scrutiny of my parents up my ass as they contemplate where they went wrong with me. *Why couldn't you be more like your sisters? Why own a diner when you could've been a doctor? Restaurants fail, you know. Doctors don't.* Merry Hell-mas to me. But I push it down. Because tonight isn't about me. Tonight's about my best friend finding her forever with her best friend. So I paste on a smile, swallow the ache, and cheer louder than anyone else in the crowd—even if my forever feels miles away.

Willa's Christmas story, Snow Strings Attached, is next in the Mount Holly Christmas series. Her fake boyfriend plan was supposed to keep her family off her back, not spark real feelings. But one snowed-in weekend at the cabin turns playful banter into something dangerously close to love—and suddenly, the line between pretend and forever isn't so clear.   https://authorgiastevens.com/books/snow-stings-attached/

Thank you so much for reading Logan and Brie's story! I hope you enjoyed their HEA. If you want more, you can download their fun and spicy bonus scene. https://authorgiastevens.com/bonus-neversleighnever

First and foremost, I want to thank everyone who picked up this book. I think I will forever be in awe that you want to read my stories.

I have to thank my husband. I don't know if I would have ever started writing without his words of encouragement. Thank you so my entire extended family. They're so supportive and read my books, and we avoid discussing the spicy scenes at family gatherings.

A big shout out to Brandi Zelenka. You were there for me every step of the way and I don't think I could have done this without you.

To my creative team, you pushed me to put out the best book possible and I am so thankful to have you on my side. Thank you to my editor, Brandi at My Notes in the Margin. I tend to give you a hot mess and you make it brilliant. And thank you to Maddie at Davenports Edits for all your extra helps on polishing this book.

Thank you to Katy Cuthbertson for all your work and support, especially your eye for commas. You've been a huge help.

Thank you Jane at Torch Lit Ink. You made everything run smoothly.

Thank you to my wonderful Sassy ARC Readers! I appreciate you so much.

Most of all thank you to all the bloggers, bookstagrammers, and booktokers for reading and sharing your excitement for this book. It means the world to me and I can't thank you enough. And of course, thank you to all the readers for reading my words. I hope I've been able to give you a fun escape for a few hours.

See you at the next book! Stay sassy!

Gia Stevens is a romantic comedy author who believes love should come with plenty of laughs—and maybe a little heat. Known for her fun, lighthearted, and spicy stories, Gia writes the kind of books that let readers escape into swoony romances filled with witty banter, quirky characters, and happily ever afters that feel both cozy and exciting.

She lives in Northern Minnesota with her husband and their cat, forever counting down the days until summer and surviving long winters with tea, blankets, and a stack of romcoms. When she's not busy writing your next book boyfriend, you can usually find her binge-watching shows everyone else finished years ago or curled up with a romance novel.

If you're looking for stories that guarantee laughs, swoons, and plenty of LOLs, you've come to the right place.

Visit my website for more information.
https://www.authorgiastevens.com

Want to read more sassy heroines, swoony heroes, and fun and flirty romance books?

Visit Gia's website to find a complete list of all her books.

https://www.authorgiastevens.com